MISTER STAND-IN

A COCKY HERO CLUB PRODUCTION

USA TODAY BESTSELLING AUTHOR

C.M. ALBERT

Mister Stand-In
A Cocky Hero Club production
Genre: Contemporary Romance

Cover by Marisa Rose Wesley of Cover Me Darling LLC
Cover Photography by Reggie Deanching of R + M Photography
Cover Model Aidan Stewart
Editing by Erin Servais of Dot and Dash, LLC
Interior by Stephanie Anderson of Alt 19 Creative

COCKY HERO CLUB PRODUCTION

Mister Stand-In is a standalone story inspired by Vi Keeland and Penelope Ward's *Mister Moneybags*. It's published as part of the Cocky Hero Club world, a series of original works, written by various authors, and inspired by Keeland and Ward's *New York Times* bestselling series.

THE OFFICIAL
MISTER STAND-IN PLAYLIST

"About Love" — MARINA
(From the Netflix film *To All the Boys: P.S. I Still Love You*)
"Addicted to You" — Avicii
"Adore You" — Harry Styles
"All of Me" — John Legend
"Animal" — Neon Trees
"Back to You" — Alex & Sierra
"Catching Feelings (feat. SIX60)" — Drax Project
"Chapter" — Christian Paul
"Deserve" — Chase Fouraker
"For Her" — Chris Lane
"Hero" — Enrique Iglesias
"I Believe in You (Acoustic)" — Tyler Hilton
"I Can't Help Myself (Sugar Pie, Honey Bunch)"— The Four Tops
"If I Can't Have You" — Shawn Mendes
"Intentions (feat. Quavo)" — Justin Bieber
"Into the Unknown" — Idina Menzel & AURORA
"Love on the Brain" — Rhianna
"PILLOWTALK" — ZAYN
"Put a Little Love on Me" — Niall Horan
"Stuck with U" — Ariana Grande & Justin Bieber
"Sucker" — Jonas Brothers
"What a Man Gotta Do" — Jonas Brothers
"You Make My Dreams" — Karizma Duo

This book is dedicated with love to my dear friends,
Heather and Deena.
My writing sisters. My strength. My laughter.
My source of growth and support
during the weirdest year ever.
Ride or die, Smuffins!
#babyyodaforever

It isn't about

Diamonds,

Fuck the

Flowers,

All she wants

Is someone to

Keep her bed warm

Every night,

And touch her

Like it's

Agony not to.

—J. ROSE

MISTER STAND-IN

CARTER WRIGHT was used to being anything *but* Mr. Right. He wouldn't exactly call himself a street rat, but his life had somehow become a rags-to-riches story—one he'd rather keep to himself. The best part about being a stand-in to some of the wealthiest a-holes in New York?

Access.

To anything, and *anyone*, he wanted.

And that certainly wasn't little Miss Moneybags, Presley Kincaid. No, he had his sights set on someone even hotter—her stepmother. But when Lauren asks him to stand in for her richer-than-sin fiancé at their rehearsal dinner, and then he's paired up with her spoiled daughter, Presley, at the wedding, Carter can do the only thing he's truly good at: Shut up. Smile. Be charming.

Be the stand-in he was born to be.

But when Presley turns out to be more than she pretends—and a one-night stand gives her more access to his past than he intended—Carter's simple, easygoing lifestyle starts to unravel, exposing the biggest lie of all. One so big Carter never even saw it coming.

Will Presley accidentally expose the Stand-In for who he really is? Or will her discovery free Carter from the street hustle he's perfected and finally help him claim a life, and *love,* that was always meant to be?

CHAPTER ONE

CARTER

"SHE WANTS ME to do what?" I groaned, hoping I'd heard my friend, Dex Truitt, wrong. I picked up the dirty tennis ball and whistled. Baby Yoda came bounding forward, her pointy ears flapping happily in the crisp autumn air.

"Who's my good girl?" I scratched behind the rescue puppy's floppy ear. Her large, dark eyes beaming up at me was almost enough to make my insides go soft.

Dex snickered. "You sure you don't want to adopt her?"

I shot him a side eye as I tossed the tattered ball across the dog park and shoved my hands into the pockets of my jeans to keep them warm. About four dogs chased after the ball, but Baby's fierce protector, Bandit—a rescued greyhound Dex adopted a couple years ago—did what he always did and growled as he stood between the ball and the other dogs. Baby plopped her cute, little, wrinkly Pug self onto the ball and chewed it with unrestrained pleasure.

"What's your deal with Lauren, anyway?" Dex asked, checking his phone quickly before shoving it back into the pocket of his expensive, black overcoat. "It's not like you haven't done something like this before. And it's easy money."

He wasn't wrong. But Lauren Kincaid was different, and this wasn't a job I wanted to take. The last thing I wanted to see was a woman I'd crushed on as a teenager marry yet another rich SOB. And worse? Stand in for said schmuck at his own rehearsal dinner because he was too fucking "busy" to make time for something so important. He didn't deserve her. Thank god he wasn't going to be there, or I was fairly sure I'd be making a scene.

I sighed, running a hand through my wavy, brown hair. I'd need a cut before Thursday if I were insane enough to do this. "How much?"

"Five."

"For *just* the rehearsal dinner?"

"Yep," Dex said, laughing when I groaned again. "The easiest five grand you'll ever make."

"Well, except for that one time," I reminded him, snickering.

"That was certainly something I'll never forget," Dex agreed. "I don't think Las Vegas will either."

"That's why I like sticking to my own stomping grounds when I can."

I grew quiet, and Dex let me have a minute to figure things out. He was busy throwing a bright orange ball to Bandit anyway. There was something I couldn't quite figure out. "Why'd she ask you and not just call my office?"

He cleared his throat. "Well, this is where is gets a little interesting," he said, rubbing the back of his neck.

"Spit it out, Truitt."

"She's marrying Richard Brash."

"As in, the CFO of Montague Enterprises? *Your* CFO?" This couldn't get any worse. "Isn't he, like, a hundred?"

Dex laughed, the deep, rich sound drawing a curious glance from a woman standing on the other side of the park. Her gaze lingered on us, and I couldn't help but flash the cute redhead my full smile and dimples. On cue, she blushed and looked away.

"He's only sixty-five, Carter. What does it matter? It's just a job, right?"

I nodded but didn't answer.

"Look, we have a critical finance meeting that night that can't be moved, otherwise he'd be there. Lauren's been to enough of our functions to know you're a friend of mine. And since you're almost impossible to book these days, she thought she'd see if she could grease some palms and pull in a favor. It's my CFO, Carter. It would mean a lot if you could make it happen. Plus, Bianca and I will be there without the kids. It'll be a good time."

Yeah, a good time. Just me, my friends, a room full of strangers, and the beautiful, leggy brunette who fueled nearly all my teenage fantasies. On the night before her wedding. What could possibly go wrong?

"Make it ten, and I'm in."

"Done," Dex said, whistling for the dogs.

We walked back to Forever Grey, the inner-city rescue center near Dex's office—the same one where he originally found Bandit. They'd since expanded and started taking in special rescue cases like Baby. Dex roped me into walking some of the dogs on a weekly basis, as a way for us to get some "bro" time in, while helping them out. Since my lifestyle didn't exactly afford a stable schedule for me to adopt one, I was happy to volunteer when I could. Being New York's elite—and *only*—personal stand-in for any above-the-board function meant I was highly sought after and always in demand. Yep. I'd spent the last four years after leaving the military being arm candy for some of the wealthiest bastards in New York. On most days, it didn't suck. The money, food, and travel destinations were exceptional. And the gig gave me access to some of the hottest pieces of ass in the entire world. Don't get me wrong. I *never* slept with a client. That was a hard no for me. I was a stand-in, not a prostitute.

But a client's sister or business partner? That was another story altogether.

Not only that, but after just a short time of running in New York's tight circle of the richest of the rich, I had more dirt on these assholes than Deep Throat had on Nixon. And it got me in a lot of doors, which is how I'd run into Lauren again after all these years. The first time she'd seen me on the arm of a super model at New York's fashion week, her eyes grew wide with recognition, and she had to do a double take. Since then, we'd brushed by each other socially many times, as the wealthy were bound to do.

I wasn't really in their circle though. Maybe that's what kept Lauren from approaching me, from seeing if that flicker of recognition was real. If the instant attraction on her part could grow into anything more. Or if I was still just the young punk she remembered from The Grove—the small coastal island where she and her first husband had vacationed every summer.

I said my goodbyes to Dex and caught a cab home.

It doesn't matter, I thought miserably as I glanced out at the bumper-to-bumper traffic. Lauren had always been out of my league. A woman like that didn't slum with the property manager's son, even if he were all grown up and could give her a run for her money now.

Shit. What could a sixty-five-year-old fart give her that I couldn't? I snorted, thinking of all the ways I'd take care of Lauren if I were given the chance. But it wasn't about that. Even I knew that. As much as I'd put her on a pedestal all these years, there was still one truth I couldn't outrun.

Lauren married for money the first time. And I was certain she was marrying for money again. Sure, I could screw her for four hours straight until she couldn't walk right or be satisfied by any other man ever again. What? I could. But the one thing I couldn't give her was the insanely wealthy lifestyle she'd been born into and would never walk away from.

Certainly not for a street rat like me.

CHAPTER TWO

PRESLEY

I CHECKED MY phone for a third time, scrolling through my inbox to see if Sylvia's edits had come in yet. Nothing. Shit. She didn't usually take this long to reply. Maybe I'd taken the wrong angle for my *Finance Times* article. Had it been too personal? I shook my head. No. Bianca Truitt had read it and thought it was perfect. And there was no one else I trusted there more than Bianca. Even though she was only with the magazine part time at best now, she'd taken me under her wing and was like a big sister and mentor, all rolled into one.

"Really, darling? Can't you step away from your work for just a minute?"

I glanced up at my stepmother. She looked gorgeous in her long, champagne-colored gown. Of course she did; she was a natural beauty. Sure, we all knew that enough money could make even the homeliest woman look like a princess for a night. But Lauren Kincaid was no princess. And she certainly wasn't homely. No, my stepmom was basically the Queen of Everything. Lauren was the kind of woman who knew her place in the world and was happy to live it in her own brand of confident style.

I pushed back my mop of strawberry blond curls self-consciously as I gave her my full attention.

"It's perfect, Lauren." I wasn't lying. The final alterations made the dress look like a second skin and would bring Richard Brash to his knees at the wedding. I just hoped he could make it through their wedding night in one piece. He was a good twenty years older if I'd done my math right. The thought of Richard in bed with Lauren made me shudder. I ran my hands up my arms and over my goose bumps. Thank god I was loaded. There was no bank account big enough for me to ride a man like Richard into the grave.

"Thank you," she said, turning this way and that in front of the three-way mirror of New York's most exclusive bridal boutique. Her perfectly round, surgically enhanced breasts swelled in the strapless dress, her light bronze skin glowing against the champagne-colored gown. The white corset top had delicate champagne boning wrapping around her thin waist, several rows of diamonds sparkling along its top seam. I had to admit, it drew your attention to Lauren's best physical assets. The soft, textured fabric of the skirt had a dreamy quality to it and flowed out from her hips like a favorite daughter birthed from petals and waves. It was exquisite and nothing less than I'd expect from my stepmom.

My phone buzzed, and I glanced down at the new text message. "Hang on, Lauren, I need to get this."

Lauren pouted prettily, used to using it as a weapon to get what she wanted in life. "If I'd known you were going to be so preoccupied, I would have brought along Sylvia."

I couldn't help but laugh. "Funny you should mention that. This *is* Sylvia, which is why I need to respond. I'm sorry—it'll only be a minute. Besides, it's your last dress fitting. It's not exactly like I needed to *do* anything," I reminded her. "I'm just here for moral support. I promise you'll have my undivided attention when I get back."

I stepped out of our private suite and into the reception area. I nodded at the personal assistant manning the front desk and quickly read Sylvia's message.

> SYLVIA: Sorry to text. In important meeting. Excellent work. Your best yet. Bailey will send over minor edits later. You may be ready for more.

I squealed, clutching my phone to my chest and drawing a curious, mildly annoyed glance from the receptionist. "Sorry," I whispered. "I just got some of the best feedback of my career from my boss!"

The woman's face relaxed and she smiled. "Will you be heading back in now?"

"I am."

"Could you please give this package to Mrs. Kincaid?"

I nodded, accepting the long, thin box with ribbon so soft and expensive it put my bedsheets to shame. When I got back in the suite it was empty. I took a seat and was about to text the good news to my best friend, Willa, when Lauren returned from the changing room, ready to go.

"All done?"

She nodded, then draped her soft, leather Hermès bag over her forearm and cleared her throat. "I do hope you'll be more present at the wedding rehearsal tomorrow night. It would look tacky for a bridesmaid to be checking her phone all evening, especially when she's my stepdaughter," she said, frowning slightly when she noticed the box in my hand. "What's that?"

"Lauren, it's your big day. I promise I won't bring my phone out once, unless it's to get a picture of you in that amazing wedding dress," I added for good measure. "Oh, and the receptionist asked me to bring this to you. She didn't say who it was from, but I could probably take a wild guess," I said, rolling my eyes. "Dick probably feels bad that he's missing his own rehearsal dinner."

"Presley!" she scolded. "It's Richard and you know that."

I couldn't help but grin as I handed her the box. "Sorry, *Mom*."

Her face softened. "You're forgiven," she said, oblivious to my sarcasm. She pulled the ribbon off and tossed it on the table next to her as if it was cheap tissue paper. The lid creaked as she opened it, and Lauren gasped. Inside was a tennis bracelet with fourteen cushion-cut yellow diamonds, each surrounded by smaller, round, full-cut diamonds.

"Wow. Dick must feel awfully guilty to send over a bracelet like that."

Lauren ignored my cheap shot, smiling as she ran a perfectly manicured fingernail over the bracelet's shiny surface. When she caught me staring at her, she quickly closed the lid and placed it in her black handbag.

"That was sweet of Richard," she murmured. "I hope someday you find a man who treats you as well as Richard treats me."

If I were ever stupid enough to fall in love in this city, it most certainly wouldn't be with a man like Dick. Instead, I thought of my father. Of his strong arms, his crinkly, bright green eyes, and a shaggy, weathered beard I'd grown up calling "spikes," since no matter how much he groomed it, it always felt a little spiky to my touch. He'd probably been the only authentic relationship in Lauren's adult life. I had to believe she'd really loved him. He'd been happy with her all those years after my mother died.

"Who knows?" Lauren said, circling my thoughts back to her wedding with Richard. "Maybe you'll meet someone this weekend? Wouldn't *that* be a story to tell?"

Yeah, some story.

Rich socialite meets even richer heir to some huge fortune at the wedding of Richard Brash, CFO to Montague Enterprises, and Lauren Kincaid, second cousin to the Kennedys.

I snorted. Not in this lifetime. The last thing I wanted was to marry into money. No thanks. I had enough of my own and didn't need a man to take care of me.

Like my father, I would marry only for love.

And with my track record, that wasn't going to be happening anytime soon.

CHAPTER THREE

CARTER

WHY THE HELL am I fussing with my tie again? It's not like she's single. I'm a fucking pro. I've got this. I grabbed a bottle of whiskey and poured a small glass, neat. Liquid courage. Isn't that what they call it? It's one night. Ten grand. Then I can lay Lauren to rest. And she . . . she can live happily ever after with the Crypt Keeper.

The Uber was a short drive over to the Excelsior. I'd been to plenty of events at the upscale hotel in Midtown. The top floor was an event space unlike many others in New York. The entire top floor boasted an elevated, retractable glass ceiling and a functioning botanical garden. In the center of the space was a large circular area where attendants bustled around as they set up for the wedding. A circular, dark brown, open-air gazebo was the showstopper, and where the vows would take place. Clumps of lush, purple flowers hung heavy from dark green vines that spilled over from the top, almost like a crown. Candles flickered in mismatched lanterns and cast a warm, welcoming light on the table at the back of the gazebo where the minister would stand.

Who just so happened to be Dex.

"You sure you're up for this?"

"Yeah. I don't know how I got suckered into this. But Bianca assured me it was legit. Bada bing, bada boom. Next thing I know, the Universal Church of Life is telling me I'm an official minister."

I lifted a brow. "You *sure* this is legal?"

"Dude. If it's good enough for Richard Branson and Paul McCartney, I think it's good enough for me." He clapped my shoulder. "Don't look now, but I think your date's here."

I turned, confused.

That's when I saw Lauren walking toward us, looking drop-dead gorgeous in a blush-colored dress that never reached her knees and clung to every curve like a lifeline. Large bands of shimmery gold cascaded down the front of the dress, broken up by a large strip of the same golden fabric circling her small waist like a cinched belt. It wasn't the dress that caught my attention though. It was her long, auburn hair, brushing her shoulders in soft waves—just how I remembered it. She hadn't aged a bit.

"So, this is the infamous Stand-In?" she said to Dex while smiling at me. She leaned in for a small hug and air kissed both of his cheeks. I could smell rich layers of floral and vanilla.

"Lauren, meet my good friend, Carter Wright. Carter, this is Lauren Kincaid—well, until tomorrow."

She reached out and took my hand, her eyes never leaving mine. "Carter Wright," she said low. "I remember you. Your father, is he Robert Wright?"

I glanced between Dex and Lauren. So she did remember me. I cleared my throat. "Yes, ma'am, he is."

Her laughter was warm and genuine and caught me off guard. "I'm hardly old enough to be called ma'am, Carter.

You can't be that much younger than me," she teased, her hand now resting on my upper arm. "I was just a baby when John and I vacationed at The Grove."

"I didn't realize you vacationed there," Dex said. "Of course, The Grove was my grandfather's baby, not mine."

"Well, yes, we did. We spent many summers there, preferring the sweet lure of the south to the same old hobnobbing circle we can't seem to escape in the Hamptons." She winked in my direction. "There was something so laid back and magical about The Grove, wasn't there, Carter?"

I thought back to the small island off the coast of South Carolina where I'd been born and raised. It was all I'd known before I went off to college, and then joined the military. But my summers weren't quite like Lauren's had been. Hers had been catered to, everything made easy and seamless. My summers? They were spent making that illusion a reality with my father and the rest of the staff at the swanky resort that Dex's family owned. One day, it would all be his. Lucky SOB.

Before I had a chance to answer, Bianca interrupted our little soiree, a beautiful younger woman in tow. "I think we're about ready to start," she said, linking her arm in Dex's. "The wedding planner is driving me nuts about our schedule."

"Perfect," Lauren said, waving over a polished, middle-aged man to our group. "Mattie, darling, please tell me we haven't stressed you out too much," she said, smoothing her hands over her flawless form.

I noticed the younger woman who'd come over with Bianca eyeing me, but she turned her head quickly when I caught her looking. I grinned, sliding one hand in my pocket. My dark brown hair was slicked back tonight, but the waves still gave it body. I'd left my five o'clock shadow, because it made me look older—and sexier. Not that I had to worry about that tonight. If there was one thing that was certain, even if she asked, my childhood fantasy wouldn't be coming true tonight. She was Richard Brash's woman now.

Mattie quickly explained what we would be doing. It was simple really. All I had to do was walk Lauren down the aisle as if I were her groom-to-be. We'd stand at the front, talk about the vows, make sure everyone knew where to stand, and then head over to the rehearsal dinner. It really was the easiest paycheck of my life. I wasn't sure why my presence was even needed. But then again, that was what my business was built on.

Show up. Look handsome. Smile. Be Charming.

I had this in the bag.

"YOU SURE YOU want to go through with this?" I asked Lauren as we stood at the head of the aisle waiting our turn. Her bridesmaids did hurried walks with their respective groomsmen, getting little chuckles from the friends and family who were present as they hammed it up.

Lauren was holding onto my arm and looked up at me with her large doe eyes. Ones I remembered being filled with kindness in my youth—even then, when most other people treated me like I was invisible unless they needed something. Lauren had always made time to say hello, check in on my father.

"Why on earth wouldn't I want to?" she asked playfully.

I switched gears as the cute ring bearer and flower girl marched down the aisle. The first practically ran, while the second clung to her mom's leg, looking out shyly at people as she went.

"So, where is Mr. Brash tonight? Seems like this is something he wouldn't want to miss," I said, glancing down at my perfectly polished dress shoes. "If it were me, I wouldn't miss it for anything in the world."

"You mean, when you get married."

"Yeah," I said, clearing my throat.

It was our turn and she beamed up at me. "You were always a kind boy—just like your father," she said. "Thanks for being here tonight so I didn't need to do this alone."

"Are you nervous?" I asked quietly as we made our way down the aisle. In all my teenaged fantasies, this was the last thing I ever imagined doing with Lauren. My gut knotted, and I felt like I was breaking out in a cold sweat.

"Relax, Carter," she teased, squeezing my arm. "It's not your wedding day."

I chuckled, releasing the tension in my body. "Yeah, right. Sorry about that."

We got to the front of the aisle and Dex greeted us. Since no one was giving Lauren away, she and her groom-to-be opted to walk down the aisle together, an untraditional move I admired. It felt right to me, like how partners should do things: together.

"This is where I greet you, then greet your guests," Dex said, looking around at the people filling a few of the ivory-colored chairs now. "Then I'll go into the ceremony portion, where I talk about love and your union. You and Richard will be facing each other during all this, holding hands if you like."

Lauren faced me, reaching for my hands. I swear, if anyone looked closely enough, they would see my boyhood crush slowly gasping for air and dying on the floor right in front of me. I willed myself to keep my face neutral. I was happy for her. I really was. It was just a naïve fantasy anyway of what my dream girl might be like one day. I raked my eyes over Lauren's smooth complexion, her white teeth. The soft curls that cascaded over her shoulder and rested just above the swell of her breasts. And god, don't get me started on her breasts.

I closed my eyes and took a deep breath, enjoying the soft feel of Lauren's small hands in mine. I zoned out on Dex's speech until he was forced to clear his throat.

"This is where you'll say your I dos and exchange rings," he said, waving his hand. "Do you Richard take Lauren, blah, blah, blah . . ."

He stared at me.

Oh, right.

"I do," I said, my voice catching. Someone in the bridal party snickered, but I couldn't see who.

"And Lauren, you'll be asked if you take Richard as your lawfully wedded husband."

"I do," she breathed out, her lashes fluttering as if saying goodbye to me.

"You'll exchange rings."

I acted like I was putting a ring on Lauren's finger, and she did the same. *I need another whiskey, stat.*

"Then, this is when Richard can kiss his bride," he winked at Lauren, then shot me a sly grin. "No standing in for this one, Carter. Sorry."

"Understandable, if not regrettable," I joked. Lauren flushed beside me, unaware of how much truth were in those four simple words.

"I'll introduce you as husband and wife for the first time, you can take hands, and then you'll head back down the aisle. When you get to the end, Mattie will be there to escort you into a private suite where you can freshen up and meet the photographer. Did I miss anything, Mattie?"

Mattie stood up from one of the pews, clearly loving his moment in the spotlight. "When you arrive with Richard at the altar tomorrow, don't forget to hand your bouquet to your daughter," he said. "And when you leave, she will hand it back to you for the march out."

Wait, what?

I scanned the row of bridesmaids, my eyes landing on the young woman I'd seen earlier with Bianca. No. It couldn't be.

I hadn't noticed her before because my focus had been on getting through this thing with Lauren. But I noticed her now. She never once waivered her cool green eyes from my own intense gaze. One perfectly sculpted brow arched, and I knew she realized I now recognized her.

Well, damn.

There—in all her glory—was bratty, little Presley Kincaid, all grown up. And she *had* grown up. Gone were the braces and unruly corkscrew curls. Gone were the dirty knees and the occasional pimple. In their place was a woman. One dressed in a slinky black tuxedo suit, the front buttoned, but with no shirt underneath. The neckline plunged all the way down, but somehow, her breasts remained tucked away, and all that was left was a smooth trail of pale skin that shimmered between her cleavage. Presley grinned, amused as my eyes did a walk of shame over the girl who once had the biggest crush on me.

The one I ignored every summer as she incessantly tried to tag along and get my attention. The girl who propositioned me when she was just thirteen, because she wanted her first kiss to be memorable—and from me.

Fuck. Why had I turned her down again?

Lauren tugged my arm, and I turned to face her, allowing her to wrap her hand around my forearm so I could lead her back down the aisle.

What a screwed-up little reunion we were about to have. At least it was just one night. I was ready to put the memories behind me and move on. To forget about Lauren—who would be sunbathing in Fiji with her new husband. And Presley, who would be . . . Well, to be honest, I didn't know what the heck little Miss Moneybags would be doing. Counting her fortune maybe? I heard she inherited almost everything from her father—and it was a shitload. I was surprised Lauren wasn't angrier about that. Who knows? Maybe that's why she was moving on to husband number two.

I waited with Lauren at the end of the aisle for the others to do their march back. Dex's wife, Bianca, met us there and gave me a little wave. "Great job, Carter."

I laughed. "Yeah, it was really hard work."

"You know what I mean," she said, swatting my arm. She looked past us, her eyes not happy until they landed on Dex. I swung around and saw him gazing back hungrily at her, too. I looked away, feeling like I was spying on something I shouldn't be seeing. I shoved my hands in my pockets and waited patiently. It was only eight thirty and I was ready to bail. Except I couldn't. I was contractually obligated to stay until ten p.m. That's what Lauren stipulated when my assistant sent over her paperwork.

At least I was off tomorrow. I couldn't wait to just kick it around my home—a spacious condo that had taken me the past four years to buy. What started off as a favor to a five-star general soon turned into my most lucrative job to date—Mister Stand-In, LLC. And it paid well enough to finally offer a cash purchase on a condo in one of the city's trendiest boroughs. So, yeah, I'd stick it out till ten.

"Why, if it isn't Carter Wright," I heard from behind me. When I turned, my eyes locked on Presley's again. They hadn't been that enticing and green when she was thirteen.

I swallowed, letting my grin raise slowly from the corner of my mouth, my eyes hooded. The look I knew well enough by now melted panties.

"Why, if it isn't little Miss Moneybags," I drawled in return. I dropped my gaze and let it caress her body, enjoying the sight, if I was honest. She was the polar opposite of Lauren. Where her stepmother was petite with curves and breasts for days, warmer complexion, dark hair, and eyes, Presley was taller and naturally fair, with strawberry blond waves tied back into submission in a long, sleek ponytail tonight.

Damn if my cock didn't kick at the sight. For some reason, the thought of yanking that ponytail and getting Presley's bratty little mouth to submit to mine made me a hell of a lot hornier than I ever imagined.

"Come back for that kiss, did you?"

CHAPTER FOUR

PRESLEY

I PACED THE length of the women's restroom while waiting for my best friend to finish changing. She'd gotten off work late and missed the rehearsal ceremony but was able to meet us for the dinner party. I was so glad, too. Because I seriously needed someone to vent with about Carter.

"As if," I sputtered. "I can't believe how arrogant he's become."

"Was it really arrogant, or just kind of take-chargey?" Willa asked. "Because a man who takes charge can be kinda hot, if you ask me."

She had a point.

But no, there was arrogance in the practiced grin, the dimples that had nowhere to hide they were so prominent. And those eyes. Warm, liquid pools of amusement as they traveled over my tuxedo jacket and down my thighs. I was wearing my kick-ass, black, satin Badgley Mischkas. They were at least four inches tall, and almost put me at eye level with Carter, but not quite.

He'd grown even taller after he'd left the island as a teenager. He had facial hair now, and I'd had to clench my fingers in my fist while we bantered, just so I wouldn't be tempted to run them over the soft growth covering his angular jaw. He was a dangerous combination now as a man—both hot as sin and with a flash of kindness behind the arrogance in those smoldering, brown eyes. I fell for it once, and he turned me down. It had burned so bad, nearly breaking my pathetic thirteen-year-old heart. There was no way I'd let history repeat itself. Even if he did smell like the ocean and fresh air and made me yearn for surfing at The Grove's hidden cove again.

"It's arrogance, trust me. I think his success has gone a little too much to his head." I pulled out my lip gloss and used my pinky to coat my full lips. He could suck it. I worked hard to become the successful woman I was today, and I didn't need a man's approval to feel validated.

I snorted. "What's he even successful for, anyway? All he does is glom onto rich people and pretend to fit in."

Willa opened the stall and glared at me. Oh, shit. I knew that look.

"Wow. You did not just say that, Pres. You sound worse than the Highrise Heiress Squad. Don't be petty. That's not who you are," she said. "Zip me up, will you?"

I pulled the zipper up her thin, brown back. "You're right. I don't know what's gotten into me."

"Not what. Who," she teased, flashing her money-making, mega-watt grin. "Well? How do I look?"

Truth? She looked like the runway model she was. "Willa, you could wear a paper bag and still be the prettiest girl in the room."

It was true. Her skin was dark brown and flawless. Her hair was in long braids this month, piled artfully on top of her head in a way that made others take notice the moment she walked into the room. Tonight, she had on a bright maize-colored wrap dress with a plunging neckline, and she was a lot fuller in the chest department than I was. Her naturally full lips were glossed but not colored, and her black, winged eyeliner was on point, drawing attention to her nearly black, seductive eyes—the ones she'd learned to "smize" with by the time she'd turned ten. I was twenty-five, and still had no clue how to do that.

I hugged Willa. "You're gonna upstage my stepmom if you're not careful."

"As if anyone could upstage the Queen," she said, laughing. "Come on, let's get to the party! I didn't come all this way to talk in a bathroom."

We held hands, and I walked into the dinner party laughing at a story Willa was relaying about a recent photoshoot where all she wore was bubbles covering her whole body. The greenscreen was a wreck and soap was everywhere. She kept trying to keep a neutral expression, all while bubbles were being blown en masse straight into her face. I couldn't even imagine.

The laughter died on my lips, though, when I saw Dex Truitt standing at the bar with none other than Carter Wright. I didn't want to go anywhere near him again, but he was the only thing between me and a drink—which I needed badly.

Willa pulled me closer to her as we headed toward the bar. "Holy shit. Is that him?"

"Shh," I snapped, which only set her into a bigger fit of giggles.

"And what are you two beautiful ladies finding so amusing tonight?" Dex asked as we approached.

"Oh, you know, just commenting on how funny it is when the people you knew as kids don't turn out anything like how you imagined they would as adults." I shrugged. "May I?" I asked, looking directly at Carter. "I'm thirsty."

That cocky grin again. "Some things are better with age, I hear," he said, lifting his glass in salute.

I traced his Adam's apple with my eyes as he swallowed, then looked back up at his wet lips. I really, *really* wish I hadn't. He may have changed over the past twelve years, but one thing didn't: how my body reacted to that sweet, sinful mouth of his.

"I'll stick to what I know," I said, which was met with an infuriating chuckle from Carter.

I'd done foolish things when I was a kid to get his attention. The Presley today wasn't so proud of those things. And she certainly wouldn't make a fool of herself repeating them.

"On second thought," I said dryly, "I'll have what you're having."

Dex laughed, watching our exchange. "Oh boy."

Carter shot him a look, then turned his attention back to me. "This drink is for big boys, *sugar*. Think maybe you should stick to—what? Let me guess. A white wine spritzer?"

My blood boiled, and I wanted to smack the smug look off his face. "I'm hardly a little girl anymore, *sugar*," I huffed, pushing between him and Dex to get to the bar. "I can hold my own."

"I bet you can," he murmured into his drink. I turned to ask Willa if she wanted the same drink, but I noticed she'd grabbed a glass of champagne from a passing waiter and was deep in conversation with Bianca.

"What's the chip on your shoulder about these days, Wright?" I asked, thanking the bartender for my honey-colored drink. "Upset that Lauren didn't choose you?"

His eyes grew dark as they pinned me over his glass, and I knew I'd crossed a line. I took a small sip and nearly gagged. It was strong and raged down my throat, threatening to tear it raw. I blinked back the shock but refused to let my eyes water as they held his gaze.

"Nah, just upset that you didn't change at all, princess. Still the same little pigtailed brat, I see."

He reached out and tugged my ponytail. Instead of anger, my body betrayed me. A flurry of lust tingled all the way from my scalp straight down to my thighs. More accurately, to what was between my thighs. *Damn him!*

Amusement filled his eyes, gorgeous little crinkles forming at the edges as they drank me in. I said nothing as I pulled my head away, smoothing my long ponytail over my shoulder while trying to gain control of my breathing.

"Well, well, well," he said low, moving closer to me. He leaned down and whispered into my ear, "Maybe I *was* lusting after the wrong Kincaid all these years."

I didn't have time to retaliate before he sauntered off.

And me?

I was left at the bar with a drink that would lay me flat on the ground if I finished it. A pulse that was racing in confusion at my body's knee-jerk reaction to his quick tug of my hair. And a pair of panties that I would most certainly find wet when I got home.

And damn if it wasn't Carter's arrogant smile that I would scratch my itch too.

CHAPTER FIVE

CARTER

"I'M SORRY, LAUREN, but the answer is still no."
It was hard to look into her warm brown eyes and turn her
down. But there was zero chance of me doing what she was
asking of me. I'd been hired to do a job, and it was over.
Now I was going home.

"Why not, Carter? Everyone will be there. You know
it's *the* social event of the month," she said truthfully. "You
could make a lot of new contacts. Besides, it would mean a
lot to me."

I took a deep breath and sighed into my glass, finishing
off my last drink for the night. It had gotten later than I'd
intended, and I noticed that Dex and Bianca had already
slipped out for the night. If I had a wife like Bianca, I'd have
left ages ago, too.

"Why?" I bucked my hips off the wall I was leaning on
and pulled on my jacket. The driver I'd called would be here
any minute and I had a long elevator ride down.

"It kind of feels like old times seeing you again, Carter.
I know I'm about to get married, and I love Richard with
all my heart, but I still miss John some days. I miss the life

we had. Those were what we call the 'good old days.' Ones I never imagined would go away," she said, her eyes growing moist. "I was so young, and so crazy in love. Raising a new daughter. Traveling with my perfect, little family. The Grove was like a home away from home, and your father was always good to us, Carter. You remind me a lot of him, you know," she said tenderly. "It would feel like having John here, if you came tomorrow. Like having a piece of my past as I step into my future."

I groaned. How could I say no to that? "I don't know, Lauren. Don't you have the table assignments all set and everything? Wouldn't it be hard to throw in a last-minute addition?"

"Don't you worry about that," she said, her grin spreading. She knew she'd won. "I have a special seat just for you."

Oh great. I didn't like the sound of that.

"I'm happy to pay you, Carter. If that's what this is about."

I ran my hand over my face, then checked my watch. "That's not it, Lauren. I just—"

What excuse could I really give? She was right. It would be an amazing opportunity to rub elbows with some of my past clients, and hopefully meet some future ones too. But it was hard enough to fake-walk Lauren down the aisle tonight. How hard would it be to watch her walk arm in arm with Richard tomorrow?

It was dumb. I knew I was being a pussy about the whole thing. The memory I had of Lauren as a kid was not the same Lauren who was standing here as an adult, asking me a small favor as an old family friend. Christ, I was selfish.

I thought about my home and how long it had been since I'd been back to see my dad. Maybe we were both feeling nostalgic. "Okay. I'll be there. I'd be honored, actually."

"Here," she said, grinning as she pressed a black- and gold-foiled envelope in my hand. "I'll see you tomorrow."

She leaned in to hug me and left a small air kiss by my ear. I closed my eyes in agony as I smelled her musky, floral scent mixed with her natural pheromones after mingling all evening. "I just wanted to thank you, Carter," she breathed quietly. I could feel her breath brush the air near my ear. "It was nice having a familiar face with me tonight, so I didn't have to face the humiliation of being at my wedding rehearsal alone. I hope we can stay friends."

And with that knife wedged deep in my heart, I nodded, untangling myself and making my way to the closest elevators.

The door was almost shut when a shimmer of black flashed between the small opening, and a *ding!* paused the doors, forcing them back open. Presley's eyes grew wide when she saw me standing there, but her friend grabbed her hand and pulled her in.

"Hey," the woman beside Presley said. She reached out a hand to me. "I'm Willa, Presley's best friend."

"Carter Wright," I said, shaking her hand. "Nice to meet you."

"That was a nice thing you did for Lauren tonight," she said, glancing between me and little Miss Moneybags, who was trying her best to look anywhere but at me as she jabbed the down button.

"Thanks. Lauren's an old family friend." I reached across the elevator and tugged Presley's ponytail again. "This one, too."

My hand was smacked away, and if steam could actually blow out of someone's ears, it would've been shooting from Presley's at the moment. I tried, unsuccessfully, to hold back my laughter.

"Oh?" Willa asked innocently. "How *do* you all know one another?"

Presley shot her friend daggers, then folded her arms across her chest. That only made things worse, because it pressed her small, firm breasts together, and I got to see what her cleavage would look like outside of the racy tuxedo jacket. I cocked a brow at her and made sure my gaze dragged downward.

"Ugh!" she huffed, yanking her jacket back into place. "Men are such pigs."

"Oink."

Willa burst out laughing. "Wow, you must know each other well. How come I've never heard of Mr. Wright before, Pres?"

"Because he wasn't worth mentioning. And I'd honestly forgotten about him years ago, until he crashed my stepmom's wedding rehearsal tonight."

"Ouch," I said, playfully covering my heart. "And for the record, I was invited."

She glanced at the floor numbers as they descended and bit the corner of her lip. Why did I suddenly have the urge to run my tongue over that spot, all hot and slow?

"For the record, I was invited back for the wedding tomorrow, too."

"What? Why?" she said, her eyes narrowing as they found mine.

"Must be because I'm great company," I said, holding the door open for Willa when we reached the lobby. Willa walked through and winked at me. "See you tomorrow, Carter."

Presley tried to sail past me, but I stepped a little to the side so our bodies would brush on her way out. I don't know why I did it. Other than to see that cute, fiery reaction again. I got exactly what I was bargaining for.

She paused in the doorway, one foot in and one foot out. The rise and fall of her chest told me she was reacting to our close contact. I couldn't help but notice the shimmery powder she'd brushed between her breasts now that we were this close.

"Did Lauren pay you for tomorrow, too?"

I stared down at her long and hard, willing her to have the nerve to meet my gaze. When she finally did, there was so much in those green eyes that I didn't understand.

"Yep, still a brat," I said. "See you tomorrow, princess."

At least I had the pleasure of watching her walk away.

CHAPTER SIX

PRESLEY

WHY DID SHE have to invite him? I asked myself this about a hundred times already. The day was flying by too fast. We'd been whisked by limo to the Excelsior with a flurry of mimosas, only to be ushered into the bridal lounge, where a hair and makeup team awaited us. The photographer and Mattie were with us nearly every moment, so it was hard for me to pin Lauren down and find out what in the hell she'd been thinking. It's not like we were really friends with the man. I hadn't seen him in over a decade, and to my knowledge, Lauren hadn't either.

But I never got the chance to ask her, and it was her special day. I didn't want to ruin it. Before the ceremony, I pulled her aside for something unrelated. Things hadn't always been easy with Lauren, and I sure gave her a run for her money when I was a teenager. But she'd seen me through some hard times and was now the only "mother" I could really remember.

"What is it, sweetie?" she asked as I hung back. Mattie shooed everyone else out to get in their procession lineup.

"You look beautiful, Lauren," I said truthfully.

"Thank you, Presley. I know this may be hard on you—"

"It's not. I promise. I know you loved my dad. I wish he were still with us, but he's not. You deserve happiness again."

"Thank you."

Mattie waved from the door for me to hurry up, but I held up a finger to say *hold on*. I turned back to Lauren and held out a piece of blue material.

"What's this?"

"It's a piece of dad's tie. The one he wore at your wedding. He told me that if you were to ever remarry, he wanted me to give it to you as a blessing. Something blue."

Lauren's eyes watered, but she blinked the tears away fast, looking up toward the ceiling. "Can't cry. I cannot cry."

"I'm sorry. I didn't mean to make you sad, Lauren. But I promised him I would give it to you. I know he would approve of Richard. Despite what others may think, I know you love him."

Lauren nodded, biting her lip.

"I'll see you out there?"

She threw her arms around me and gave me a warm, gentle squeeze. "Your dad would be proud of the woman you've become, Presley. It means everything to have you stand up with me for my wedding."

"Of course," I said.

It wasn't until I was in line standing next to a stranger with a receding hairline that it hit me. After this, she would be Lauren Brash. And another part of my dad's memory would be erased.

The soft, melodic sound of a harp let us know it was time. That and Mattie, who was barking out in a hushed stage voice to us, *"Go. You're up next. Walk slow! Go, go, go."*

The man I was paired with smiled down at me. "Ready?"

I nodded, forgetting his name. I'm sure someone told me it at some point. All I knew was it was a brother of Richard's. Luckily, he was married with about eight kids. No weird wedding mishaps to worry about here.

As we walked slowly down the aisle, I noticed there were far more seats filled than last night. There were easily over two hundred people in attendance. Yet, somehow, Lauren and Mattie managed to make it feel intimate. Maybe it was the potted trees that surrounded us, or the walls of climbing flowers. Jumbo-sized pots overflowed with cascades of purple aubrieta. And the candles. They cast a warm, intimate glow over the crowd. I couldn't help but smile.

When I got to the front, the mystery balding guy gently released my arm so I could stand beside Sylvia. We were all in mulberry-colored, one-shoulder dresses. The waists were high, and the asymmetrical chiffon material flowed effortless over the diverse body types of Lauren's six bridesmaids. The strappy, silver, high-heeled sandals were open-toed, and our freshly painted toes matched our dresses perfectly. Mattie hadn't missed a single detail.

When the "Wedding March" started, the room grew quiet. Everyone rose from their seats and turned toward the bride. That is, everyone except Carter. His eyes were on me, and they were even darker and harder to read from this distance. I glanced away, keeping my focus on Lauren. She looked like Aphrodite floating on her wave of sea foam as she sailed down the aisle, radiant on Richard's arm.

When they got to the front, she handed me her bouquet as Mattie had instructed last night. Dex greeted the crowd, but his words faded as I looked down, seeing that Lauren had tucked the piece of dad's blue tie into the handle of her bridal bouquet. I bit my lip, willing myself not to cry.

The ceremony was over before I knew it, loud applause erupting all around me as people whistled and clapped. I looked over and saw Richard dipping Lauren backward into a deep and thorough kiss. I looked away, and unfortunately right into the eyes of the last person I wanted to see.

Carter stood there stoically, his arms clasped in front of him. He looked hotter than sin in a monochrome suit and shirt of the same matching midnight blue. His dark hair was gelled back, and for reasons I didn't want to admit, I ached to kiss those smug lips of his. I licked my lips without even realizing it, unable to look away. I only moved when Sylvia nudged me with her elbow, letting me know it was my turn to head out.

The next few hours went by in a blur as we freshened up, took endless pictures, and headed into the reception area. The sky above was an inky black, and they'd opened the glass roof for the evening. Heaters were staged around the garden, so no one felt the chill on this cold September evening. Guests mingled at a makeshift bar before they opened the dining hall for a full sit-down dinner. Willa was off somewhere, supposedly getting us drinks. But she was a beautiful woman and often got waylaid by well-intentioned men. I shivered, wrapping a light shawl around my shoulders as I huddled next to one of the tall heaters.

"Cold, princess?"

I turned, wishing it were anyone other than Carter. I hated to admit it, but it was torture seeing him again after all these years. The man had aged ridiculously well, making it even worse. He'd been fit at seventeen with washboard abs from surfing and hours of hard labor. But now? He'd not only gotten taller, but he'd filled out. His arms were much larger than I remembered. His shoulders too.

"No," I lied, gratefully accepting the tall flute of champagne he handed me. "Just enjoying the view." I looked up at the night sky, and a few stars winked back at me. "So, you actually came. I wasn't sure you were going to show up."

"Now why would I miss something as big as this?" he asked. "Besides, I couldn't pass up a chance to see Dex marry his first couple. Now that was something!"

I grinned. That was a sweet thing of Dex to do for Lauren and Richard. Even though he was important and busy with Montague Enterprises, he was never too busy for a friend. It was inspiring, really. Bianca was a lucky woman.

"You think he'll ever do it again?"

"Never say never," Carter said and shrugged. "Maybe he can do your wedding next."

"Don't hold your breath," I said, laughing.

He cocked his head and examined my face, his dark eyes drinking me in. I felt so uncomfortable under the scrutiny of his gaze. No—not uncomfortable. Vulnerable.

"So, what? You're telling me little Miss Moneybags doesn't have a boyfriend, then?"

God! I hated when he called me that. "I'm too busy for a relationship right now, Carter," I snapped. "My career keeps me busy."

"Which is what?"

"I write for the *Finance Times*."

"Isn't that cute," he said. "You're a journalist."

"I'll have you know I graduated at the top of my class with a double major in finance and international business." I don't know why I felt the need to justify myself. Well, yes, I did. It was Carter. And I'd spent many years trying to impress him and get him to notice me. Old habits die hard, I guess.

"What about you?" I tossed back. "What did Mister Stand-In do before he was arm candy?"

Carter smirked, and I wanted to wipe that damn smug look off his face. "Does it matter what I did before?" he asked. "I'm here now."

"So, who was it tonight?" I asked, looking around. "Which one of these lucky ladies gets an evening with the much-desired Carter Wright?"

"That would be you, princess."

CHAPTER SEVEN

CARTER

PAYCHECK OR NOT, the look on Presley's face was worth it. She sputtered prettily, then narrowed her eyes at me.

"You're barking up the wrong tree, Wright. I don't need a stand-in for anything," she said suggestively.

"That's not what *she* said."

I thought Presley might actually slap me. If I were being completely honest, it kind of turned me on. I chuckled as she opened and closed her mouth, debating on how to retaliate. But the "she" in question joined Presley at her side, wrapping an arm around her waist.

"There you are! I've been looking all over for you," Lauren said. "We're about to line up to enter the dining hall for dinner. Come," she said, reaching out for my hand and pulling the two of us along with her.

"Wait," Presley said, stopping in her tracks. "Why is he coming with us?"

"Because, he's sitting with you at the head table, darling."

Presley's eyes darted between mine and Lauren's and the tick in her jaw was absolutely adorable. "And *why* would Carter be sitting with the wedding party?"

"Because I invited him. PJ had to head home. He and his family have a long flight back to Amsterdam."

"Who the hell is PJ?"

"Seriously, Presley. Do you read any of the emails I send you? All of this was outlined by Mattie in the bridal party memo I forwarded weeks ago. We were lucky he could make it at all, but the finance meeting made that possible. Now, with him heading home this evening, it leaves us with a dreadful hole in the table seating arrangement. And Carter was gracious enough to fill in as your date so the tables wouldn't look all lopsided in pictures," she said, wrinkling her nose as if that offense were too distasteful to bear.

"So, let me get this straight. You *hired* me a date, so *you* wouldn't feel embarrassed about what others think if I happen to be sitting without a partner by my side? Does my singleness offend you that much, Lauren? And why didn't I get a say in any of this? If I knew I *needed* to bring a date, I would have!"

"Presley, this is very unbecoming of you. It's Carter we're talking about, not some random stranger. You two practically grew up together."

Presley threw up her hands, her exasperation bubbling over and getting the best of her.

"And for the record, Carter offered to do this for *free*, as a wedding gift."

"Oh, well wasn't that charitable of him," she said, glaring at me. "Couldn't you have just bought her a crystal vase like a normal person?"

I laughed hard. "Come on, Presley. I'm not *that* bad to walk in with, am I? Aren't you the one who called me 'arm candy?'"

I swear I heard her snarl under her breath.

"Fine," she said, "but I am not dancing with you. This is not a date. This is us sitting and eating side by side. Understood?"

Lauren glanced between us, a satisfied smile on her face. "There. Now that wasn't so hard, was it? Chin up when we walk in. Act like you like each other. And smile, for heaven's sake, Presley. Pictures last forever."

We lined up with the rest of the wedding party in pairs of two, and our names were announced as we entered the dining hall. All other guests had already been seated at their assigned tables. The room was awash with a warm, golden tone from the candlelight, and a mixture of white and saturated purple flowers spilled from tabletops, fireplaces, and large floor urns. The dance floor's smooth, dark surface beckoned me, and I knew, without a doubt, that I was getting a dance in with little Miss Moneybags before the night was through.

I offered her my arm, and for a minute, I didn't think she'd take it. Then she glanced up, saw Lauren, and sighed as she slid her hand around my arm. It was the first time we'd touched as adults, outside of me pulling her ponytail. I think she was as surprised as I was by the feel of her fingers on my arm. Even through my dress shirt and jacket, I could *feel* her energy. Her fingers felt *right* the way they fit around my arm. I pulled her a little tighter to my side, curious how *more* would feel.

I nearly groaned at her closeness. How was bratty, little Presley Kincaid stirring up these kinds of feelings? She smelled like champagne bubbles and springtime, her scent far lighter and more favorable than Lauren's.

"Come on, Mister Stand-In. We're up," she muttered.

We stepped into the room to the sound of the DJ's deep, melodic voice saying, "Mister Carter Wright and Miss Presley Kincaid."

That's when the photographer stepped in front of us for a quick picture of us walking in. I didn't have time to think. In fact, I didn't think at all.

I spun Presley around, wrapped my arm under her, and dipped her back as my lips found hers. The entire room broke out in applause as I kissed that sassy mouth of hers. I knew I'd pay for it later, but when she relaxed against me, and her lips parted, I knew it would be worth the cost.

And I had no doubt she'd make me pay.

CHAPTER EIGHT

PRESLEY

"WHAT IN THE hell was that?" I fumed to Willa later. We'd found a small area within the garden that had a bench, a fountain, and best of all—privacy.

"It was hot, that's what it was!" Willa said, laughing. She took a puff of a small cigar someone had handed us. She offered it to me, and I wrinkled my nose. "Guess he's more take-chargey than you thought."

"That wasn't being in charge, Willa. That was arrogance again! He knew I was stewing, and he took that opportunity when I couldn't very well make a scene to catch me off guard. But what's his end game? I don't get it."

"Maybe his end game is you," Willa said simply, blowing cherry-scented smoke into the air.

"I'm pretty sure you're not supposed to be smoking in here," I said.

"Presley, loosen up. This is a Kincaid/Brash wedding. There's not a person in the Excelsior who will say no to anything we want to do tonight. I bet we could strip butt naked and dance a conga line down the hallways and they'd ask if there was anything else we needed."

I chuckled. She was right.

"Sooo?" she said, letting the OOOs do the talking.

I knew damn well what she was asking, but there was no way I'd admit what that simple kiss did to me. Grown-ass women with master's degrees and financial minds didn't get weak in the knees, or feel "butterflies," or actually *swoon*— ack!—when a man kissed them. I hadn't in twenty-five years. And I certainly wasn't going to let one tiny, delicious, tantalizing kiss ruin my track record.

"It was okay," I lied, shrugging. "It happened so fast I hardly had time to experience it. Maybe I should call him Mister Slip-In instead, since he just slipped right by me and stole that damn kiss."

I huffed, not realizing what was so funny until I looked over at Willa. She was clutching her sides and laughing hysterically. "What?"

"Mister Slip-In? Really, Presley? Mister Slip-In?" Willa wiped a tear from the corner of her eye. "That sounds X-rated, if you ask me."

"What? No—that's not what I meant. Eww . . ."

"Mmm-hmm," she said, pursing her full, purple lips together. She snuffed out the cigar in a discrete bin near the bench and looked me dead in the eye. "I know when you're lying, Presley. You forget how long we've been friends. All I know is that man gave you one little peck and your mind is already in the gutter. I see where this is headed. I think you need to scratch this itch, girl. You know—get him out of your system."

"Oh, my god! Willa! This is not headed anywhere. It was a peck. Not even worth all those childhood fantasies."

"Liar," she said as we headed back to the reception. A waiter walked by, and she gracefully lifted two champagne flutes from the tray and handed me one. "To many more nights of X-rated shenanigans with Mister Slip-In."

"Willa!" I hissed. But I couldn't help but laugh. I lifted the glass to my lips and swallowed, knowing I really needed to get back to the party. They would be cutting the cake soon, and if I missed that, I'd never hear the end of it from Lauren.

"Excuse me, ladies," I heard from behind us. I turned and found Carter leaning against a wall, his eyes glued to mine. "Mind if I steal your friend for a bit?"

"No—"

"Absolutely! I was just going to find my dance partner anyway," Willa said over me. "Meet you on the dance floor later?"

With that, she was gone, leaving me alone with Carter— the man who slipped in and stole the first kiss I'd waited twelve years to get from him. I wasn't sure if I could forgive him.

"What do you want now, Carter?" I asked and sighed. My feet were tired from running around in my strappy, four-inch heels. I bent down and tried unfastening one, eager to take them off.

"Here, let me," Carter said, surprising me. Damn if the man didn't take a knee and start unfastening my sandal.

His dark brown hair was slightly tousled, and for the first time I noticed how big his hands were. They were strong, capable hands—tempting me with their skill as he lightly brushed his fingers over my calf. He let my foot down gently and started on the other shoe. I had to close my eyes and bite the inside of my cheek. Seeing Carter on the ground like that in front of me brought all kinds of naughty scenarios into my head. Maybe Willa was right.

My eyes were still closed when he stood up in front of me, his body way closer than necessary. "Presley," he whispered, "open your eyes."

What? I blinked, looking up into eyes I could lose myself in for days on end.

"Here," he said.

Hmm?

"Here, what?" I asked, mesmerized by the way his lips were formed. The way his teeth were near blinding they were so white. What would he taste like? If I just ran my tongue over those lips, past those teeth and really *tasted* him?

"Your shoes," he said lightly.

Oh, right. My shoes.

I took them from his outstretched finger that they dangled from by their long, complicated straps. When I did, he grabbed my wrist and pulled me closer, until I was flush against his chest. My breathing accelerated, and I wasn't sure how to react. Should I joke and push off him? Close my eyes and let him kiss me again?

He put his hand under my chin and lifted it, forcing me to look at him. "You think too much, princess. Has anyone ever told you that?"

All the time.

"What are you doing, Carter? Ha-ha. It was very funny to catch me off guard and embarrass me like that in front of a room full of people earlier. You got me. But the party's almost over, you'll get paid, and you'll never have to see me again."

"Is that what you think I want?"

His voice was low, and it pooled warm in my belly. I bit my lip, daring to meet his eyes. "I don't know what you want. We're not kids any more. But you certainly never wanted me then. I know you had a crush on Lauren—everybody knew that."

His silence told me what I suspected. His jaw clenched, and he pulled me even closer. "You were only thirteen then, Presley. Thirteen. But you're not anymore," he said huskily. "And Lauren has nothing to do with this, princess."

"Stop calling me that!" I finally huffed.

He chuckled, and I could feel the vibration through my chest. What would his skin feel like if I just placed my hand on his shirt, under his open collar?

"Thank god we're not kids anymore."

"Why?" I croaked.

"Because back then, I couldn't do this," he said.

His hand wrapped around my neck and cupped the back of my head, sending goose bumps racing across my arms. The shawl I had earlier long disappeared at some table or another. His other hand trailed up and down my bare skin, making the goose bumps worse, not better. Then his head dropped, and I was ready this time.

My pride wanted me to turn my head, give him my cheek. But my heart had other ideas, giving over to the soft sweep of Carter's warm lips. I may have moaned as his mouth brushed mine again, his tongue making slow, confident strokes and wetting my lips. I parted them, giving him permission this time. I heard the low chuckle as his hand tightened on my neck. That small act skipped right over goose bumps and sent tsunamis of lust straight to my lady bits. My hands snaked up under his coat until they found his waist. I clung to his belt as he deepened the kiss, this time pressing his tongue forward and searching out mine. He tasted like whiskey, warmth, and bad decisions. I knew I should push him away, leave it at one kiss, and be grateful I even got that after all these years.

But I couldn't.

I wanted more of Carter now that I'd tasted him. My hands slid up his strong back, running my fingers over his dress shirt and moaning into his mouth as he owned me—literally owned me—with his lips, his tongue, his hands in my hair. Then the kiss slowed, his warm tongue sensuously teasing mine, giving my bottom lip a sexy tug that made me want to do very naughty things.

But he gripped my hands and pulled them out from under his coat and backed up, putting a little distance between us. Confused, I looked up at him, in a daze of lust as memories swirled together in my mind. The sun-kissed skin of his youth, all bronze and wet with humidity. Watching the strength in his legs, torso, and back as he surfed near the cove. Listening to him laugh with his friends as they built some of the newer houses, getting all hot and sweaty under the strong Carolina sun.

He was still gripping my hands, holding them together between our bodies. Our breath rose and fell together.

"Presley—"

"Wow. I can't believe I just did that," I said, trying to back up. I'd practically thrown myself at him the minute he gave me the time of day. What was I thinking? "Look, Carter, I gotta go. I have to get back to the party."

"Fuck the party, Presley," he growled.

"No. I can't," I said, touching my swollen lips. They still tingled and tasted of Carter and whiskey.

"We're not done with this, Presley," he said low.

"There is no this, Carter. It was just a kiss. Right?"

I backed away, not waiting for his answer. It would be easier to walk away now after just one kiss than to let this slow burn catch fire.

I knew, with every ounce of my being that if I let Carter in, I would go up in flames in no time. And if being rejected by Carter as a kid was tough . . . Well, I wouldn't take that risk again.

Not even for a first kiss that made my legs buckle and butterflies take flight in my belly.

CHAPTER NINE

CARTER

"YOU ALL RIGHT, man?" Dex asked. I was at the bar staring into my tumbler, swishing the liquid around. I wasn't going to find what was making me thirsty in a glass.

"How well do you know Presley?" I asked.

His silence was deafening. I could feel his eyes taking inventory before he cleared his throat and finally answered. "I've known the family for some time. How come?"

"Because the last time I saw Presley Kincaid, I was seventeen. It was my last summer at The Grove. She was skinny, had braces, and was annoying as hell," I said, taking a sip.

"And now?"

"Well, she's still annoying," I said. "But she certainly grew up."

"So, what's the problem?"

"She was thirteen that summer, Dex. But I'd seen her around the resort since she was just a kid. Seven maybe. She was just an annoying brat who seemed to show up wherever I went. Remember the summer you came to visit with your folks? It was my last summer there, and you were older than me. I looked up to you so much. You were so much cooler than I was. I barely had my shit together."

"That was a fun summer," Dex said, chuckling. "We got into some good trouble."

"Yeah," I said. "I was a punk back then, Dex, but I knew my place. All summer long that year Presley tried to make small talk with me. I was polite, but she really had some sass, you know? I was trying to be all cool around you and the guys, and I had this scrawny girl following me around with moony eyes. All the guys gave me shit for it."

I shook my head. "I knew she was into me. It was pretty freaking obvious. But she was thirteen, Dex. Even if she'd been a local, I wouldn't have touched her with a ten-foot pole. She still wore her hair in those damn braids. Do you remember those?"

I groaned, my mind swapping the memory of her back then with the woman Presley was today—wishing I could be so lucky to see her in a bikini and braids again.

Dex laughed. "I'm guessing you don't see her as an awkward thirteen-year-old kid anymore?"

"How could I? She's a freaking bombshell. All that soft, shiny hair. And those sexy green eyes. Christ." I ran a hand over my face. "Did you ever know I had a crush on Lauren when I was a teenager?"

Dex's eyes bulged wide as he gaped at me. "Lauren Kincaid? No shit. Is that why you got so weird when I asked you to stand in for Richard?"

I nodded. "Presley wasn't even on my mind when I said yes. I honestly forgot all about her—didn't think she might've actually grown up and grown into herself. I was just thinking about Lauren. How fucked up is that?"

Dex chuckled. "It's not. Not really. I mean—Lauren has always been hot. Some might say she's a little old for you, but I can't say I blame you." Dex nodded toward the dance floor where Lauren and Richard were slow dancing. Her body sensually swayed from side to side, her whole back bare in her wedding dress. We could see the muscles in her shoulders and the definition in her upper arms as they draped around Richard's shoulders. She pulled his head down and whispered something so private in his ear that when he looked up, his face looked as if it was on fire. Lucky bastard.

"Here's to Lauren and Richard," I said, raising my glass to clink against Dex's beer bottle. "And to looking forward, not back."

THE PARTY WAS winding down. When Dex and Bianca said their goodbyes, I was ready to call it a night too. I'd met several new prospective clients, and already had four jobs booked over the winter. But that's not what made the wedding worthwhile.

Presley had taken me completely by surprise. That kiss on our entrance? Completely spontaneous and impulsive. Yeah, it was a jerk thing to do. I'd be in her stepmom's wedding album forever now—our kiss sealed in time. That peck was supposed to put Presley in her place and nothing more. Instead, it fanned something inside of me. And I didn't know why. I'd never thought of Presley this way before. Not ever.

But after that kiss in the garden. . . all I wanted to do was find her again, pin her up against the wall, and drop to my knees. I could still smell her on my clothes. Light, citrusy, sexual. She was so sassy and bratty when she was a kid—trying to run with the older local boys on the island. She never wanted to hang out with the girls who came with their parents, and she always managed to get under my skin somehow.

Twelve years later, and she was under my skin again. Only this time, for very different reasons. I had two choices. I could write Presley off forever, just as I had to write Lauren off. Or I could go find her. Take another taste. See if she was worth taking home.

I drained the rest of my glass and stood up, determined to find her. But she was literally nowhere to be seen. I walked the gardens, checked the dance floor, scoured the bars. I was ready to throw in the towel and leave when Willa staggered from the kitchen, one of her long braids coming loose from the intricate updo she was rocking.

"Hey, Willa," I said as she passed by. She hadn't seen me, so she stopped, trying to focus on me. "Are you *drunk*?"

She giggled. "I might be. Maybe. Just a little."

"Can I get you a ride home?"

"Oh, you're such a gentleman, aren't you, Carter?" At least, I think that's what she said. Her words were a little slurred. "Look. I have to go to the little girl's room. Would you be a doll and go check on Pres?"

"Uh, sure," I said, looking around. "And she'd be where, exactly?"

"Oh," Willa said, laughing again. She pointed to the double doors she'd just exited, then stumbled toward the ladies room.

Oh boy. I just hoped Presley wasn't in as bad of shape. When I pushed through the swinging doors, there she was, sitting on a kitchen prep table, her chiffon dress hiked up around her knees. She had a cigar dangling between her lips and a set of cards in her hands.

"Uno!" she called out triumphantly.

A guy in a white kitchen uniform and a high-and-tight buzz cut swore and drew a card. There were five people playing, and a dozen beer bottles lining the counter behind the sink. Presley laughed when she saw he didn't get the card he wanted and had to take a swig from a communal bottle of tequila I just now noticed.

Two others laid their cards down, then looked at Presley expectantly. She still hadn't noticed my arrival. Her strawberry blond curls had come undone from the fancy half-updo she'd had earlier. Her rhinestone hair comb was sitting on the table in a pile with about fifty dollars in cash, a watch, and a pack of Reese's Peanut Butter cups.

I didn't dare ask.

I leaned against the wall and crossed my arms, enjoying this new side of Presley I'd never seen before. She was cutting loose and having fun! Presley threw down her last card—which looked like a Wild card, meaning there was no way she could've lost—and she hollered. She stood on the table and I noticed she'd never put her strappy, sexy sandals back on. She was barefoot and happy as she tossed back the tequila bottle and took a victory guzzle.

"Presley! Presley! Presley!" they all chanted. She laughed, tequila dribbling down her chin as she spun in a circle with her arms out. Then she saw me. I ran over just in time. She wobbled, off balance from the spin, and started to fall. I caught her in my outstretched arms like she was a sack of flour someone just tossed to me. She threw her head back and laughed wickedly. I wanted nothing more in that moment than to lick the tequila off her chin and plunge my tongue into her sexy mouth, muffling her laughter and turning it into a pleasurable moan. She was so dangerously sexy like this.

"Come on, princess. You've had too much to drink."

"Boo!" the others shouted at my retreating form.

"Yeah, yeah," I muttered, not giving a shit that I was taking their fun-time girl from them. "Where are you staying tonight?"

"Willa and I . . . we got a room together. I think. Where's Willa?" she asked, looking around. "Willa!" she called out louder.

"Shh!" I said. "Your mother will kill you if she finds you like this."

"She's not my *muther*," she slurred. "She's my stepmom. So it's okay if you liked her, too. Right? It's not like it was my *mom*," she over emphasized, laughing hysterically against my chest. Oh boy. This was gonna be a long night.

"I don't *like* Lauren, princess." I sighed. "Willa is in the restroom, I think. Want to go get her?"

"You can't go in the ladies room!" she chortled. "Hey, do you know your five o'clock shadow overslept?" She rubbed my jaw. "It's half past ten already." Then she dissolved into a fit of giggles again.

Thankfully, Willa came out of the bathroom just then. "Presley! I was looking all over for you!"

No, she wasn't. She'd been in the bathroom. I wanted to roll my eyes and was seriously doubting my sanity. How in the world did I end up with a drunk Presley in my arms at almost one o'clock in the morning? And it wasn't even in a *good* way.

"We need to go back to the room," Presley said. She bucked her body in my arms. "Giddy up!"

Willa snickered. "Nah, girl, I'm headed home tonight."

I shook my head. "No. No way. You are too drunk, Willa."

"Take it easy, *Dad*," she said. "My roommate is here. See?" She pointed into the reception area, and I saw a young lady grinding up against an older man on the dance floor.

"You sure she's going to your place tonight?" I asked, skeptically.

"For sure," Willa said. "I pinky promise."

She reached out her pinky and stared at me. "Go ahead," she said, nodding toward her finger.

I had no clue what in the hell she was doing.

"Just wrap your pinky around hers. It's a binding oath she can never break," Presley said solemnly. *Oh, Christ.*

I wrapped my pinky around hers and "shook." She pulled a key card from her clutch and handed it to me. "We're in room 1111. Oh, and guess what?"

"What?" I asked, losing patience. Not to mention Presley was now running her fingers over my ears and it was hella distracting.

"It's on the eleventh floor," Willa said, laughing hysterically.

"Thanks, Willa. I think we'll be able to find it."

"Take care of my girl, okay? No monkey business. She doesn't need you to break her heart again."

Huh?

"I mean it, Mister Slip-In. No slipping it in tonight, got it?"

"Oh my god, Willa!" Presley said, suddenly aware of her friend again. "Go!"

I burst out laughing and glanced down at Presley. Her legs dangled over one of my arms, and her back rested against the other. Her one-shoulder dress covered her cleavage tonight, and I could feel the warmth from her body as she curled into me.

I made sure Willa made it back into the reception area. When she was successfully with her roommate, I made toward the elevator.

"If I set you down, can you stand?" I asked as we entered the small space.

"Hmmm?" she said, eyes closed, half asleep.

"Never mind."

We got off on the eleventh floor and it was completely silent in the hallway. Thank goodness she'd closed her eyes in my arms and wasn't still hollering it up at the top of her lungs like a sorority girl gone wild.

Somehow, I managed to get the keycard in the door without banging her head into it and pushed it open with my dress shoe. It was late, and I still had to catch a ride home. My jaw dropped when I entered the massive suite. This wasn't a "room." It was bigger than most of my old apartments. The walls were painted rich, matte black, and large crystal chandeliers were scattered throughout the space. The sitting area had two trendy, low-back sofas, a conversation set of chairs, a dining table, and finally, a stunning set of gold, highly arched French doors leading to the bedroom. I hoped. The walls were ornate with woodwork and on the opposite end of the room were floor-to-ceiling windows that ate up the entire wall.

Fuck. Presley really was Miss Moneybags if she could afford a suite at the Excelsior for the night. It made me wonder if Lauren and Richard were staying here, and if so, what the presidential suite looked like.

The sleeping area was at least painted a more muted tone, but the headboard was a rich, tufted gray monstrosity that reached all the way to the ceiling. The bottom of the bed was black, as were the two leather sitting benches at the foot of the bed, and the low-back sofa facing the wraparound windows. Presley's bedroom was on a corner, which would let in beautiful daylight in the morning. Right now, the bright lights of New York's skyline twinkled all around us.

I laid Presley gently on the bed, realizing she was already sound asleep in my arms. When I tried untangling myself, she nuzzled in closer, wrapping her arms around my neck. "Stay," she whispered.

Dear god, help me.

"Pres—"

There was no way I was staying with her in this condition. She was too vulnerable and too . . . nuzzley. I wasn't a strong man. And it was bad enough I'd stolen our first kiss. There was no way our first fuck would be one where she was loaded and wouldn't remember it in the morning. No, if I were to take Presley to bed, I would mark my territory, and she would remember every fucking second of it. That was for damn sure.

"Just hold me, then? While I fall asleep?"

I sighed. How could I say no when she asked me so nicely? I gently ran my hand over her hair, letting my fingers trail over the small of her back, until she finally fell asleep. I must have accidentally dozed off, too, because when I woke, my arm had fallen asleep from the weight of Presley curled over it, and she was snoring lightly. Somehow, she made even sleeping and snoring look cute.

I eased my arm out and held my breath. When she didn't wake, I walked over to the blinds and closed them, then found a pad of paper and scrawled a note so she didn't panic in the morning. I got a glass of water and left it on the bedside, along with two Excedrin I found in the bathroom.

I glanced back at Presley before I left, unsure how I'd been so confused about being around Lauren just the night before. Now, here I was, sneaking out of Presley's hotel room at three in the morning, feeling like she had me wrapped around her finger already.

I knew I shouldn't have taken this damn job.

CHAPTER TEN

PRESLEY

MY TONGUE STUCK to the roof of my mouth and I licked my lips. Where the heck was I? I sat up straight, then lay right back down. The room was still spinning. What time was it? And where was Willa? I glanced around, seeing I was still in my bridesmaid dress. *Crap!* Did I leave my makeup on too? Why couldn't I remember getting back and into bed? I guess I should count my lucky stars I wasn't naked with a stranger lying next to me.

I glanced at the bedside table, seeing a glass of water and two Excedrin there. From Willa? That was sweet. I took a greedy swallow of water, thankful to get some of the sticky taste from my mouth. What all did I drink again? I took the Excedrin and lay back down. I'd figure it out later.

When I woke for the second time, the room was still dark, the heavy black-out curtains closed tight. But I could see thin slivers of light around the edges, so I knew it was time to get up. I looked around the room for my purse, or my phone. I found neither and cursed silently. Did I leave it downstairs? *Crap!*

That's when it all came flooding back to me.

Carter Wright.

I'd actually kissed Carter. Then I panicked. And Willa and I went into the kitchen to say hello to her friend, Rack. A bottle of tequila came out, we started playing Uno, and then—I was dancing. I won! I remember looking up into Carter's eyes. I was in his arms last night. *Oh crap!* It was bad enough I'd kissed him back in the garden and was almost ready to take him home. But if I'd been that drunk . . . what had I said? Done?

I rolled over and pulled the cover over my head, burrowing under the soft, down comforter. Then I remembered feeling his lips warm on my temple and him gently rubbing my hair as I fell asleep.

A shrill ring had me throwing the heavy cover off and sitting straight up in bed. I reached over and grabbed the white, scrolled handle of the old-fashioned telephone. "Hello?"

"Good morning, Miss Kincaid. This is the wakeup call you requested."

I had? I had! Oh, shit! I had to get home and finish an article for work. *Why did I drink so much?* Oh, yeah. Carter.

"Thank you. Can I please have breakfast sent up?"

"Absolutely. The usual?"

"Yes, please."

"Would it be acceptable for us to send up your things from last night, as well?"

"Please," I said gratefully, hoping one of those items was my clutch, and that the other was my phone.

"It's our pleasure. Will there be anything else?"

"What time is it, again?" I asked, groaning.

"It's ten thirty, ma'am."

"Thank you. Can you have a car pick me up at noon, please?"

"Certainly. Have an exceptional day, Miss Kincaid."

Exceptional? The only exceptional thing I'd be doing is nursing this hangover and crying over my regret from the night before. That, and maybe eating a pint of Ben & Jerry's Chocolate Fudge Brownie ice cream once I got home.

I made my way toward the large walk-in shower and peeled off my bridesmaid dress on the way there. When I was done, I quickly dressed and packed my belongings while waiting for room service. That's when I spotted a note in neat, slanted handwriting.

Presley,

I hope you don't wake up too hungover. Don't worry. I didn't take advantage of you. 😌 When I last saw you at The Grove, you were upset with me because I wouldn't give you your first kiss. I'm still glad I didn't. (I mean, then you would've been pining over me for the past decade!)

Well . . . it was worth the wait. But for some reason, you didn't seem any less upset afterward. I know. It took me by surprise too.

Kissing you was the last thing in the world I imagined doing, Presley. But now that I have, it's the only thing in the world I want to do again.

So now it's your turn, I guess. You can either chalk this up to a mistake or call me. We can't change the past. Don't be mad at me for the punk I was as teenager. Or for my schoolboy crush on Lauren. I was just a dumb kid. And I promise, you'll like this guy better.

I pinky promise to stop being an arrogant asshat if you pinky promise to put away the boxing gloves. Because I want to see you again. Taste you again. Taste you more. Soon.

You have my number. (See it? There below?) I'm leaving whatever this is, or whatever this could be, in your court. Besides, I play a mean game of Uno myself. Let's make it a date?

XO, Mister Stand-In

Was this for real? My hands shook as I reread his letter again. The kiss *had* caught me off guard. One minute I wanted to smack that damn cocky smirk off his face, and the next I wanted to devour his mouth whole, investigating every inch of it. Tracing his lips with my tongue. It's what I'd always wanted, right? But maybe he was right. Thirteen was a long time ago. Would I have even appreciated or understood a kiss like that at thirteen? Not if I could hardly wrap my head around it now at twenty-five.

I set the letter back down only when room service knocked at the door. I gladly accepted and devoured breakfast, texting Willa that I *had* to talk to her ASAP. Though, if I knew my friend, she wouldn't be rising from the dead until well after noon. The car ride home was short, which only gave me time to worry over the kiss . . . and Carter's note. I *had* to talk to someone.

When I got home, I called Bianca.

"Hey, girl!" she said cheerfully. I could hear the clatter of dishes behind her and a warbly, off-key rendition of a Disney song.

"Oh, hey. Did I catch you at a bad time?" I asked, laughing.

The warbler was Georgie, and she was belting out "Into the Unknown" from *Frozen 2* as if she were auditioning for the *X Factor*.

"Nope. Not at all," Bianca said, with all the calm and confidence of a seasoned pro. "Just finished loading the dishwasher. Let me find somewhere quiet where we can talk. Hang on."

She closed a door and then released a hefty sigh. "Ah! It feels so good to sit down. My feet are killing me after dancing in those heels last night!"

I laughed, knowing exactly how she felt.

"It was a beautiful wedding, don't you think?" she asked.

It had been. I knew I should be more focused on my stepmom's happiness than my own. But I never thought I'd see Carter again, let alone twice in one week. And I certainly didn't expect the attraction to be tenfold. If I thought he'd been cute as a teenager, I would have melted over the man he'd grown into.

"It really was. Lauren seemed . . . content. It makes me happy to know she was able to find love again."

"It's the happiest I've seen her in a long time," Bianca admitted. "Who knew Richard had that in him?"

Then I really belly laughed. "Don't get me started on that," I said. "My mind just *cannot* go there."

"So, what's going on? Are you calling about the new article Sylvia has for you?"

Umm . . . "What new article?"

"Oh. Shit. She didn't find you last night? She said she would."

"Not as far as I can remember," I said. "Do you want to tell me what it's about?"

"Why don't you go first," she said. "Pleasure before business. I want to hear the good stuff. Speaking of good stuff—I saw you and Carter chatting it up a few times."

"Ugh!" I moaned. "That's why I'm calling."

"Well, that certainly doesn't sound like a good thing. Everything okay?"

"Yes. No. I don't know," I admitted. "I knew Carter when we were younger. From The Grove. My dad, Lauren, and I used to vacation there every summer for almost an entire month."

I closed my eyes and saw Carter's arrogant grin. Remembered the way the muscles of his back felt under my hands when we kissed. Even the sound of "princess" as it rolled off his tongue made weird things happen to my body.

"We kissed," I blurted out.

"Wait, what? When? Last night?"

"Yep."

"You mean, other than the smooch he laid on you when he dipped you on your entrance?" she teased. I would never live that one down thanks to Carter.

"Yeah," I said quietly. "I'm not sure how it happened. I— there was tension between Carter and me from when we were kids. And we were at each other all night. When we bumped into each other in the garden . . . I don't know. It was like he was baiting me one second, and then kissing me the next."

"Sounds like tension, all right," she said. "The best kind. So, was it as good as you suspected?"

"Better!" I groaned, making it sound like that was the worst thing in the world.

"So, what's the problem? You gonna see him again?"

"I don't know. It's just—weird. He used to have a crush on Lauren when he was a teenager. That's kind of weird, right?"

"Not really. Most boys fantasize about beautiful, older women who are out of reach. He doesn't *still* have feelings, does he?"

"I don't think so," I said. "He wants to see me again."

"That's great! Sounds like there's no reason to make it an issue then."

"I suppose."

"Am I missing something?"

"No. Maybe." I bit my lip. It was one thing to admit this to Willa, but another thing all together to say it to Bianca. "When we were younger, I asked him to be my first kiss."

"Oh, no!" Bianca said, chuckling sympathetically. "And was he?"

"No. That's the problem. I felt like such a fool. I was thirteen and he was almost eighteen. But I was so sure he *saw* me, despite all his goofy friends mocking him about me. I guess that rejection hurt more than I realized. That and feeling like I didn't quite measure up to Lauren all these years."

"Oh, Presley, those are two separate things. His being a horny teenager and fantasizing about Lauren had nothing to do with your worth. And his saying no to your first kiss was noble, in my opinion."

"How so?" It sure didn't feel noble.

"You were thirteen, Pres. He was older, and probably more experienced. It would've been easy to take advantage of that—especially if you were making your intentions known. Some boys would've. But trust me when I say, back then, it would've crossed a line. Especially with his father working at the resort. That age difference is nothing though, now that you're both consenting adults."

I sighed, knowing she had a point. But I'd felt so grown up at thirteen. I was traveled. I'd survived the loss of my mother. I had even seen a naked boy already by then (though he didn't know that!). I *felt* ready to be kissed by Carter. There hadn't been a single thing I didn't like about him then—except for the fact that he wouldn't give me the time of day.

"I guess it's silly to hold on to something that happened so long ago. You're right. He's a grown-ass man now. And I—I'm completely different now, too. "

"Maybe you owe it to yourself to find out?"

"You're right. Maybe I can find a reason to see him again. See if it was just the champagne, or if the chemistry was real."

"Well," Bianca said dramatically, "I *may* have a chance to make that happen."

"Bianca?"

"Hear me out. Remember that article I mentioned?"

"Yeah?"

"Well, you'll want to get the specifics from Sylvia, but she mentioned last night that she had a brilliant idea for a 'rags to riches' article to publish online."

"And?"

"And apparently Lauren asked Sylvia to do a piece on Carter. You know—because he didn't come from much, even though his dad works for one of the most prestigious resorts in the southeast. He rose up from next to nothing, graduated college, went on to join the military—"

"He was in the military?"

"Yep. Then he came to New York and started his business—Mister Stand-In. He keeps a small, wealthy clientele, and that business model seems to work for him. He's estimated to be a millionaire already, and he hasn't even turned thirty yet. The *Finance Times* is doing its biannual feature on the top thirty millionaires under thirty and what makes them so successful. And Sylvia wants you to write a featured article about Carter for this."

"I can't do it, Bianca. Especially not now. It's a conflict of interest."

"Not if you do the interview first—before you get too involved. I can attest to that," she said, chuckling.

I bit my lip. Could I actually do this? "Why is he on the list though? If his company is privately held, how did he make such a prestigious list?"

"Well," Bianca hedged, "it probably had something to do with Lauren cornering Sylvia last night at the reception. Who knows? It doesn't matter, though, because he deserves to be on that list."

I dropped my head to my hands. A few days ago, Carter Wright wasn't even on my mind. Now, he was showing up everywhere, and . . . *complicating* things.

"This will be a huge billing for your resume, Presley. Your first full-feature online article. When Sylvia asks, just be prepared. This is a make-it-or-break-it career move. Do the story, then if you're still interested, pursue the guy."

"Was that what you did? With Dex?"

Bianca chuckled. "Not exactly. Though I tried to stay as neutral as possible until the article was published. For journalistic integrity. But I'd be lying if I didn't admit that my interest had been *more* than piqued beforehand. Like the time he sent me a pic of him half naked and stretched out on his bed. Man," she said, whistling. "To be fair, though, I didn't know it was Dex at the time."

"Maybe more than I needed to hear," I said truthfully. Dex was like a big brother to me. Yeah, he was attractive. But no. Just no. The problem was, as soon as she said it, all I could imagine was seeing Carter lying in bed, half naked, looking at me with those soulful brown eyes of his.

"Okay, well I guess I'll wait to hear from Sylvia, then decide how to proceed." It was all I could do. I'd waited over a decade for Carter Wright. If I needed to write this piece, he could wait a few more weeks for me.

"Keep me posted, okay?"

"Will do. And Bianca?"

"Yeah?"

"Thanks."

"No problem, P. I've been there. I know how conflicted you feel. I believe everything will work out as it's meant to."

"Yeah, me too," I said before hanging up.

I'm not sure who I was trying to convince though.

CHAPTER ELEVEN

CARTER

KARMA'S A BITCH, plain and simple. Waiting for Presley to call was the worst form of torture. I'd never once in my life waited by the phone for any woman. Yet I couldn't stop from checking my screen every thirty minutes or so.

I went and walked Baby Yoda on my own, since Dex had a fire he had to put out at work, what with Richard gone on his honeymoon. I only had one gig this week, and it was an easy one. I was accompanying a rising new painter to her first gallery opening, so she had someone by her side. We'd already been introduced through a friend of a friend, so it wouldn't feel awkward or look like it was our first time being together. Hopefully, it would feel more natural for her. And that's what I provided my clients. A friend to stand in so they didn't have to do something alone. True, some of my clients weren't quite that wholesome. Some simply hired me because I was good eye candy to beef up their social media. But most really needed someone to just be there for them.

Like the young woman whose college graduation I attended with a group of my friends, cheering so loudly I thought they'd escort us out. Because she was gay, her parents disowned her, refusing to attend their only daughter's graduation ceremony. Or the kid whose mother hired me to help him learn how to do things that his father would have taught him, if he hadn't died in combat. (That one I did for free.)

The gig Wednesday night with Chelè would be fun, and most of all, easy. I needed that after this weekend. I hadn't meant to get involved. It was supposed to be an easy in, easy out gig. Brush my hands clean of the Kincaids.

"And then I saw Presley," I said to Baby, who was sitting at my feet on the bench. Without Bandit to watch over her, I think she was afraid of the other dogs. I scratched behind her favorite ear and she leaned into me. "Has that ever happened to you? Where you just saw someone and *knew*?" I found myself asking the dog. Then I checked my phone again.

"Of course you didn't. You'd have to smell their butt first," I said, chuckling. Baby hopped up into my lap and curled up. It was going to be one of those kinds of days. I sat there in contented silence, enjoying the sunny afternoon while eating my lunch. I fed Baby a few pieces of chicken, even though the center advised us not to. How could I say no to those big, round, puppy dog eyes? It was unfair that she was so damn cute.

When the phone rang, I nearly dropped Baby from my lap I reacted so quickly. But it wasn't Presley. It was my dad.

"Hey, Pops. How's it going?"

"Well hey, Carter. How are you doing these days? It's been a while."

I knew he hadn't meant it as a dig. The guilt was all my own. "Doing okay. You'll never guess who I ran into last week."

"Oh? Who's that?"

"Lauren Kincaid and her daughter, Presley. Do you remember the Kincaids?"

"How could I forget them, son? They were some of the kinder guests I've met over the years. How's that sweet Presley doing these days? Isn't she your age?"

"Are we remembering the same girl?" I asked, chuckling. "I think you forget how she used to hide lizards in my toolbox and purposefully tripped the breakers so I'd have to come reset them for the building."

"Innocent fun," my dad said. "And Lauren? She still as foxy as you remembered?"

"Pops," I warned, "the reason I ran into her is because her husband passed away several years ago. Presley's father. If you recall, Lauren was her stepmom. And she just remarried."

"Oh, right, right. So, who's she hitched to now? Anyone I know?"

"I don't think so," I said. "Richard Brash? Dex Truitt's CFO at Montague Enterprises?"

"Oh, yes. Richard. Huh," he said, then grew quiet. "Sounds like she'll be taken care of at least."

"No doubt," I said.

"And Presley?"

"Still as mouthy and perplexing as ever."

Pops chuckled. "So, she's turned into a looker, has she?"

"Maybe," I conceded. "So, what's going on with you? How've you been feeling?"

"Well, that's why I'm calling," he said.

I stopped cold. *No.* "Pops, what's wrong?"

"Nothing yet, I don't think. Just, maybe a few polyps they're concerned about."

"As in cancer?" I stood up, the puppy sliding from my lap and staring up at me from the bench.

"Well, let's not rush the gun yet. Just some polyps they think they can remove fairly easily. Not sure how many. Not sure if they'll need to do anything else. Not getting too excited about it yet."

"Dad," I said. I rarely called him that. He was always Pops. But I was worried. My throat felt like it was closing, and I had to put Baby back on her leash and start walking or I'd do something embarrassing like cry on a bench in the park.

"If it gets worse, I'll let ya know. I promise."

"When's the biopsy?"

"Oh, they've done the biopsy. These are precancerous. They're removing the polyps next Tuesday."

"Do you need me to come down?" I was going down regardless of his answer.

"Nope. You stay home and I'll keep you posted. This ain't life or death, you know. Everyone gets a few polyps now and again."

Did they though?

"Who's bringing you? Making sure you get home okay?"

"Oh, you know Veta is," he said, speaking of his long-term partner. They'd not gotten married, and they still lived apart, but they had an understanding and treated each other like husband and wife. She took care of him—cleaned his house and cooked him meals. And he mowed her lawn and fixed things around the house. Yet they both said their arrangement worked fine the way it was. No need messing with something that wasn't broken.

"All right. I'll keep in touch with her then. I was planning on a visit soon anyway."

"You don't need to bother, Carter. I'm okay."

"You're not a bother, Pops," I said affectionately. "I miss seeing you. It's been too damn long."

"Yeah, I suppose it has."

"All right, good luck, old man. You'll do great."

"Yep. All I gotta do is lay there and hold still."

I covered my eyes with my hand. "Dad, I'm pretty sure you'll be under, right?"

"I'm just teasing, Carter. They're pros. Do this stuff all the time."

"All right. Love you, Dad."

"Love you, too, son."

I didn't say anything about the catch I heard in his voice, and he ignored mine. I picked up Baby and held her in my arms all the way back to the shelter. I know it was for my sake more than it was hers. I needed something to hold on to when I had no control over my dad's fate.

I dropped my little buddy off at the rescue center and Suzette at the front desk smiled up at me. "How did she do today, Mr. Wright?"

"You know, Baby," I said. "Always the life of the party."

"Have you heard the good news?"

I stood up straighter. "No, what good news?"

"We finally found her a home. She's being adopted next Wednesday."

My heart sank. I'd never get to see Baby again? I knelt and scratched her ears.

"You know the outpouring of interest spiked after we released a picture of her on the news. Everyone wants the puppy who looks like Baby Yoda. But we found her a good forever home with kids and a big yard. Someone who could take care of her specialized health needs."

I stopped listening. Baby stared deep into my eyes and blinked up at me, as if saying, "It's okay. I'll be fine."

I petted her back one more time and tugged gently at her floppy ear. "Good luck," I whispered. She licked my cheek, and for some reason, it made me want to cry more than laugh. She followed Suzette back to the kennel with a hop in her step as if she knew everything was going to be okay.

"It's okay," I said after her. "I'll be fine."

CHAPTER TWELVE

PRESLEY

"HAVE YOU HEARD anything from Sylvia?" Willa asked as we munched on salads in the park. We sat in our favorite spot outside the dog park. It was a prime place for cute dogs and even cuter men.

"Not yet. We have a meeting when I get back."

"And have you called Carter?"

I shot her the world-famous Kincaid stink eye.

"Girl, what are you waiting for? If that fine piece of ass left me his number after a kiss like that—I'd be all up in his business by now."

I rolled my eyes. "It's only been three days, Willa. Isn't there some girl code about how fast you're supposed to call a guy back?"

"I forget how inexperienced you are sometimes."

It was true. I'd prioritized my school and social activism efforts far more than my dating life. I figured there was time for that once I was more settled, and I already knew what I wanted in a partner. Sure, there had been boyfriends. But nothing serious. Nothing long term. And nothing worth losing my virginity over. Like I said—I hadn't even believed in the butterflies until Friday night. Hell if I was giving my V-card to just anyone.

"Don't remind me," I groaned. "That's exactly why I'm afraid of Carter."

"You think he's gonna care about something like that? Shoot, girl. Most guys dream about that."

"Wait, what? They do?"

"Where have you been Presley? Do you not read any of the romance novels I've loaned you?"

I blushed. I had. But most of the women in those books had already been experienced. The only thing I had in common with them is they all seemed to be described as having a tight hoo-ha. I had no doubt mine was nice and tight since there were iron doors at the entrance. Don't get me wrong, I took care of my own business. But always with my fingers, and never the sleek vibrators Willa tried to get me to buy. I mean—just no. The math didn't add up.

"Yes, I've read them," I said, "but I have no clue what men really expect or want. The types of guys I dated in college didn't prioritize sex, Willa. I know this is foreign to you. But they weren't guys like Carter, that's for sure. Those types of men weren't looking at a woman like me."

"What's that supposed to mean, Presley? Have you not looked in the mirror lately? You could model with me, girlfriend. And I'm not just saying that. I know models who would kill for those cheekbones and that perfect, tiny booty."

I rolled my eyes. "I'm sure a man like Carter who has openly admitted to being attracted to Lauren would never find me even remotely attractive for long. I have none of the qualities that she does."

"You're talking physical appearances only, Presley. Give the guy a chance. He didn't seem shallow, even though you insisted he was arrogant."

I sighed. She was right. He hadn't made me feel unattractive, despite Lauren looking her most beautiful both nights I'd spent with him. In fact, his heated gazes and long inspections had made my skin burn and my insides ache. The guys I was with in college had never done that. They'd either respected me too much or didn't have the game to openly lust after me.

I had to admit, it was kind of nice to feel beautiful for once. I knew I wasn't *un*attractive. I just didn't see myself in quite the same light as my delusional best friend did.

"I guess you're right," I admitted. "I just don't know if I should call him for personal reasons when I suspect I may need to call him for professional ones very soon. That seems—icky. Calculated."

"It's not if you don't make it that way. Besides, you haven't gotten the assignment yet. Maybe Bianca was wrong. Maybe they're assigning it to someone—" she stopped, her eyes fixated on something in front of her. "Presley, don't look now, but Mr. Wright is headed our way."

"Huh?" I asked, not knowing if she meant Mr. Wright or *Mr. Right*. I swung around on the bench to look where her gaze landed. Sure enough, there was Carter, busy on a phone call, the most adorable little puppy trotting alongside him. He was fast walking and distracted.

"When's the biopsy?" he asked as he flew past us.

I waited a beat. "Did you hear that, too?"

Willa nodded. "Call him, Presley. See how he is. See if he's okay. Even if it's as a friend. You owe him that."

I did. I'd known his dad, Mr. Bob (as all the kids called him), most of my life. Even after Carter left for college, we'd gone back to The Grove. That is, until my father died. Then Lauren couldn't bear to be there with the memories floating like ghosts all around us. We tried that first summer after he passed, and we both agreed in three days that we couldn't be there without him.

Willa and I parted ways with a hug, and I promised to call her after I'd spoken to Sylvia. The problem was she got pulled into an emergency and was holed up in the Brain Quad, as we called our "think tank" room, for most of the day. It wasn't until I got a "ping" close to six o'clock that I realized she'd quietly changed our meeting time on my calendar app. I sighed, packing up my things for the evening.

I enjoyed a class of hot yoga, then grabbed Greek takeout on my way home. I plopped down my laptop bag on the sofa when I entered and set my food on the coffee table. Jar Jar wrapped himself around my calf, so I scratched his tan head, stroking the one ear he had left. Jar Jar was the cat no one wanted at the animal control shelter. He'd been injured and had the most annoying meow. But it was love at first sight for me. And we soon realized the reason for that annoying meow—he had a misplaced bone in his femur from a break no one was aware of. A nasty infection had already taken hold by the time I adopted him, and the poor guy was in all kinds of pain. One operation later, and his leg was fine. But he still only had partial hearing in his one remaining ear.

I changed into my evening uniform of pj's after taking off my bra. *Ah! Sweet relief!* It was getting chillier at night, but I was too stubborn and cheap to turn on the heat. It didn't matter if I could afford to pay the entire city block's heating bill. If I could make do with a sweatshirt and blanket, I did.

It was something my father instilled in me from the time I was a kid: don't squander money just because you can. That's how the rich lose everything. By believing it will never go away and wealth is inherently their birthright. It wasn't. Which is why he'd also taught me about social activism and helping those less privileged than myself—and not just with money (though I did that too), but through acts of service, love, time, and knowledge. He always said the way to raise someone else up is to pass on the knowledge you acquired, so they could do it themselves alone someday.

Damn, I missed him. I grabbed my phone and scrolled through some pictures of my father that I'd posted to my social media feed in the past. "Hi, Daddy," I said quietly.

That's when I noticed a new friend request. From Carter, no less. I swallowed, daring to open his account. *Fuck me.* The man was wearing thick, dark glasses in his profile picture, and the nerd in me about had a nerdgasm on the spot. I clicked the picture to see it in full. My nipples tightened at the sight of him with his bright blue shirt opened a few buttons, his hands casually shoved into his pockets like he did all the damn time, and those freaking glasses.

I knew it was masochistic, but I curled up on the couch and flipped through the pictures of him in his news feed. Carter at a charity fundraiser in a tux. Carter volunteering at a local, inner-city school. Carter sitting in a hammock, reading a book. Could my loins get any wetter? Then I landed on Carter at a beach with water so blue and clear I could see the sandy bottom. He was in nothing more than a pair of swim trunks, holding the largest conch shell I'd ever seen over his head.

Yep, I could get wetter.

His stomach was perfection in ways I never even knew existed. His chest was solidly chiseled, his small brown nipples catching my eyes despite the tan he was sporting. And his shoulders . . . who knew men had muscles that did that? His dog tags hung around his neck proudly, his dimples framing that genuine smile that lit up his whole face. A half-sleeve tattoo covered his lower arm that I didn't know he had because he'd been clothed both times I'd seen him as an adult. I had to admit . . . it was sexy as hell.

I'd forgotten all about my salmon kabobs and Greek salad as I drooled over Carter's godlike physique instead. I knew it would only bring me agony, but god help me, I saved the pictures of Carter in glasses and Carter on the beach to my phone. I would be imagining what that happy trail of dark brown hair on his tummy and the deepest V I'd ever seen led to. Surely there was a treasure at the end of that hunt.

I swallowed. Did I have the nerve to do this?

Before I could stop myself, I dialed Carter's number. I'd already added it to my phone the morning after the wedding. Just in case.

"Hello?"

My mouth ran dry as I thought about Carter's abs, remembered the way his hips felt under my fingers when we kissed. How I'd wanted to wrap my hands around him and cup those tight buns of his.

"Hello?" he said again.

It was now or never.

"Hi, Carter. It's me, Presley."

CHAPTER THIRTEEN

CARTER

I WAS SITTING at my desk in my home office when she finally called—three days after I'd left my number for her. Not that I was counting. Her voice was soft and hesitant. Not at all the sassy, loud, confident Presley I knew.

"Hey, princess," I said, deeply. "Thought maybe I'd scared you off."

"Well, no, I was just busy."

"But now you're free?"

She cleared her throat. "Yes. I was calling to take you up on your offer, actually."

"And what offer was that?"

I was going to make her work for it. I *needed* to know she wanted me.

"Carter, you know damn well what I'm calling about. I don't need to say it."

"Why? Does it make it too real? Is Presley Kincaid afraid of where that kiss was gonna go if I'd had you alone?"

It had been all I could think of these past few days. The bare shoulder that was exposed in her bridesmaid's dress. The way the front swished as she walked, and then parted to reveal long, smooth legs that were so sexy they could make a grown man cry.

"No," she replied, though I could hear the uncertainty in her voice. That was interesting. The Presley I knew at thirteen had all but demanded a kiss from me. This one? After I'd already kissed her? She seemed hesitant. Unsure of herself.

"I just don't usually kiss on the first date—and that wasn't even a date. Not only that, you kinda stole our first kiss from me with your whole asshole move on our entrance."

I chuckled. There was the Presley I knew.

"And yet, when I got you alone, you kissed me back. Not only that, but you clung to me, Presley. You pressed your sweet little body against mine and moaned into my mouth."

She gasped, which made a deep chuckle rumble low in my belly. "Have you been having the same naughty dreams about me that I've had about you?" I pressed.

"First of all, I did not *moan* into your mouth. I would never do that. Second of all—"

"Oh, but princess, you did. It was the hottest little whimper I've ever heard." My cock swelled in agreement.

"Carter! That's not why I'm calling. You asked me on a date. If I don't kiss on a first date, I most certainly don't have sex on one either. If you want a date, you can have a date. Nothing more."

I contemplated her words. Did I just want to see Presley again because she was a complicated puzzle I wanted to figure out? A series of contradictions I wanted to unwrap? Or was it because she'd grown into one of the most beautiful women I'd ever seen?

I thought of her light freckles across the bridge of her nose that were covered when the wedding started, but that I noticed when I tucked her into bed after a long night of dancing and wearing her makeup off. The way her long, strawberry blond curls framed her head on the pillow. The way her hips curved in her soft, silky dress, and how she'd fit perfectly in my arms as the little spoon.

I most definitely wanted more. But I would go at her pace. For now.

"I can agree to that," I said, "on one condition."

"And what's that?"

"That I see you soon. I'm headed to The Grove next week, and I'd really like to see you before I do. Does Friday night work?"

She was quiet, and I could just imagine her biting that damn lower lip of hers, worrying it. "Friday works fine, Carter."

"Well, don't get too excited about it or anything," I teased.

"No, I am excited. I just—Carter, my friend and I were in the park today. And we saw you rush by."

I didn't say anything. I knew exactly when that was.

"Is your father okay? I overheard what you asked him."

The level of concern in her voice almost leveled me. *Damn it.*

"He's fine," I said shortly. I don't know why I did that. I just wasn't ready to talk about his surgery yet. Not to Presley. Not to anyone. "He'll be fine."

"Okay. Well, if he's not, will you let me know if I can help?"

I swallowed, closing my eyes.

Sweet baby Jesus. She was sexy as sin and worried about my dad. If I wasn't careful, Presley Kincaid would break my fucking heart.

THE GALLERY OPENING went flawlessly, and Chelè's art sold like wildfire. Her work was important too. Her paintings were a combined message about racial inequality and environmental destruction—if you looked closely enough. She'd been easy to talk to, and we exchanged information so we could keep in touch. I'd most certainly be buying a painting of hers in the future.

Friday was here before I knew it. I didn't know why I was so nervous. Maybe because Presley could buy my entire building, and here I'd been so confident and proud of myself when I'd finally scraped together enough to buy this one condo. I looked around, trying to imagine what it would look like through Presley's eyes. Would she judge me? I'd seen pictures of Lauren's home in *Architecture Today*. If Presley was used to growing up in that . . . well, my place would be low rent in comparison.

I shook off the doubt. She'd agreed to a date. Which meant maybe she didn't care so much about money as I thought she did. I cringed, thinking how I was so quick to pass judgment and called her little Miss Moneybags the first time she got under my skin. It was an easy shot, and one I regretted.

The buzzer chimed, letting me know she was in the lobby. I called down to the bellman and asked him to escort her up. Then I glanced in the entryway mirror, running a hand over my scruff. I shrugged. Good enough.

I wasn't prepared for the sight of Presley when I opened the door. It wasn't the fact that she was wearing skintight jeans, low-heeled grunge boots, and a Ruth Bader Ginsburg "Not Fragile Like a Flower, Fragile Like a Bomb" T-shirt under her black leather moto jacket. I couldn't imagine a more fitting T-shirt for Presley. She *was* about as fragile as a bomb, and I had the feeling she was about to blow my heart to smithereens.

But it was the smile on her face that stopped me cold. She was grinning from ear to ear at something the bellman said, laughing as she exited the elevator. I'd never seen a smile that big on her face before. Ever. And damn if jealously didn't kick me in the gut and make me wish I'd been the one to light up her face like that. I glanced at the man who'd been our building's bellman since the beginning of time. He was probably my father's age, but still. He winked at me and waggled his bushy gray eyebrows. I couldn't help but chuckle as I escorted Presley into my condo.

"So," I said as she looked around, her eyes wide and her smile returning, "can I take your coat?"

"Sure," she said, shrugging it off. She handed it to me and flushed when she caught me watching her. "Your home is beautiful, Carter. Not at all what I imagined it would look like."

"Um, thanks?" I said, hanging her coat in the entryway closest.

"No, it's just . . . more grown up than I expected. I thought it would be more bachelor pad than an architectural wet dream. It's a little Brad Pitt meets Mies van der Rohe."

"Wow. So you really know your stuff," I said. "I don't even know who this Mies character is."

"Oh, sorry. The geek in me takes over sometimes. He was a German-American architect. Minimalist. Less is more kind of stuff. Ludwig Mies van der Rohe. He basically invented the open-floor concept. Used plate glass windows and structural steel walls as room dividers, like you have over there," she said, pointing to my office space.

"Where does Brad Pitt fit into all this?"

"Oh, he designs as well as builds. You have an eye for his aesthetic," she commented, glancing around. "Not everyone knows that he builds homes for those in need. I was lucky enough to volunteer on a project of his once."

I looked at Presley with new eyes. She was a ball full of surprises.

"You worked side by side with Brad Pitt?" I asked, jealousy fanning its wicked flames again. How could I compete with fucking Brad Pitt? Wasn't he single again?

She laughed. "I wouldn't say I worked side by side with him. But I did get to meet him. He was really nice."

Yeah, I bet he was, I thought.

I led the way into the kitchen so I could grab us some wine. I was gonna need it tonight. Presley was determined to keep me on my toes with much more serious conversation than I was used to having with women. Not that I couldn't. I just didn't.

She accepted the glass of wine I handed her. She took a small sip and smiled. "Delicious," she said. "A little sweet, a little dry. Just how I like it."

I couldn't help but stare at her mouth as she talked. Her lips fit the rim like a second skin, and I was suddenly envious of the wine for having all the fun in her mouth.

"What?" she asked, oblivious to my reaction to her.

"You're just—" I didn't know how to finish. She'd said she wanted to take it slow. Yet here I was, wanting to tear her damn clothes off less than two minutes after she stepped through the door. "You're complicated. In a good way. Not like what I expected."

She grinned as she walked toward me. She was close. Too close. I could smell cloves. Something like cinnamon and oranges. The two smells might not have normally gone together in my world. But on Presley, they drove me fucking insane.

"Carter, I feel like some of this is my fault. Can we sit?" she asked, batting those large, green eyes up at me. She had little to no makeup on and, quite frankly, didn't need a stich. But her eyelids shimmered, and her lashes were long and black. They reminded me of the mossy green ponds on the island.

How could I say no?

We made our way to the living room, and I watched as she soaked up the architecture there, too. "If you love design so much, how come you didn't go into it?"

"I loved numbers more. What about you? What did Carter end up studying in college?"

"I'm not sure I would have called it studying per se," I joked. Though, I'd done a lot better than I imagined I would. "I double majored in business and communications and minored in marketing."

She nodded, running her fingers over the exposed brick wall behind the seating area that faced the large, floor-to-ceiling windows. I suddenly wanted to use the built-in privacy shading so I could pin her up against the wall and grind against her until she moaned into my mouth again.

But Presley was not like the other women who had come in and out of my life. None of whom were serious. All of whom were a bundle of fun and easy to part ways with when the fun times were over.

She curled up on the cream-colored couch and patted for me to join her. I sat down, my arm draping over the back of the sofa as she turned to face me, one leg tucked under the other. I loved how she made herself comfortable here. She was starting to loosen up around me.

"I'm sorry I was so bratty when I was a kid," she said, her eyes twinkling. She didn't look sorry at all.

"Oh yeah?" I said, running my fingers over her shoulder. Her body responded with a small shiver and I grinned.

"But you were kind of arrogant. Still are," she said, raising a brow at me.

"Arrogant in a sexy, I-want-to-rip-his-clothes-off kind of way?" I asked hopefully.

"No, as in—confident. I can see now that it's more confidence than arrogance, really."

I didn't feel so confident when I was around Presley for some reason. In every other aspect of my life? Sure. I'd built my life from the ground up, and I was damn proud of it. Nothing had been handed to me. Not that it was Presley's fault that her father dumped his mammoth fortune on her. But every part of my success was mine.

"So, you were military?" she asked, nodding to the dog tags that rested on my chest. I'd opted for simple tonight, too. Jeans and a black T-shirt.

"Yeah," I said quietly. I didn't really like talking about it. I'd gone into intel, and I'd learned more about the human condition than I ever could've imagined. And none of it was the rainbows and butterflies kind of life Presley had lived. We'd stopped terrorist movements and threats to US soil on a daily basis. And they weren't all from people like the ones who are portrayed in the media. It was hard to know sometimes who was the real threat: outsiders, or the dangerous men living within our own borders.

But it sure as hell wasn't something I was discussing on night one with Presley. I'd never discussed it with a woman before and wasn't sure I ever would.

Presley saw that I'd put up some walls, and her eyes softened. She reached out and took my hand, moving closer to me on the couch. "It's okay, Carter. We don't have to talk about it."

I nodded, shoving down the anger, hurt, and betrayal I carried around with me. I didn't want to talk about it later. I wanted to taste her again.

I needed to taste her.

"Presley, I know you wanted to take things slow, and I completely respect that, but I—"

She didn't let me finish. She'd inched closer and wrapped her arms around my neck. The soft fabric of her T-shirt brushed my skin, and she was just inches from my lips. I didn't move. I needed her to take this at her own pace. Otherwise, I'd fuck things up. Because the truth was—I wanted everything she had to give me.

Her mouth brushed mine, her velvety soft tongue sliding over my hungry mouth. She kissed my lips again and again, asking me with her body and her tongue to open the fuck up. I could taste a hint of the cinnamon I'd smelled earlier, and I wanted to swim in it.

I groaned, making Presley giggle.

"Something funny, princess?" I asked, opening my eyes.

She playfully bit my lower lip and climbed in my lap. It wasn't what I was expecting, but I loved the way her sit bone burned into my thigh. She trailed kisses off my mouth and to my cheek, holding my jaw in her hands as she kissed up my neck and to my ears.

I was about to fucking explode, and all Presley did was giggle again.

I grabbed her hands and pinned them down, her body stilling in my lap. I could hear her quick, shallow breaths close to my ear. "All right. What's so funny, P?"

"Oh, nothing," she said casually. "But, for the record, who's moaning into who's mouth now?"

I was screwed.

In that moment, I knew I didn't just have to worry about my heart around this one. If I wasn't careful, bratty, little Presley Kincaid was going to be the actual death of me.

Death by fragile bomb.

CHAPTER FOURTEEN

PRESLEY

TO SAY I was disappointed when Carter lifted me off his lap and plopped me solidly onto the couch was an understatement. I was hoping for more of those delicious kisses I'd stolen this time. And, boy, did it feel good to be the one in charge. I think I caught Carter completely off guard because he seemed flustered after that. I'd never had a chance to take my sexual power for a test drive, and I suddenly saw the appeal.

He fed me dinner—takeout from a favorite steakhouse that he had delivered. Between the baked sweet potato drizzled in a honey, cinnamon, and butter sauce; the long, crisp spears of asparagus; and the tender, bacon-wrapped filet with au jus sauce, my taste buds were in overdrive and my tummy was in heaven. We sat and talked some more about life and what we'd both been up to the last ten or so years—minus the military years, of course. Which was okay by me. I suspected the responsibility and aftermath of service could weigh heavy on even the strongest soul. I would let him share more in his own time.

When we were done, I looked at him across the table and smiled. The night had been easier than I expected. I was pleasantly surprised.

"So," I said, knowing I should probably go before I did something I would regret. And I was one breath away from doing just that.

"So," he said back, winking at me. "I have something fun planned if you can stay a little longer."

He got up and took my hand, leading me into a small library off the living room. It, too, had a steel wall separating it from the living space. He pulled me inside and I inhaled, smelling the rich binding of floor-to-ceiling books. My kryptonite.

"Oh, yeah? And what's that?"

"Tell me you'll stay," he said, staring at my mouth, "just for a little longer."

He hooked his fingers into the belt loops of my jeans and yanked my hips closer to his body. I knew I shouldn't stay a minute longer. I'd already gotten the assignment from Sylvia, and I'd been too chicken to mention it yet.

He reached one of his hands up and cupped the back of my head, forcing me to look up and into his dark brown eyes. They were full of amusement and heat. He slowly backed me up until my shoulders met the steel wall. I was pinned between a solid slab of steel and a solid slab of muscle. He slid his knee between my legs, pressing them open just a bit. My breath caught when both of his hands pressed against the wall on either side of my head, and he grinned, moving even closer to my mouth.

"Well, princess?"

Say no. Say no.

"Yes," I breathed out, praying he would lower his head and kiss me again.

Instead, he pulled back and took my hands in his. My heart was still rapid-fire beating out of my chest from his closeness and my anticipation when he backed away from me.

I closed my eyes, feeling like a damn fool.

Until he led me over to a card table, where a bottle of tequila and a deck of Uno cards were waiting. Holy shit. I was in trouble.

OF COURSE I killed him at Uno. I was the Queen of Cards! By the time we were done, I had tears of laughter spilling over and a sweet buzz burning through my veins. I'd never spent so much time with Carter, and I was finding the more I did, the more I liked—beyond just the surface.

"Well," he said, trying to remain composed, "don't I get to see your victory dance again?"

I lost it, laughing so hard. "Oh, god. No. Please tell me I didn't do my victory dance?"

"But you did," he said. He leaned back in his chair, his ankle crossed over his knee. He nodded toward the tabletop. "Up you go."

"You want me—to get up there? And dance?"

My mouth went dry.

He nodded, his eyes penetrating.

Oh, screw it.

I shucked off my boots and used the chair to climb on top of the solid oak table. I kicked the cards off with my socked feet and started boogying. It was silly at first, like I'd just made a touchdown. But when I met Carter's eyes, my insides burned with the way he was watching me. I'd never felt sexier in my entire life.

I held his gaze, then slowly started swaying my body. I'd had enough shots to loosen up and lose some of my normal inhibitions. I crossed my arms over my torso and ran them up and down my sides as I moved to the imaginary music in my head. Then I grasped the bottom of my T-shirt and found myself pulling it up over my head before I had time to second guess myself.

Heat pooled in my belly when the look in Carter's eyes went from heated to primal. I didn't really have anything to compare it to, but I knew he wanted me. I knew if I gave him the green light, he would devour me. His eyes dragged from my gaze, down my neck, to my collarbone, then trailed to my flimsy lace bra. I was smaller than Lauren and Willa by a landslide. But the way his tongue traced his bottom lip as he watched me made me realize he didn't care in the least. He was enjoying what he saw.

I turned, shimmying my butt as I glanced over my shoulder at him. Then I slowly unhooked my bra, dropping it to the card table. Carter groaned, but I didn't look at him. Instead, I closed my eyes and lifted my arms straight in the air. I clasped my hands together, slowly swaying my body side to side as I dropped down into a squat and slowly rose back up again. The tequila was doing wonders for my self-confidence.

"Presley," he warned, "you're gonna need to stop."

I swung my hair off my shoulder as I turned back to look at him again. This time, he was standing. His cock was rock hard in his jeans and he did nothing to hide it.

"Or what?"

He walked forward, sliding his hands up the front of my thighs as he rested his cheek against the back of my legs. "Or I'm going to give you a whole lot more than a kiss on our first date."

I don't know where the instinct came from, but I reached up and cupped my breasts as I pressed my backside farther into Carter's embrace. Before I knew what was happening, he'd spun me around, yanked me off the table, and had me in a fireman's carry over her shoulder. I couldn't help myself. I giggled in delight.

He grabbed the bottle of tequila and handed it to me as he marched out of the room.

"Wait—where are we going?"

"We're moving this party," he said gruffly, smacking my ass.

"Ouch!" I cried out. But dear god, why did it make my insides ache for more? What was happening to me?

He flopped me down onto his massive, low bed. The room surprised me. It had the modern aesthetic of the rest of his house, but it was darker, moodier. Thick slabs of reclaimed wood lined the wall behind his bed. The headboard itself was low and dark gray. The furniture was sparse, but richly made. Masculine, but understated. Just like Carter.

He yanked me to the edge of the bed and my body shook under his gaze. My breasts were exposed, and I reached up to cover them. He pulled my hands away in one swift movement, pinning them above my head. We breathed deep like this in each other's space, his lips so close I could swear I felt them brush mine.

"Stay exactly like this," he said. "Don't move."

I wasn't sure I could if I tried.

Yes, I'd had men see me naked before during clumsy foreplay in college. But I never let it go too far. It was more curiosity and heavy petting than desire or outcome. And the chemistry hadn't been so . . . intense. All consuming.

This fucking burned me alive from the inside out.

He took my chin in his mouth and sucked, his tongue tasting my skin. My nipples pebbled, and I moaned somewhere deep in my throat. I wanted to close my eyes, but I also wanted to see this demigod as he paid tribute to my body. How could I do this to him? Make him want *my* body this way when he could have anyone?

His warm mouth trailed down my neck, suckling the soft indentation where it meets my collarbone. He stared down at my breasts, and I had to force myself not to turn my head away under his intense scrutiny.

"Goddamn, you're beautiful, Presley."

I closed my eyes then. I couldn't focus on the words, the heat, the feel of his mouth all at the same time. My skin ached for his touch in ways I didn't understand.

He cupped my breasts, kneading them with his large, firm hands. His thumb and pointer finger rolled my nipples like an expert, and lightning shot to my core. I knew if I touched myself, I'd be wet.

Something cold hit my nipples, dripping down the side of my body. I opened my eyes to find Carter grinning wickedly before he flicked his tongue over my wet bud.

"What was that?" I gasped.

"Tequila," he said, drawing my nipple deeper into his mouth and sucking it hard. I ached to bring my hands down so I could run my fingers through his dark, tousled hair. But he took his time, running circles over my nipple with long, wet strokes of his tongue, until I thought I'd lose my mind with need.

"Carter," I cried, unsure how much more of this I could take. Or when I should put an end to it. *If* I should put an end to it. I was a grown adult. Maybe it was time to stop hiding behind my virginity.

As he suckled, he massaged my other breast, gently tugging upward on the nipple as he pinched it hard between his fingers. *Oooh! There!* I wanted to cry out. But I didn't. I let the heat pool between my legs as I pressed my eyelids closed, my body panting as stars exploded behind my lids.

Oh. My. God.

So that's what an orgasm from someone else felt like.

His kissing slowed, and he let my nipple pop from his mouth, wet and swollen. I would have love marks on my breasts later—something I'd never had before. The idea thrilled me.

Still, I wasn't sure if I was doing the right thing, rushing into things with Carter. "Is this really a good idea?" I asked.

"Why wouldn't it be?"

His mouth moved lower.

He flicked that warm tongue of his inside my belly button, his hands gripping my hips. Then I watched as he poured a small puddle of tequila onto my stomach. I gasped, trying not to wiggle and have it spill all over the bed. "Your skin tastes fucking delicious, Presley. We're both adults. Besides, I'm just finishing the 'loser's shot' you told me I needed to take."

He bent his head, his fingers digging into my flesh as he sucked up the warm, brown liquid. Goose bumps covered my body from head to toe. His tongue didn't stop after the shot, though. He traced my belly button, kissed my stomach, nibbled on my hips. Then he lowered his head, pressing his forehead just below my belly button and groaning. The pressure of his head there—just above my pubis bone—made me press my hips up off the bed, urgently needing to get closer to Carter. I grabbed his hair in my hands, not sure why or what I was asking for. I just knew that my insides throbbed like never before.

He took my hands from his hair and pinned them to my sides as he stood. "I said to keep your hands where they were. Did you listen?"

I was so shocked I didn't know how to respond. He'd been serious?

"I—it just felt so good. I needed to touch you."

I'd never been so forward with a man. But then again, I'd only been with boys, if I was being honest with myself. Not one of those boys knew how to do anything like what Carter was doing to my body. And damn if it didn't make me want more.

"Do you need a spanking, Presley?"

My eyes grew large and I bit my lower lip, remembering the feel of his hand on my ass earlier. I shook my head slowly, saying no. But my insides screamed, *Liar!* I gripped the bedspread so I wouldn't move my hands again, but I wasn't sure what Carter wanted. What he was going to do next.

He slowly lifted his shirt over his head, and I thought I was going to pass out. His abs, and that damn V, were even more deadly and sinful in person. My pussy was full-on throbbing now, not sure what it needed, but knowing what it liked.

And what it liked was Carter.

He unbuttoned his jeans, letting them fall to the floor. He was wearing short, black, cotton boxer briefs, and they conformed to his strong thighs. But it wasn't his thighs my eyes were focused on. His erection stood straight up, and I could see the outline of it through the material. It was not like any I'd ever seen in my college forays.

He leaned over, unzipping my jeans and yanking them down my legs in one swift movement. I felt so exposed lying there in my black, lace thong and nothing else. But I didn't dare move my hands again. He grinned, seeing the war play out behind my eyes.

"Good girl," he said. Then he dropped to his knees in front of me and yanked me down the bed until my butt was almost hanging off. He slowly poured a little more liquor just above my panty line, and held my gaze as he lowered the pour, straight between my legs so it dripped down the center of my underwear and coated my thighs.

I had to bite the inside of my cheek when I felt his hot tongue slide slowly over my stomach, my legs shaking as he drank up the liquid, sucking and massaging my skin as he went. I sucked in my stomach on reflex, which raised my hips and my mons even closer to him.

He looked up at me, met my eyes, and then slid his tongue down over my thigh, biting it as he edged closer to the space between my legs. I'd never had anyone's mouth that close before, and a million thoughts raced through my mind.

"Relax, Presley," he said, his hands holding my hips down as he dragged his tongue straight up the center of my crotch over my underwear. *Holy. Shit.* He bit my clit through the material and chuckled when I whimpered. "Close your eyes, princess. Let me take care of the winner the way she deserves."

My eyes fluttered closed and I waited, the silence deafening. Carter's hands wrapped under my ass and squeezed before gripping the thong and yanking, hard. I cried out as the material gave way, my eyes unable to stay closed. He threw the torn material to the floor and raised a brow at me, then dropped his chin and licked me *there*. I threw my head back, every nerve ending in my body celebrating.

How did I not know how *good* this felt?

Carter flicked his thick, warm tongue over my swollen clit and chuckled knowingly when my thighs spasmed and clenched in response. He splayed my legs up higher on the bed, and I was wide open in front of him. I tried not to think about what I looked like, or how wet I was. He would know how much he'd already turned me on, and I would look like such a novice.

Not that I wasn't. I just didn't want him to know that.

He breathed in my scent. I could feel him hovering over my opening. What was he waiting for? Then his tongue reached out, made contact, trailed up the center of my wetness where no one had ever kissed before. He groaned, wrapping his mouth around my clit and sucking hard.

My hips bucked, but he kept working it. There was no way I could leave my hands like this. I whimpered, near my breaking point. Then sweet relief as he slid his tongue back down my slick opening. He lapped me like that several times, the noises of him slurping mortifying me as he made love to me with his mouth.

I thought he was done, but then his greedy little mouth found my clit again, biting it between his teeth as he tugged at it. Pleasure like nothing I'd ever experienced ripped through my core. "Carter," I panted, clutching his comforter in my hands.

"Yes?" he asked, now using his fingers to rub the sensitive nub as his tongue traced my opening with reverence. "You're so fucking wet for me, Presley."

"You like that?" I asked, genuinely unsure.

"I fucking love it," he said. Then he slid a finger inside me. I couldn't help but cry out in surprise. It felt *so* good. Sure, I'd masturbated before, but never this deep. Whatever he was doing inside of me made me want more.

My body rolled with waves of pleasure as he moved his finger back and forth. Just when I was getting used to the rhythm, he slowly slid a second finger inside me. I turned my head, biting the sheets. It burned for a minute as I stretched to fit them, but then I found my body adjusting, becoming slick enough for him to move them back and forth as he brought me closer to the brink.

My thighs shook, clenching his hand as I let him fuck me with his fingers. On our first date. But *oh my god!* I didn't care. All I wanted was more. More of Carter. More of his mouth. More—pleasure. His mouth found my nipples again as he continued to play with me down there. His fingers were slick with my juices, and he used it to coat my clit, then he rubbed it along the outer lips of my pussy before plunging his fingers back inside. My eyes rolled to the back of my head, and I couldn't take it anymore. He was sucking my breasts, one then the other, biting and tugging the nipples as the intensity of everything peaked. I wasn't sure what was going to make me come first: his fingers, or his teeth.

His fingers won out, arching inside me and finding some ancient place I didn't know existed. I probably should have read more of Willa's books. I realized that now. I free fell inside my body, and I didn't feel tethered. My insides tightened around Carter's fingers, and my thighs shook as my climax ripped through me, and I came.

"Fuck," he growled, his lips crashing onto mine. He swallowed my cries of pleasure and my hands finally found his hair again, pulling him tighter against my mouth as my hips pressed all the way against the flat of his palm, holding his fingers deep inside my body as I shook. I never wanted them to leave.

"Jesus, Presley," he said into my ear, "that was so fucking hot."

My laugh was shaky, because I honestly was too spacey to answer at the moment. He slid his fingers out of my pussy and rubbed them against my clit again. I jerked each time he pressed it, the aftershocks racking my body.

I didn't know what to do next. I wouldn't know how to return the favor if I tried. Sure, I'd seen porn before with friends in college as a joke. I knew *what* it entailed. I just wasn't sure how to get from here to there.

I tried to sit up, but he pressed my chest back down.

"I'm not done with you yet, princess."

CHAPTER FIFTEEN

CARTER

EVERYTHING WITH PRESLEY felt new. Her body was so responsive to every stroke, every flick of my tongue, every touch. I thought I was going to blow my load a couple times, she was so hot. She held an air about her that made me feel special, as if no one had ever made her feel this way before. Which was ridiculous. She was Presley fucking Kincaid. One of the wealthiest heiresses in the world. She could have her pick of men—all kinds of entitled assholes who were nothing like me. Rich. Cultured. Stuffy. And boring as shit. No wonder she was responding the way she was. I bet they were the type of men who ate a pussy and then brushed their teeth afterward.

Not me. I kneeled next to Presley on the bed and licked each finger, my eyes trained on hers. They were a stormy sea of green. They widened as she watched each digit slide into my mouth, and I savored her musky taste. God, I could do nothing but lick her sweet pussy all night long. But now that I'd gotten a taste of her, I was selfish. I wanted—no, I needed—to feel Presley wrapped tightly around my dick.

I leaned over and grabbed a condom from the bedside table, then flipped Presley onto her stomach. She moaned, her body writhing against my comforter as if every sensation were new and a turn-on. Her body was made for me to fuck.

I pulled off my boxer briefs and slid the condom down my swollen cock. Then I leaned over her, my arms supporting my body weight. I licked her back, kissed her shoulders. She sighed, rolling her neck so it was exposed to me. I slid my tongue up it, tasting salty, little beads of sweat. I crashed my lips onto her mouth, needing to taste her. She moaned into me as my fingers slid between the cheeks of her ass to feel for her slick opening and coat her in it. My fingers pressed down around the outside of her lips as they slid back and forth. She was fucking swollen down there from her orgasm, and I couldn't wait to slide deep inside of her.

If just my fingers had fit that snuggly, her pussy would feel like a second skin wrapped around me. I positioned myself at her opening, rubbing the thick head of my cock in and out a few times to prep her.

"Did you put the condom on?" she asked quietly.

"Of course," I reassured her. "I don't mess around that way."

She nodded against the sheets, gripping them with her fingers by her head.

I nudged the tip of my cock into her opening and coated it. I could see my own precum through the clear rubber. I teased her for a moment, popping the head in and out, getting it nice and wet.

Then I pressed my hips forward, eager to bury myself inside of her. Holy fuck, she was tight. She wasn't dry, that was for sure. But I had to ease in slower than normal. Maybe she'd never been with a larger guy before. Not to brag, but I was well above average. I pulled my hips back, knowing she would stretch enough to take all of me soon enough. Then I went for it. I threw my hips forward, pressing all the way in, fast and deep.

Presley screamed out, grabbing the sheets. She was tight. Too tight. She whimpered, her eyes pressed closed.

No. *No!* I stopped moving, but the damage was done. I was already buried balls deep inside her. There was no taking this back.

"Presley," I growled.

"What? Why did you stop? Don't stop—please. Keep going."

"Are you a virgin?" I ground out between clenched teeth.

She opened her eyes to look at me. "Yeah? So?"

"Good god, woman. That's something you have to tell a guy before you let him split you open. Not to mention, if I'd known—"

"Exactly! If you'd known, would you be inside of me right now? Would you have given me a chance?"

"What do you mean a chance?"

She sighed. I didn't want to yank myself out and hurt her again, but I knew I should.

"I'm not experienced. I know that's a turnoff."

I leaned forward, my cock still lodged inside her. "Look at me," I demanded.

Her eyes fluttered open, and I saw they were wet.

Jesus. What did I do?

"Nothing with you is a turnoff, Presley. There's just— bigger implications—with taking your virginity. Ones I'm not sure I'm ready for. Either way, I should've known, so it at least could've been more—I don't know. Special."

"Carter, I'm exactly where I want to be. I'll get better. It'll be easier and won't hurt as much if we keep going. I promise. Just—please don't stop," she begged. "Please."

I closed my eyes and took a deep breath, torn between what I thought was the right thing to do and Presley's sexy-as-fuck whimpers as she asked me to keep going. "Are you sure? I mean, a thousand percent sure?"

She nodded, looking up at me bravely.

I kissed her lips slowly, letting my body weight fall on my forearms. I reached under her and cupped her breasts as I slowly started moving back and forth. Gentle, easy. Just little rocks of the hips to make sure she was wet and could handle me. I'd never fucked a virgin before and had no clue how to make it *not* hurt. But I would do my best.

I massaged her chest and kissed her neck. She turned, finding my lips and swirling her hot, little tongue inside my mouth. She sucked my tongue in and my dick kicked inside her. We kissed passionately like that as I ground my hips slowly, easing my cock back and forth until she was slippery enough to move more easily.

"There," I said, quietly by her ear, "does it hurt less?"

She nodded.

"If anything hurts, you tell me right away. Do you hear me, Presley?"

"Yes," she breathed out. "Just, keep going. Please?"

I chuckled. She wasn't just brave. She was enjoying this. It was too late to turn back now, so I would make this a first she would never forget.

"Does it feel good having my cock buried deep inside you?" I said low, next to her ear.

I started moving my hips more rhythmically now. She was still hella tight around my cock, but it was now coated with her pleasure and made the slide back and forth much easier.

She whimpered, but it was one of pleasure—not pain.

"Does my filthy mouth offend you?"

She shook her head from side to side. "No one's ever said anything like this to me before," she admitted. Her lip curled into a half smile. "But I kind of like it, coming from you."

"Good. Because your fucking pussy makes me want to wax poetic it's so goddamn tight."

She groaned, pressing her butt back against me.

"That's it, Pres. Take me deep. Feel each stroke, baby. Tell me what you like, okay?"

She nodded and I sat up more, pulling myself to my knees as I brought her hips back to take me all the way in. She gasped, crying out my name.

"The pain will get less intense, princess. I promise. You're just having to adjust to me every time I move. Different positions can feel more intense and be deeper than others. And you're stretched farther than you probably ever have been."

"I—"

"What is it, P?" I asked, moving my hips back and forth as I watched my cock sliding between her butt-cheeks. Her legs were pressed together, and I was gripping her hips. I knew I wasn't even as deep as I could be from this angle, but I'd give her a moment to adjust before really working her body over.

"You, you're so big," she said, shakily. "I just . . . I like the way it feels, the whole length of it, when you slide it back and forth."

"Like this?" I asked, curling my hips so I brought my cock nearly all the way out, then slowly rolling them forward, pressing back deep inside her.

"God, yes," she said. "Just like that."

"I love hearing you ask for what you want, Presley. It's a huge fucking turn on."

I pulled back and slowly curled my hips, nearly unhinging as she stretched and clenched around my cock each time. I *needed* to see it.

"Do you trust me?" I asked.

She nodded, so I pulled out slowly, letting the walls of her pussy contract back to normal. Then I turned her over onto her back so I could see her face fully. She was so damn open and trusting right now. If I'd known she was a virgin, I never would've tossed her onto her belly like that. Her first time deserved better.

I leaned over her, taking her nipple back in my mouth and sucking hard. She seemed to like that because her nails clawed at my biceps each time I gently bit down. I rolled my thumb over her clit, helping her desire bubble to the surface again. The slicker she was, the less it would hurt when I slid back inside.

"You sure you want me to keep going?"

"Carter, I will kill you if you don't," she said, laughing. That was the Presley I knew.

I looked down at her, sprawled out on my bed, her shiny, strawberry blond hair framing her face. Her cheeks were flushed, and her eyes were bright with unequivocal lust. The tears were done. She reached for my cock, surprising me when she stroked it back and forth.

"I want you back inside me, Carter."

God. Damn.

I parted her legs so they were bent and sprawled open wide, letting me see her gorgeous, pink pussy glistening for me. "Open yourself for me, baby," I groaned.

"What—what do you mean?"

"I mean, take your fingers, slide them down your pussy, and show me your opening."

She swallowed hard, her eyes trained on mine. But she slid her hand down, spreading her fingers around her swollen clit and down her wet lips. I nearly came watching her tentative fingers spread herself open for me. I could have done it myself, but it was far sexier watching her do it, and it bought me time.

I pressed the swollen tip of my cock to her opening and held her gaze. Then, slower this time, I urged my cock forward, inch by inch. She was much wetter now, and her eyes rolled back, closing. When I was buried back deep inside her, she sighed, smiling with her eyes closed.

"What is it?"

"You fit so perfectly inside me. Is it always like this?"

"No, Presley. Your pussy was made for my dick."

She gasped as I pulled back and pressed forward again, starting the slow motions of fucking her. I pinned her knees down against the bed, so she felt every single inch of me as I drove deep inside of her. I was afraid she wouldn't stretch again to hold me, but she did, and I nearly lost my mind with how snug she fit around me.

"That's it, baby," I said, thrusting my hips back and forth.

"Carter—shit! That feels so good."

"If it doesn't, I'm not doing it right."

I drove slow and deep, bottoming her out with each hard thrust of my hips. She cried out, her hands instinctively finding her tits to prevent them from bouncing.

"Play with them," I ground out between clenched teeth as I pumped faster.

She cupped her perfect tits. They were round and high, and the sight of her playing with her nipples and writhing beneath me was too much.

"Christ, Presley, you're too perfect."

I sat back farther on my heels and yanked her ass off the bed until her thighs brushed my abs. Her eyes opened wide, wild and crazy with her desire. I lifted my hips and drove into her over and over again until Presley was screaming out my name and gripping the comforter.

"Come for me, princess," I said. "I'm not coming until you do."

"I—I don't know if I can."

"Oh, you can." I coated my thumb with her juices and rubbed her clit as I fucked her. With each thrust she bounced against me, whimpering for a release I knew would soon be hers.

"Fuck. Carter!"

"That's it, baby. Come for me."

"I—oh, god . . ."

Then her hips lifted, and she clenched that tight pussy around my cock, her legs shaking violently. She closed her eyes and moaned, "Oh my god, oh my god."

I watched as she rode the wave of her orgasm, her eyes pinned shut as she gasped out my name. I slid my thumb into her mouth and her lips wrapped around it. "Suck it," I growled, and she did.

Her tongue was tentative, but she drew it in, her cheeks hollowing as she sucked. I about lost my damn load. She bobbed her head up and down my thick finger, finding a rhythm with her tongue and drawing it all the way into her throat.

"God that mouth on you, Presley," I said, slamming my hips forward.

I didn't want to be too rough and leave her too sore to walk in the morning, but my cock was aching to own every inch of her pussy before it unloaded. She clenched her walls around me again, and I thrust a little faster and harder than I should have, sweat beading my brow line as I drew closer.

Those lips wrapped around my thumb were like sweet torture as I thought of how'd they feel around my thick cock. I closed my eyes, the tightening of my balls letting me know I was about to explode. I gripped her hips, my head falling back on its own accord as I growled out like an animal, releasing deep inside her.

I fell forward, careful not to crush her with my weight. I eased my finger from her mouth and peppered her swollen lips with gentle, sweet kisses. She looked like a fucking sex goddess in my bed—which was ironic considering this was so new to her. I knew I didn't deserve her—or deserve that special gift from her.

But I knew that before the night was through, I would go back for seconds. And thirds.

I would take as much of Presley Kincaid as she would give me.

CHAPTER SIXTEEN

PRESLEY

"COME ON, PRINCESS," he said before I even had time to think about what I'd just done. Oh my god! I wasn't a virgin anymore! I couldn't wait to tell Willa.

Carter hopped off the bed and held his hand out to me. I was mortified, afraid to look down and see the evidence of what we'd done. There was a small red stain on the comforter, but not as much as I thought there would be. Thank god he had a dark bedspread! Carter scooped it off as if it were no big deal and carried it with us to the bathroom. He tossed it in the hamper in his large walk-in closet and turned to face me. It was stupid, after what I'd let him do to my body, but my instinct was to cover myself. Not because I was ashamed of my body, but because I just wasn't used to being naked in front of a man.

"Presley," he said, moving my hands away and stepping closer, "you are fucking perfect. Please never cover yourself in front of me."

"Why are we in here?" I asked, looking around the large space.

"Because your body is going to be sore, beautiful."

He ran water in the bathtub, adding some Epsom salt to the mix. "Here," he said, pointing to the large soaker tub. "Get in."

"In front of you?" I asked, gaping at him.

"No," he said, stalking toward me and scooping me up. "With me."

I shrieked as he stepped over the rim of the tub, then slowly lowered himself into the warm water. I sank against his chest, my back to his hard abs, and closed my eyes. The warm water *did* feel soothing. My vagina ached, if I was being honest, and my legs felt like Jell-O.

"Thank you," I said quietly.

"For what?" he asked, his fingers running trails on my arms as we talked. I could feel him beneath me, but he wasn't being sexual. He was just all man. I felt small and protected in his arms. It was a nice feeling, and I let myself sink deeper into relaxation.

"For not stopping. For being gentle," I said. Then I thought of the way he'd thrust so deep and hard inside of me, making me beg for more. "Well, most of the time," I chuckled.

"I wish you would've told me first, Presley," he said, nuzzling my neck.

"I didn't think it mattered, Carter. I was honestly hoping you wouldn't even know because I didn't want to make a big deal out of it."

"But it *is* a big deal, isn't it?"

I thought for a minute. How could I explain this to him when it didn't even make sense to me?

"It's not like I ever intentionally stayed a virgin, Carter. I just—didn't have time in college for much fooling around, and the guys I did get intimate with, there was just something missing," I said as I swirled the water around with my hand.

"I wasn't kidding when I told you I didn't normally kiss on a first date," I said, laughing. "I don't know. Maybe it's because I've known you for so long, but it didn't feel like a first date. I just—you were doing things to my body that I've never felt before. So, yeah, I guess it was a big deal. Because for once, it *felt good*—and I mean, really good. But don't let that go to your head, mister," I teased.

Carter nibbled my earlobe in response, and I had to stop myself from dropping my hand beneath the water and searching for him.

"I felt like a woman, tonight, Carter. And not just what people think about me in the public eye. Does that make sense? I'm not a party girl. I don't sleep around. I don't even open myself emotionally to most men because I don't know who I can trust. But I feel like I can trust you. And, I don't regret it. So, yeah, it was pretty damn special, I guess."

Carter groaned, nuzzling my neck with his mouth as he pressed up against me. He kissed the indentation there, and I was surprised when my nipples immediately hardened again. He chuckled, bringing his hands around and cupping my breasts in the water, massaging them. I leaned back instinctively, turning my head and letting his lips find mine again. His mouth was warm, but softer this time, as he explored my mouth slowly.

It was like my body was on autopilot as I pressed my bottom down, grinding against the long length of his cock. I couldn't possibly be intimate again. I was too sore. But my body didn't get that memo. His tongue plunged deeper, forcing me to open wider for him. My pussy ached even more, but not from soreness this time. From desire.

I didn't know if he was wanting to be intimate again, or if he was just enjoying kissing me. I was so damn new to all of this. I didn't wait for his lead. I did what I'd been tempted to do a moment ago. I reached my hand back under the water and wrapped my fingers around him, feeling him pulse and grow even bigger in my grasp. I stroked him back and forth as I slid against him in the water. I wanted to see him, touch him, kiss him down there. I turned in his arms, crawling into his lap.

"Carter," I said.

"We don't have to do this again so soon, Presley. You just— damn. You felt so good against my chest. I thought I could just wash you and get out. How fucking stupid was that."

He gripped my breasts, tugging at the nipples as I ground against his lap. I didn't understand how it could feel *that* good just from having him play with my nipples. "God, you're so sensitive."

He popped a nipple into his mouth and moaned as he sucked enthusiastically. He licked up and down the hard bud, my body arching against his mouth and cupping his head to my chest for more. When he bit down, I cried out in a confused mixture of pleasure and pain.

"Do you like that?" he asked. He tugged my nipple with his teeth again, and my pussy constricted. I nodded. He bit down a little harder, and I caught my lip in my teeth the pleasure was so raw. "I'm going to have a lot of fun teaching you a thing or two."

"I want to taste you, Carter."

He gripped my hips, then stood with me still wrapped around his waist. I lowered my legs, assuming we were getting out.

"Wash yourself first," he said, handing me a washcloth.

I blinked.

He sat on the side of the soaker tub and gripped his cock. I hadn't really *looked* at it yet, but there was Carter, challenging me. Looking me dead in the eyes. I glanced down at his cock, swollen and long. It was straight, and beautiful. He was covered with brown hair from his lower abs all the way down.

"Wash yourself so I can eat your pussy again, princess," he said, slowly stroking himself.

I quickly grabbed the soap and washcloth and washed the blood off between my legs. It wasn't much, but the rest of me was viscous, too, from coming so much—which, before today, I wasn't even sure I could do! After I was clean, I walked toward him, my eyes focusing on his cock. He was so goddamn sexy leaning back on the rim of the tub, his hand sensually sliding back and forth.

Carter was big, even I knew that. I wrapped my hand around his and pumped with him, our strokes matching in time as we squeezed his length with our fingers. He groaned, encouraging me. I knew I was still too sore to have sex again any time soon, but I could do this. He kissed me as I rubbed him, encouraged by the sounds of Carter's pleasure. They guided me when I did something he really liked. I broke the kiss, our eyes meeting. Then I dropped between his legs and kneeled in the water.

I didn't know what to do, exactly. But I'd seen enough in college to try. I wrapped my lips around Carter's thick head and took him into my mouth. He tasted salty and musky. I ran my lips around the tip while I got used to it, then slid my mouth down around his shaft. He was too thick for me to take him all the way in, but I did what I could, swirling my tongue around his shaft. He groaned when I bobbed my head, taking him in and out of my mouth the way I'd seen Willa do once when she'd forgotten to tie a ribbon around our dorm room's knob back in college.

I wrapped my fingers around his thickness, stroking him in rhythm with my mouth. Eventually, I lost track of who was moving—him or me. His hips pressed forward, and I took in more, my mouth stretching to accommodate him just as my insides had. He gripped my head and groaned as he held it in place. He thrust in and out a few more times before he caught himself, then pulled out of my mouth before I could stop him.

I was in a sex haze, somehow so turned on again already. I wanted more of him. All of him. He pulled me to a stand, then drew me into an embrace as he kissed me deeply, passionately. My toes curled as he held me against him, barely touching the tub's surface. His hands were all over my body, and I shivered against him.

"God," he said, stepping back, "you're cold. Come on."

He stepped out, then helped me over the side. He wrapped me in a large, warm towel then draped one over his hips.

"Why did you stop me?" I demanded.

He looked down at me and grinned. "Because you have no idea what power you have, P. If you didn't stop, I would've come inside your throat. And I was this close to doing just that."

The idea that I could push him that close to the edge flooded over me, thrilled me.

"Besides, you just lost your virginity. I think we need to give you a rest. You're already going to be sore."

"But it feels so good," I said truthfully.

He lifted my chin. "And it will feel good again. I promise."

I nodded, not sure what to do now. Should I get dressed? Call for an Uber?

"Come on," he said, pulling me into his closet. He tossed me a pair of sweats and a T-shirt.

"What are these for?"

"Well, I tore your underwear, and I'm not the kind of guy who keeps women's underwear lying around," he said, chuckling. "But you can't eat cheesecake naked."

Then he paused. "Well, you could . . ."

"Did you say cheesecake?"

"I may have."

My buzz was long gone, and the cheesecake sounded delicious.

"Race you to the kitchen," I said after getting dressed in his clothes. They were several sizes too big, but right then, they felt like the most comfortable things I'd ever worn.

He caught up to me in no time, wrapping his arms around my waist and pinning me to the kitchen island. My laughter died against his mouth as he devoured me. His tongue swept my lower lip and then parted them, searching for more. I gave it to him, standing on my tiptoes and letting myself fall into the vortex that is Carter.

CHAPTER SEVENTEEN

CARTER

"HOW BAD IS it?" I whispered into the phone. Not that it mattered. Presley was still fast asleep in my bed. And man did it feel good to think about going to wake her lazy ass up. It was nearly eleven, but I didn't have the heart to wake her. She'd given everything and more to me last night—things I didn't even know I needed, until I snuck out of bed and felt the absence of her punch me in the gut while I did some paperwork this morning.

"Oh, Carter, you know your dad. He's a stubborn old goat," Veta said. "He had a little blood in his stool this morning. I was surprised he even told me about it. Which, I suppose, is what made me worry even more."

"Can they move up the surgery date?"

"It's only three days away, Carter. Not much closer it can get. He'll be okay. I just want you to know what's going on."

"Well, I appreciate it. You call me if anything changes, okay?"

"You still coming down on Tuesday?"

"Yeah. I won't make it in time for the surgery because I have a work commitment here in New York Monday evening. But I promise I'll call as soon as I get onto the island."

"You know you're welcome to stay at your dad's place, sweetie."

Sweetie. I can't remember the last time I'd heard someone call me something like that, with the love and care that only an older relative could do. It was kind of nice.

"I appreciate it, Veta, but I'm staying at the resort this time. I have a job I'm taking while I'm down there, so it works out better this way."

"You know if you tell them you're Bob's son, they'll let you stay for free."

It was sweet that she was looking out for me. "That's okay, Veta. I can afford it now. I don't want to take advantage of my friendship with Dex and his family either. They've done a lot for me over the years."

Had they ever. I didn't tell many people this, but Dex Sr. helped me get into my first pick college. I wasn't sure my grades were really up to snuff—but he'd made a call and boom. My application was fast-tracked, and I'd been accepted early.

It was the only thing I ever wished I'd done differently. It made me feel like I cheated the system somehow. Would I be where I was today if I didn't know the Truitts? It's not something I liked to consider—because my friendship with Dex was as real as it came. He was like a big brother to me. To be honest, he may not even know the favor his father did, come to think about it.

I felt a hand wrap around my waist, and I turned, pleasantly surprised to see Presley standing there in nothing but an old workout shirt of mine that said Beast Mode across the front. I could fucking eat her right up. I looped her into my arms and snuggled into her neck, planting a kiss right where her shoulders started. She giggled quietly, but apparently it didn't escape Veta.

"Sounds like I need to let you go, Carter. You have company?"

"Yeah," I said, grinning. "I have a friend over."

"A friend, huh? Sounds like she might be more than just a friend."

"Veta," I teased, "how in the world could you discern that from just one giggle?"

Presley was now wrapped around my body, her arms linking behind my neck. She was making it damn near impossible for me to wrap up this conversation with my dad's partner. I'd been rock hard all morning thinking of Presley snuggled up in my bed. It had taken all my will power not to wake her up by pressing my dick against that sweet, round bottom of hers. She made the most delicious noises while she slept.

"Call it a woman's intuition, Carter," she said, laughing. "Well, I'll let you go. Fly safely, okay?"

"You got it, Veta. And hey—maybe don't tell dad I'm coming? You know how he gets. I don't want him to get stressed before the surgery."

"Sure thing, Carter. I'll see you soon. Say hi to your lady friend."

As soon as she hung up, I tossed my phone across the room onto the couch and spun Presley around, lifting her onto my kitchen counter. "Morning, sleepyhead," I said, running my hands up her outer thighs.

"What time is it?" she asked, looking around for a clock.

"Almost noon."

"Oh god!" she moaned. "Why'd you let me sleep so late?"

I cupped her ass and pulled her closer. "Because, if you seem to forget, I kept you up till almost five a.m. Thought you could use a little sleep."

She blushed. "I do feel more rested. Thank you, Carter."

"Are you sore this morning?" I asked. It was something I was genuinely concerned about. Talk about beast mode. She'd awoken an animal in me last night. I couldn't seem to get enough of Presley. I knew I'd pushed it—and tried several times to keep my damn hands off her. I was afraid it was too much too soon, given that I'd just taken her virginity.

She shrugged. "I'm a little sore, but in a good way."

Being a guy, I had no clue what that even meant. But she'd been just as fired up as I'd been—instigating several of our intimate moments. Including that damn blow job in the bathtub. I would never be able to shower again and not think of Presley kneeling in front of me, her green eyes filled with an insatiable lust as they stared up at me.

"Too sore?" I asked, my fingers sliding over her thighs toward her hot center. I *had* to taste her this morning. My fingers brushed her bare pussy. *Fuck.* She had nothing on under my T-shirt. "Please tell me you aren't too sore."

We were forehead to forehead. My thumb started making lazy circles around her clit, slowly waking her up. Presley's breathing hitched.

"I'll take that as a no," I said, chuckling.

I slowly alternated between rubbing her clit and dragging my thumb up and down the center of her legs. She was getting wetter with every pass.

"Is it always like this?" she breathed out quietly.

"Like what?" I asked, pressing my thumb inside her hot opening. She groaned, pressing forward into my hand. As hot as this was, I wanted more. I pulled my thumb out and turned my hand, easing one finger, then two, into her tight pussy. "Sweet Jesus you're so fucking tight."

"Is that good thing? Doesn't it make it harder?"

"Oh, it makes it harder all right," I said, sliding my fingers back and forth. "Presley, you have no idea what you do to me, do you?"

She shook her head, her hips wriggling against the counter to match the stroke of my hand.

"And for the record—no, it's not always like this."

She stilled.

"Is that because I'm so new at it? Was it . . . bad?"

I pulled back, looking her directly in the eyes. "God no. It's because I've never wanted so badly to fuck the same woman so many times in one night. It's because I went to bed with the smell of your pussy on my face, and all I dreamed about was getting my tongue back on you."

Presley moaned, her head falling back as she rode the sensation of my busy fingers.

"And because no one has ever felt so fucking amazing wrapped around my cock before. No one," I said. I bent over, pulling Presley's legs over my shoulders. "And that fucking scares me, P. Because I can't stop going back for more."

I pressed my face between her thighs, inhaling her musky, aroused scent. Then my tongue found its way home, flicking her sex lightly, and getting the response that drove me absolutely wild—the shaky thighs, her hands clinging to my hair. That delicious, soft whimper that made my cock kick even harder.

Her noises let me know she was close to climaxing. I stood up, sliding my fingers back inside her slick opening. I found her lips, melting as her arms snaked around my neck and she kissed me back hard. It was half pant, half moan as her tongue swirled with mine. I was so fucking hungry for more, but I wanted her to come first. I found I was living for the sound of her orgasms.

"Yes," she said as we kissed.

"Yes what?"

"I'm—I'm so close," she cried out.

"You like this?" I asked, driving my fingers in as deeply as they'd go and curling them.

"Oh!" she screamed out. "Oh my god!"

"That's it, princess," I coaxed, knowing exactly where I was stroking her and how fast it would make her come. Her body shook, her thighs tightening around my hand. She buried her face in my shoulder and cried out as her orgasm ripped through her. My hands didn't slow until her thighs relaxed and she chuckled softly.

"So much for me playing it cool this morning," she said, her voice shaking.

I pulled my fingers out, then helped her off the counter. "There's no need to ever play games with me. Okay, P?"

She nodded, almost shy to meet my eyes.

"Hey," I said, lifting her chin.

She glanced back at me, as if not knowing what to do with herself now that she'd come all over my kitchen counter.

"There's no need to play it cool with me. I meant what I said earlier. I don't care that you're new to all this. In fact," I stood back, letting my eyes graze down her body, "it turns me on way more than I would've imagined. You asked if this is normal? I don't know, Presley. But it's not for me. This is anything but normal. But normal's fucking boring."

"Okay," she said, nodding. "I just—I didn't know that once I did it, I wouldn't be able to get enough. You know?

I can't stop thinking about everything you did to my body last night. And . . ."

She twirled that damn hair of hers.

"And what, princess?" I demanded, my hands going to her hips and fisting them.

"Am I going to turn into a nympho or something?"

I burst out laughing.

"A nympho?"

She nodded, as if this were a real concern of hers.

"First of all, no one really says 'nympho' anymore. Second of all, god I hope so."

She laughed, looking up at me with those huge, green eyes of hers. "I'm serious, Carter."

"Are you saying I've ruined you for all others, already?" Why did the thought of that excite me so damn much?

"I don't know since I don't have anything to compare it to. Maybe I should find out?" she teased.

"Like hell you will," I said, lifting her into my arms. She squealed, then held on tight as I walked back to my bedroom.

"Carter! Put me down! I need to get dressed and head home. I have to work today!"

I tossed her onto my bed, then lowered my jeans, showing her just how much she turned me on. Her eyes trailed down my stomach and saw the bulge in my boxer shorts. She bit her lower lip.

"As do I," I said, low and heated, "but it can wait."

I slid my boxer briefs down my hips and grabbed a condom from the bedside table. She watched as I rolled it with one hand down my long, thick shaft.

"Time for something new," I said, lying on the bed next to her, on my back. "Come here."

She rolled onto her side and curled up next to me, trailing her fingers over my torso and playing with the dark curls that surrounded the base of my cock. "Are all men this big?" she asked.

"God damn, you're good for the ego, Presley."

She rolled her eyes. "I'm serious."

"I don't want to talk about the size of my cock, princess. I want you to feel it."

I pulled her up so she was lying on top of me. She was breathing heavy, and her hooded, lust-filled gaze told me everything I needed to know. "Bring your pussy up here and sit on my cock."

She pressed into a sitting position on my upper thighs. Presley wrapped a hand around me and squeezed, before slowly stroking up and down. I didn't think I could get any harder, but seeing her spread open like that, over my thighs, her wetness slicking my bare legs . . . I was about to lose it.

"Shouldn't I wet it first?" she asked innocently.

Dear Lord.

"I think you're wet enough for the both of us, Presley," I said, lifting her hips and positioning her right above the tip of my cock. "All you have to do is slide down it."

She didn't hesitate. Her green eyes were locked onto mine as she slowly lowered her bottom. My head pressed in, and yeah—I was right. She was soaked from coming earlier. Presley gasped though when she was just halfway down. It would feel bigger like this, I knew. But I also knew once she got the hang of it, Miss Bossy Pants would love the energy that came with being in control. And god did I want to see her take control over my cock.

"It's okay," I said quietly. "Just take it slow. Pull back up a little, then ease back down. Keep doing that until I'm all the way in, and it gets easier to move."

She nodded, following my directions. I wanted nothing more than to grab her hips and slam my cock straight up inside her, bottoming her out. But that could wait until she was ready. Little by little, she eased her way down. She groaned when she reached the bottom, shifting her hips against my stomach.

"Oh my god!" she cried out softly. "Why does it feel so much bigger like this?"

"Remember what I told you last night? Every position feels a little bit different. Different angles have different advantages."

"Ooh! Can we try them all?" she purred, rolling her hips and sliding against me.

I laughed. "Yeah, Presley, we can if you want. It might take a while though."

"I didn't mean today!" she said, laughing.

"No time like the present," I said, gripping her hips. "Now ride me, princess."

Her body's natural instincts took over, and she began rocking her hips back and forth on my stomach, her body arching with the movement. The pure ecstasy that was written all over her gyrations had me on edge. Watching Presley fuck me was like observing living art. She was a goddess on my cock. A real-life Lady Godiva. I couldn't take it anymore.

I gripped her hips harder, holding her still. She glanced down at me, and I could see the worry flash over her eyes. "Don't worry, P. You were doing everything right. Too right. But now it's my turn," I said, flexing my cock inside her tight channel .

"Do you want me to get off?" she asked.

"Don't move a muscle," I ground out between clenched teeth as I slammed up inside her.

She moaned, then let me continue setting the pace as I lifted and lowered her ass over my cock, meeting her each time I slammed my hips up, pressing deep inside her. She cried out in unrestrained pleasure with every thrust, and I knew I wasn't going to last long like this, listening to her.

"Fuck, fuck, fuck!" I cried out, my pace quickening. Presley's head fell back in pure abandonment, and her small tits bounced with every thrust. She had no idea just how fucking sexy she was, which just made it even more torturous.

As soon as a guttural cry tore through Presley and her insides clenched my cock in release, I let go, too. I pressed my hips up, and stiffened, my body arching back against the bed as I exploded inside her. When my balls were finally empty, I lowered my hips, pulling Presley down on top of me.

We lay pressed together, our bodies sweaty and worn out, as we caught our breath. I ran my hand over her hair, trying to figure out how to get more time with her.

"What if you worked from here today?" I suggested, laughing.

She climbed off the bed and sauntered to the shower. I wasn't sure I had the energy to follow her. Didn't matter. The view was phenomenal. At the last minute before she crossed the threshold to my bathroom, she turned and met my heated gaze.

"I might be able to swing that," she teased, her eyes bright from our morning tryst, "only if you agree to take a few breaks and show me some more of these positions you promised me?"

God damn.

"I've never had sex in a shower before," she said playfully before disappearing into my bathroom.

My feet had never hit the floor so fast. I think we both knew work was a euphemism. At least, I hoped it was.

I had at a minimum of five more ways I wanted to be a first for Presley, and she was a very quick learner. My cock was already hard again before I closed the shower door behind me and melted into Presley's giggle as she began to roll my balls with her fingers.

This woman had no idea what was in store for her. Or maybe she did. She literally had me in the palm of her hands, ready to give her whatever the hell she asked of me.

But it wasn't me who gave this time. It was my sexy, little nympho princess. How in the hell had I gotten so lucky?

CHAPTER EIGHTEEN

PRESLEY

THE DAY FLEW by so fast I could hardly believe it. Shower sex led to kitchen sex, which led to library sex, before we finally had a late lunch/early dinner. Carter drove me home so I could grab my laptop, shower alone, pack an overnight bag, and add more food to Jar Jar's automatic feeder. He nearly choked on his coffee that we'd stopped and grabbed on the way over when I told him my cat's name. Turns out the rescue dog he walks was affectionately nicknamed Baby Yoda, and it kinda stuck.

I'd snuck in a text to Willa with about ten exclamation points, but I wanted to tell her the BIG news in person if I could. It wasn't every day a girl lost her virginity.

We were back at Carter's place, and he was busy cooking something sinful on an indoor grill that was built into his large, commercial-grade stove that I swear was nicer than mine. I was supposed to be doing background research—on Carter no less—in prep for the upcoming article. I felt like a little sneak. I could probably ask him directly, but that would be hard to explain to Sylvia, and this wasn't supposed to be the interview itself, just context I needed to turn in so she could help shape the direction she wanted the story to take.

As I looked around Carter's spacious, open condo, I was in awe of the man he'd become. I thought back to the scrappy teenager I'd crushed on and realized he'd been right not to kiss me back then. I could finally see that now. Beyond our age difference, I couldn't help but wonder what would've happened if he had, and neither of us liked it. Would I be sitting here today? Fate has a funny way of pulling strings and working on her own damn fickle timeline.

I grinned. *Carter Wright.*

I couldn't believe I'd given my virginity to the same man who turned down my first kiss. Never in a million years could I have seen this coming a week ago. And those fucking butterflies? Never mind those. I didn't even have words to describe the fluttery feelings I had when Carter kissed me. Or the way he made my toes curl. Hell, I didn't even know I could have multiple orgasms, because in all the times I'd pleasured myself, I'd mostly stuck to the outside surface. And oh my god! The things I'd been missing out on!

But I wouldn't trade it for the world. As sore as I was today, and for as long as I'd waited, it had been worth it. Even if this—whatever the heck this is between Carter and me—is temporary, it will have been worth it. Because now I *knew* those feelings existed, and not just in Willa's romance novels either.

> WILLA: What's up, girl?
> PRES: OMG! Willa! I went out with Carter last night!
> WILLA: Can you call? I want the dirt!
> PRES: I can't actually.
> WILLA: Because?

PRES: Because I'm kinda still with him?

WILLA: Shut your face!

PRES: I know! I can't wait to tell you everything.

WILLA: Just one question.

PRES: Yeah?

WILLA: You still pure as the winter snow?

PRES: . . .

WILLA: . . .

PRES: Well, I mean, how do I answer that? Our snow here in NYC is kinda dirty, isn't it?

WILLA: You telling me you're DIRTY now?

PRES: Maaaaybe . . .

WILLA: HOLY SHIT! The man has corrupted you already! Go, Carter!

PRES: Hey . . . what about Go, Presley!

WILLA: Go, Presley! 😏

PRES: Thanks, I think?

WILLA: I can't wait to hear all the deets. When?

PRES: Well . . . I'm kinda staying over again tonight.

WILLA: Wait—what? How many times did you do it, girl?

PRES: Um . . .

WILLA: I mean, are we talking you can count the number on one hand? Two?

PRES: I don't know. I mean, I kinda lost count?

WILLA: Never in my wildest dreams did I think I'd be living vicariously through you!

PRES: Right?

WILLA: Just tell me . . . was it worth all that damn waiting?

PRES: A thousand percent.

WILLA: 😌

PRES: Let's meet for dinner tomorrow. I need my BFF!

WILLA: Sounds good, doll. And P?

PRES: Yeah?

WILLA: I'm happy for you. For realz.

PRES: Thanks, Willa. Me too.

WILLA: Just don't go getting your heart broken, okay?

PRES: Don't worry. I'm not pretending it's anything more than just hot sex at this point.

WILLA: And you're okay with that?

PRES: Am I ever!!!

WILLA: Hahaha!

PRES: Later, gator.

WILLA: In a while, crocodile.

PRES: I love you.

WILLA: I know.

What could I say? That was our thing. The way we always signed off with each other. We'd been best friends for a long, long time—since our freshman year at Brearley, a private, all-girls high school. I couldn't wait to talk with her tomorrow night. I had so many questions—and they were questions I couldn't ask Carter, no matter how comfortable I felt with him.

I stood up and paced the room. That was part of the problem. I was already too comfortable with him. A week and a half ago, I was bickering with him at the rehearsal dinner. This week, I was riding naked, cowgirl style on him. And I unabashedly wanted *more*.

I looked at the pictures Carter had set up around the living room. They were all in black and white, even recent ones. It was hard to tell when they were taken. My favorite was a picture of Carter standing with his dad as adults, their arms around each other in front of The Grove's main resort. There were other free-standing cottages around the island that you could rent for more privacy, but if you wanted to be seen, you stayed at the resort.

The front entrance was grand, with a dual staircase sweeping up to the main landing, which was a giant balcony leading to massive double doors. It was the resort's signature showstopper piece, and anyone who stayed there knew those stairs. They'd probably even had family pictures taken on them at some point like we had.

There was also a picture of Carter when he was younger with his dad. That was the Mister Bob I knew! He'd been the nicest man. He always gave us kids tokens for the ice cream parlor on the pier. You could only get them from Mister Bob—your parents couldn't buy them for you. He wasn't stingy with them though. He loved seeing the kids and passing them out. Sometimes he'd make me "work" for one—something easy like feed the fish in the koi pond or sit up all the chair backs on the pool loungers. I did that in the early morning before anyone else was up. Sometimes I'd help him put out a rolled towel on each chair, too, or he'd let me help him weed the entrance when no one was looking.

One time, he even let me go on rounds with him on the golf course. He talked to me about the island's history, and all the secrets it held. It always fascinated me when I was younger. I didn't know if there was buried treasure there, or what. But I'd always ask more questions, trying to sleuth out the truth. He'd just smile and say, "Someday, Miss Presley, someday. Today's not the day."

I grinned, moving on to the next picture. Hmmm . . . that was interesting. It was an older one. Despite it, too, being in black and white, the clothes were clearly from a different era. It appeared to be a reprint from a newspaper clipping. I didn't know who all was in the picture. There were two young men in their late twenties, early thirties, I'd guess. They were standing in front of what looked like The Grove's front entrance—recognizable only by the start of that grand staircase behind them. It was an active construction zone, but there was a ribbon in front of them, and one of the bored boys at their side was holding a giant set of scissors to do the ribbon cutting. Behind them was a sign that caught my attention. It looked like a builder's sign—large, wooden, proud. I couldn't make out the name on it. It was longer than "Truitt" though, and Dex's family owned both the resort and island. Maybe they'd contracted out the construction back then. Montague Enterprises wasn't in the business of building real estate anyway.

I took a quick snapshot of the picture and texted it to my graphics partner at work. Rico could sniff out anything and had way better equipment than I did. He'd not only be able to zoom in on the image, but probably find the exact newspaper it was originally printed in.

At least, I hoped so.

I mean, why would Carter have a picture of the men who built The Grove in his apartment unless one of them was related to him? And that wasn't Carter as a boy in the picture, clearly. I squinted, looking closer. Was that, Bob? It was hard to tell.

"What are you looking at?" Carter asked, making me jump.

"You scared me!" I said, laughing.

"Dinner's ready."

"Oh, good. I'm starving."

"Well, get some calories in, princess, 'cause you'll be working them off really soon," he promised.

We dined on the most delicious bacon-wrapped, blue-cheese burgers I'd ever eaten. I polished the whole thing off, along with a chop salad and a bottle of beer.

"You spoiled me with dinner, Carter."

"I needed to make sure you had enough energy for later," he said playfully.

"Oh yeah, and why's that? You think you're gonna get lucky again?"

His dimples flashed and heat filled his eyes just like that. We'd gone from fairly benign dinner banter to wickedly naughty conversation in the blink of an eye. I didn't know if this was normal or not, but I loved Carter's filthy mouth and all the delicious ways he promised to corrupt me.

"Oh, I know I am," he said confidently. Cocky almost.

"Want to wager a small bet?" I asked, raising a brow.

"Oh yeah, and what's that?"

"A game of war. If you win, you get lucky."

"You mean, if I win, *you* get lucky," he said and winked.

"Well, true," I conceded.

"And if you win?"

"You have to watch me pleasure myself, but you don't get to touch me for the rest of the night."

"No."

"Afraid to lose?"

"No, but I'm not taking any chances."

"But either way, you win. You either get to have my body or get to watch me being pleasured. Win-win, right?"

"Wrong," he said, pushing his chair back and stalking toward my side of the table. "There is no way I can watch you play with yourself and not touch you."

He pulled me up from my seat. "If you play with yourself, Presley, it'll be because I asked you to. And I will watch. But I couldn't stop my mouth from finding that pussy if you paid me."

"I think a little self-control would be good for you, Carter."

"You really want a lesson in self-control, princess? You have no idea what you're asking for."

The way he said it made my skin break out in goose bumps. His eyes were dangerously dark, and I knew there was so much to Carter I hadn't even scratched the surface of yet.

"Show me," I whispered.

He walked forward, pushing my body back until it collided with the glass wall overlooking the city. His body was hard and sexy as fuck against mine. He leaned down and sucked my bottom lip in, leaving me in a puddle of my own wetness. I pressed my legs together, willing myself to not be so weak around him.

Carter stepped back, walking to the coffee table and picking something up. It was a remote control, and he used it to darken the glass windows so no one could see in.

"Take off your clothes," he ordered.

He stood across the room from me, his hands in his pockets.

"Now?" I asked, looking down at the city on the other side of the glass.

"Yes, princess. Now."

"But . . .we haven't cleaned the dinner dishes up," I squeaked.

"Fuck the dishes, Presley."

"Nah, they're not my type," I said, stalling.

"Clothes. Off."

My body gave me no other choice. I was so freaking aroused with his bossiness.

I stared directly into his eyes and rolled the straps of my dress over my shoulders and down my frame. Carter's eyes raked over my body, his jaw clenching when he realized I'd been naked beneath my dress all evening. The thrill that gave me, of knowing he wanted me just as badly as I wanted him, made my body shiver all over. All I wanted was for him to rush across the room and have his dirty way with me.

Why did I press him on patience and control again?

Carter didn't storm over. He patiently lowered himself onto his couch and stayed fully clothed as he watched me. The large bulge in his dress pants gave away his desire though. He grinned when he caught me eyeing it. "Like what you see?"

I nodded, already dripping wet with the idea of having Carter sliding back inside me. I mean, how many more positions could there be? I shivered in anticipation.

"Touch your breasts, Presley. I want to watch you play with them."

I reached my hands up and cupped them, my eyes still trained on his.

"What do you like when I play with them?" he asked.

I swallowed. I would not demure around Carter and lose my edge. "When you tug on them."

"Show me."

I pinched the nipples as Carter had done to me many times now and tugged them up until my breasts were like triangles. The combination of pinching and pulling sent a wave of pleasure straight between my legs.

Carter grinned. "That's my girl. Now walk over to me, Presley."

I walked as slowly as I could to show him that I had patience and control too. But it was bullshit. I just needed to feel Carter thick inside me. God! I'd gone completely wanton.

I stopped when he told me to, next to the glass coffee table. It had a large, glossy, real wood base, made from an ancient-sized tree trunk. The large oval top twinkled up at me in the reflection of the overhead lighting.

"Lay down, Presley."

I looked down at the table, then back up to him. Was he serious? He nodded toward the table. I blinked, swallowing my pride as I sat on the cold glass.

"All the way down."

I reclined until my back was flat. My nipples were rock hard and standing straight up from the cool, teasing sensation of the glass beneath me. He finally stood up and walked around the table, looking down at me.

"Do you do this with women often, Carter?" I asked, flushing at being so open and vulnerable with him.

"Never," he whispered reverently as he openly worshiped every inch of my body with his eyes. "You seem to bring out the beast in me, Presley."

I shivered against the glass in anticipation.

"Touch yourself. Like you said you would."

"But we never played the game, Carter. I said I would if I lost."

"We're past that now, aren't we, P? Now touch yourself. Show me how you like it."

I swallowed.

Then I reached my hand down. I'd never played with myself in front of a man with the lights on before. Sure, a guy and I had done that a few times together when we were in college, and I hadn't been ready for anything more than some heavy petting. So, to relieve the itch, we both pleasured ourselves. But it was always in the dark, and under a blanket. Now, here I was, just a few years later, with my legs wide open on a glass table under the watchful, heated gaze of my biggest crush—the one I never thought I would have.

My, how times had changed.

I didn't know how long they would last, and I wanted to soak up every experience with Carter while I could before he grew bored with the novelty of an inexperienced lover.

I closed my eyes and let my hands slide down my body, to my stomach. One beer had not been enough to give me courage for this. I imagined I was alone, so I wouldn't worry about doing it "right." I did what felt good. What made me release when I was alone. My fingers parted my folds, teasing the entrance, which was wet under Carter's intense gaze. I could feel his eyes burn over me as I worked my clit, my legs parting farther.

My breathing grew heavy, and I wanted to slide my fingers all the way inside, but I'd never done that before. Not like I wanted to now. Not as *deep* as I needed to silence that slow burn aching to be released. My body arched and squirmed on the table as my legs shook, looking for a release I knew I couldn't get like this.

I shuttered my pride and slid two fingers down, pressing them between my folds. I arched, whimpering with the relief of feeling them inside me. It wasn't enough, but it was a start. I slid them back and forth, ignoring the slick sounds my pussy was making. I was so close, but I didn't think I could get there myself.

"I need help," I groaned, my fingers frantically trying to achieve what Carter could do in one second, it seemed.

"Tell me what you want, my naughty princess."

"Your mouth."

"Where?" he demanded.

"On me. Between my legs."

"I don't know," Carter said, considering. "Maybe a little self-control would be good for you, Presley," he teased.

"Carter!" I cried. "Don't make me beg. Please . . ."

"Well, since you asked so nicely."

He was on me in a flash, his arms gripping under my thighs and tugging me to the edge of the table to his waiting mouth. "God you taste so fucking good."

The sounds of him licking me, the suctioning of his mouth over my clit, the moan against my pussy as he applied pressure with his clasped hands that pinned me down—it overwhelmed my senses to the point of nearly blacking out. I saw lights spark behind my lids as my body convulsed, shuddering like it never had before with an orgasm under Carter's mouth. And I'd had plenty over the last twenty-four hours.

I felt a flood release within me, and I nearly sobbed in relief.

Carter scooped me up and carried me to his bedroom, where he continued giving me lessons in both patience and control. I'd gone from being a virgin to a sex-craved maniac in less than two days, thanks to Carter. And I didn't mind it a single bit.

We were both restless that night, and we found ourselves in each other's arms more often than not. It was as if we were both reaching out to one another even in our sleep, still aching to be closer, closer. Sometime before dawn, I finally fell into a deep and heavy sleep, a smile on my face before I crashed into a dreamless slumber.

CHAPTER NINETEEN

CARTER

IT WAS WELL after noon by the time I woke up. Lucky for me, it was to the smell of fresh bacon. I hopped in the shower but didn't take time to shave. I don't know when or how the hell Presley had crawled under my skin so fast, but she was like a fucking drug. I just wanted more of her.

I made my way to the kitchen and nearly came at the sight of her standing at my stove in a pair of the skimpy, black shorts women sometimes worked out in. She had a workout bra on under a loose tank top, the sides dipping low and revealing a large portion of her soft skin. It gave me all kinds of naughty ideas.

"Morning," she said with an easy smile before turning back to the stove. "Hope you don't mind, but I was starving after last night, so I helped myself to your kitchen. Hope you're hungry."

I peered over her shoulder at the French toast she was flipping. It smelled like cinnamon and heaven—in other words, like Presley. "Damn those look good."

I moved her hair over her shoulder and kissed the bare spot near her clavicle. I wasn't used to such sentimental gestures, but it had somehow become one of my favorite things to do. "Did you sleep okay?"

"I did, actually. Slept like a baby. Well, you know. After the last time we . . ."

"Fucked?" I said suggestively. Clearly, I couldn't get it off my mind.

"Yeah, that."

I was grateful to see that Presley was a coffee girl, too, and poured myself a large mug from the Keurig. "Mmm," I said, closing my eyes. "Good choice on the coffee. Man, do I need this today."

"Same," she chuckled. "I actually have a lot of work I have to do, unfortunately. So, after brunch, I've gotta head out."

Well, shoot. I'd been hoping to have another lazy day of making love to her. There were still so many positions we hadn't tried out. And Presley was . . . insatiable. I freaking loved it. The more we tried, the more she wanted. She was completely at ease with anything and everything we'd done so far. She was every man's wet dream, if I was being honest with myself. How I had ever been attracted to Lauren all these years was beyond me. She had nothing on Presley. And that felt damn good to say.

It was more than the sex though—and it was everything else that scared me. She was smart as fuck. Educated and thoughtful. Curious. Presley was interested in my answers, too. She had a smart mouth and made me laugh more times than I could count. The best part was she gave it just as easily as she took it.

I was doomed.

"So, what are you working on?" I asked as she handed me my plate. We went and ate at the smaller breakfast table by the windows.

"Well," she said hesitantly, "it's something I actually need to talk to you about."

"Oh yeah?" I asked, shoveling a mouthful of French toast into my mouth. "Damn. These are amazing. When did you learn to cook like this?"

"My dad taught me, actually," she said quietly. "In the summer, when he'd vacation with us, he spent time showing me how to cook his favorite meals. He didn't get a chance to cook often when we were back at home because he was so busy with work. But the summers were my favorite time of year. That's when I actually got to spend a lot of one-on-one time with him."

I nodded. I remembered Presley's dad well. He'd been a good man. Not like some of the other douche bags who vacationed at The Grove. "He taught you well. These are amazing!"

She didn't answer, so I knew something was worrying her. I caught the way she nibbled at her lip instead of her breakfast. She cupped her mug of coffee and used it as a shield as she sipped.

"Spill it, P. What's up?"

"Well, just know this was not my idea. Okay?"

"Uh, okay."

"Lauren somehow got the idea to do an article on you. I think she saw it as an opportunity to share your story with the world, while 'helping' a family friend," I said, doing the air quotes with my fingers. "She spoke to my boss, Sylvia, who then spoke to me. We just so happen to be spotlighting the top thirty millionaire bachelors under the age of thirty. So, the bottom line is that *Finance Times* wants to do an online feature article on you for it."

Well, that wasn't where I thought this was going. *Shit.* I set my fork down and rubbed my temples, deciding what to say and how to say it. "Presley, that's awfully kind of Lauren, and of Sylvia. But I'm gonna have to say no."

She lowered her fork, her eyes holding fast to mine. "I'm sorry. You're going to have to say *no?*"

I nodded, decided. "You heard me. First of all, there's a conflict of interest now. How can you be unbiased when you've let me bury my face in your—"

"Okay, okay. I get it. Is there a second of all?"

"Second, and most important of all, I don't want the whole world to know my goddamn story. There's nothing special to tell. I'm a simple guy who runs a simple business. The whole idea is not to have it broadcast, so that people who choose to use my services aren't embarrassed. I'm not an escort, and I don't want to put any of my clients in an uncomfortable situation."

She wiped her mouth with her cloth napkin. "I should have said something sooner, Carter. Before I let things get this far with us. I meant to. On Friday. I had—I had no intention of sleeping with you. You know that. I can recuse myself and get another writer to cover the story. But I don't think it was a question. I think Sylvia wants to cover your story now. And she doesn't need your permission to do a piece—it would just be helpful if she did so that you could be presented fairly and accurately. So you're *not* written off as an escort. I know that's not what you do, Carter."

Fuck. This was the last kind of attention I wanted to draw to myself. "Why? I just don't get it. I'm nothing special, Presley. I'm just a guy who came from nothing. Yeah, I'm doing okay by my standards. But compared to the Kincaids and the Truitts of New York, my portfolio is a joke."

"That's not true, Carter. Most people will never become millionaires in their lifetimes. You've managed to do that before you even turn thirty!"

"Yeah, well, the clock's ticking on that too."

"I know," she said. "Which is why we want to do the article ASAP, before your thirtieth birthday."

"That's less than a month away," I pointed out.

"There's time, especially with it being an online exclusive."

I sighed. My heart and my head were at war with themselves. "Fine. But I won't do it unless you agree to a few terms."

"I'll have to run them by Sylvia, but I'm open to hearing them," she said as she set her napkin on the table. "Should I get something to take notes on?"

I laughed. "You're something else, Presley. I think you'll be able to remember them. First, I won't cooperate unless you write the article. Period. Conflict or not."

She nodded but said nothing.

"Secondly, I'm getting ready to go to The Grove for a work event and to see my dad. He's having surgery Tuesday, and I need to be there when he wakes up."

"I'm sorry to hear that," she said.

"Yeah, me too. He's going to be okay though," I said, more confident than I felt. An idea started brewing as I considered my options. "If you want to interview me, you need to come with me on this trip. You can get a lot of one-on-one access to ask whatever you want. But I'll only answer questions while we're away. When we get back, the interview is over. Then it's just me and you again. I don't want work interfering."

"Interfering? With what?"

"With us."

SOMEHOW, BY THE grace of god, Presley agreed to my terms. Though she said we'd talk about "us" when we got back. My hands felt clammy as I helped her pack up her bag to bring her home. I wanted her to stay all weekend and was afraid if she left, it would all be just a dream. I don't know why I felt that way. Maybe because Presley feels out of my league. Even as a bratty thirteen year old, she still knew her place on the island. Felt the comfort of her privilege.

I just wanted one more day with her. Now, I'd have five or six.

When she was done gathering her things, I saw her standing by my pictures again. She'd been there yesterday, too, looking at the same one.

"Whatcha looking at?" I asked, over her shoulder.

"I noticed this picture yesterday," she said. "Do you know who these men are?"

"Is this Presley asking, or Miss Kincaid, investigative reporter?"

She made a snarly face at me and I laughed.

"Fine. I never asked my dad, so I'm not a hundred percent sure, but I think the boy holding the scissors is him. I found this newspaper clipping in my grandpa's old journals."

"Did they say anything about the picture?"

"I don't know," I answered, honestly. "I haven't read them yet."

"How come?" she asked, looking at the rest of the pictures on my built-in bookshelves.

"The situation's complicated," I said, shrugging. "Guess I never felt the need to."

I shoved my hands in my pockets, thinking about the interview and how much I wanted to share with Presley. "He wasn't exactly grandpa of the year," I admitted, finally. "He abandoned my dad when he was a kid—not long after this picture was taken. Just up and ran off."

She turned, placing a hand on my arm. I didn't want to see the pity that was in her eyes.

"Where was your grandmother when your grandpa took off?"

"She'd passed away already by then in a car accident. She and my grandpa went off a bridge. My grandfather walked away from it, but just barely. Dad says he had a limp after that and couldn't remember much about the accident. Didn't talk about it anyway."

"I'm so sorry, Carter. Do you think he mentions it in the journals at all?"

I shrugged again. "Not sure I care."

"But it's your family's history! How can you *not* want to know?"

I thought about what she was asking. Sure, I'd wondered before when I was a teen. I'd pestered my dad with questions that he wouldn't, or couldn't, answer. But I'd grown up and left all that behind me when it was clear I was getting nowhere. With dad being sick now, though, maybe I *should* talk to him about it. It was definitely a wake-up call that my time with him could be cut short. And someday, my own kids might have questions. I'd sure as hell like to be able to answer them—unlike my dad.

"Yeah, I guess so," I said, rubbing the back of my neck.

She flushed. "I'm sorry, Carter. I don't mean to be nosy. I really don't. I just—look at the sign behind those men. Does

Dex's family own that company? Didn't his grandfather build The Grove himself after purchasing the island?"

"I don't know, not for sure really. I was told growing up that his family owned the place. They didn't run it though. A trust does. That's how my dad got paid. But everyone knew it was owned by the Truitt family. They could've subcontracted it out back then, I guess. Makes sense. They aren't in the commercial real estate business that I know of."

Presley nodded. "Is the man behind your father your grandpa then? I see a little resemblance," she said, eyeing me.

"Maybe. I see my dad a little in him, but I don't know for sure. I never saw a picture of my grandfather. Not sure why he'd be in a picture like this though. He was a mailman, I think."

Presley nodded, as if thinking. "Have you asked your dad about the picture?"

I shook my head. "I can when I'm down there, though."

Her eyes were bright, curious. I loved to see how the wheels in her head were spinning. I hoped it was for personal interest and not just because of the article. But I'd take any excuse I could get to spend more time with Presley.

I cleared my throat, looking at the picture one last time and wondering what brought my dad to the island that day for the ribbon cutting. "After my grandpa took off, a local family who knew the Truitts adopted my dad. They ended up working for the resort, so when my father was old enough, he started working at the resort, too. Made his way up to being the property manager with a lot of hard work. Even though he had a pretty rough go of it, he never let that stop him or hold him back," I said, proudly. I shook my head. "He might not be a millionaire, but stories should be written about men like him. Not me."

"I disagree," Presley said, taking my hand in hers.

The sexy look in her eyes made my chest puff out in pride and was entirely too dangerous. If she kept looking at me like that, I'd never get her home.

"Come on," I said, gently rubbing my thumb over the back of her hand. "It's getting late, and I know you need to work before your dinner with Willa."

She smiled. "Thanks, Carter. I really appreciate it."

I would move heaven and hell to make that woman smile like that more.

"You gonna tell Willa all about our wild weekend?" I teased, winking at her.

Presley's face flushed an adorable shade of pink.

"Just make sure you mention what an overachiever I am."

Presley laughed, squeezing my hand. "Some things I might want to keep to myself."

"Fair enough. Maybe just slip in somewhere that I have a huge—"

"Carter!" she yelled playfully.

I swooped down and kissed her, silencing that hot little mouth of hers. One kiss became two. And before I knew what was happening, our clothes were off, and I was showing Presley yet another fun position—this time in the entryway.

Based on her reaction, this might be her new favorite.

CHAPTER TWENTY

PRESLEY

"STAWP!" WILLA NEARLY screeched as we hid behind our menus and giggled hysterically. We were grabbing dinner at our favorite Vietnamese restaurant, a little hole in the wall that had the freshest ingredients in New York. Willa took a sip of her wine and nodded. "But go on—tell me more!"

I laughed as we handed the menus back to the waiter. I gave her the highlights of my weekend until the food arrived. Then we dug into our shared dish of brown rice, fried tofu, grilled pineapple chunks, and steamed organic veggies. We split the same thing every single time. I dipped mine into their house-made peanut sauce and moaned. "I don't think I've ever tasted anything better in my life."

"Anything?" Willa teased. "Even after this weekend?"

I nearly spit out my mouthful of food. "Willa!"

"Come on," she begged. "I want *all* the juicy details!!"

So, over dinner, I spilled the beans. It was all so new to me, and I was still kind of in shock at myself. "So, is that normal, then?" I asked, pushing the food around my plate. I was stuffed. "Wanting it even more after the first time? I mean, it's literally all I can think about right now. Everywhere

I look, my mind drifts off, and I'm daydreaming about Carter's mouth, or the things he's said to me, or the way he manhandles my body in all the right ways."

Willa sighed, looking at me dreamily. "I am so jealous right now."

"Don't be! I'm miserable!"

"You are not. And why would you be?"

"Willa . . . I slept with Carter, even though I knew I shouldn't because of work. I crossed ethical lines. And now? I'm cursed with him being my first. I mean—who's ever going to top Carter? And worst of all, he has me all wound up like some nymphomaniac! I'm gonna have to call up Charlie Sheen and find out the name of his sex therapist, for heaven's sake!"

Willa clutched her sides and was laughing so hard others were starting to look at us. "What's so funny?"

"Girl. You are," she said, wiping a tear from her eye. "You're not a sex addict. It's called being horny. And Carter unleased your inner sex goddess. That is nothing to be miserable about, I promise. Enjoy the ride while it lasts!"

That was the problem. How long would this last before Carter tired of me? Before he decided I was still the bratty girl he remembered from childhood? Or worse, that the sex wasn't really that good and he could do better? Ugh! Sex just complicated things—which is why I'd avoided it for so many years.

"I guess so. I'm just worried, Willa. I mean, it can't always be this good, right? Like, every time?"

"Define every time."

"What do you mean, define it? I mean, every time we've had sex. Surely there's going to be a time when it's just a flop, right? Statistically speaking—"

"No, girl. No. Statistics have nothing to do with chemistry. Leave them out of the bedroom."

"God! You're right. What is wrong with me?" I nearly jumped out of my skin when my phone vibrated on the table. I never answer it during my Willa time, but I was waiting on a return call from Sylvia. "One sec, let me just see who this is and make sure it's not work."

I picked up my phone and grinned.

It was Carter.

I quickly read his text. *I cancelled my job Monday night, so we're flying out at noon tomorrow. I'll be by to pick you up at ten. Pack something sexy.*

My ears burned bright red, which happened sometimes when I got flustered. It didn't escape Willa's attention.

"So, when are you seeing him again?"

I glanced up, sheepishly. "Uh . . . tomorrow?"

"Wow, girl. You two are moving fast. I don't think you have anything to worry about with him growing bored with you."

"It's not like that," I said, explaining what happened with the article and how he'd made me agree to go with him to The Grove. "It's for work. We just happen to be going together."

"Mmm-hmm. And aliens aren't real."

I laughed. Aliens were Willa's baseline for everything. "Fine," I conceded. "I might be hoping to get a little lucky this trip. I mean, he did tell me to pack something sexy."

"And?" she pressed, paying for the bill when it came before I could grab my wallet. "Do you even have anything sexy?"

"Define sexy . . ."

"I'll take that as a no. Come on, girl. We're going shopping. I know just the place!"

TWO HOURS AND two grand later, I had a sexy number for every night of our trip. You know, just in case. I also bought a few matching bra and panty sets, because my old grannie panties just wouldn't cut it if I wanted to keep having sex.

Me. Having sex.

I squealed inwardly as I packed for our trip. When had I become *this* girl? I get laid once, and now I'm jumping up and down over a guy? I needed to snap the fuck out of it. I called Bianca to ask for some advice, but it went straight to voicemail. She and Dex had met because of an exclusive article she'd gotten to write about him. Not only had that article been a game changer career-wise, she'd also ended up meeting the love of her life—even if it hadn't felt that way at first. Not that Carter was my soul mate or anything. Sheesh. But these waters were tricky to navigate, and Bianca had sailed this ship before. And here I was, floundering out in the deep end with no life jacket.

I needed to get to sleep, but first I wanted to pop over to The Grove's website and see if I could get any info about when it was built and who was at the ribbon-cutting ceremony when they broke ground. It was coming up on its sixty-fifth anniversary of being open. The website mentioned little about the Truitt family, which was odd. It just showed a Limited Liability Company's name in fine print at the end of The Grove's "About Us" section. Other than the resort itself, there was no additional contact information. Maybe Dex would know?

I checked my phone. It was after midnight, and I had to get up early to work and then head to South Carolina with Carter. I'd call Dex tomorrow. I jotted down a few strings I wanted to tug, though I wasn't sure why I was bothering with this.

Sure, Carter's dad had been in the picture. But maybe that's all it had been. A cute photo op. It had nothing to do with the story I was writing, so I probably just needed to let it go.

I climbed into bed, grateful for my cold sheets. When I reached for the phone to set my alarm for the next morning, I noticed a missed call from Rico, and a text from Carter. My insides definitely did a little flip and a little flop. I rolled my eyes. I was *so* becoming that girl.

It was too late to call Rico back, so I snuggled down with Jar Jar and opened my texts from Carter with a shit-eating grin on my face. The cat meowed, then plopped down on his pillow next to mine and started kneading.

> CARTER: Hey, princess. Don't forget to bring a swimsuit.
> CARTER: And something sexy. Did I mention that already?
> CARTER: I know it's uncool to text so soon after our first date. But since we kinda threw all our first date rules out the window, and I've known you since you were in pigtails, I figured a text or two the day after wouldn't hurt.
> CARTER: Am I right? Hello?

We certainly *had* thrown all first date rules out the window. And second, and third, and fourth. Good god, the things I'd unabashedly let that man do to my body. I was a heathen. A happy heathen. But a heathen, nonetheless. Might as well text him back.

> PRES: You're forgiven. On one condition.
> CARTER: Oh yeah? What's that?

PRES: You score an ice cream token for me.

CARTER: I might know a guy. Any other conditions?

PRES: Come to think of it, I might have a few more . . .

CARTER: Presley, are you flirting with me?

PRES: Maaaaybe.

PRES: Unless that's uncool. Then I'm totally not.

PRES: I'm not. Truly. I mean, we're keeping this week professional, right?

PRES: Though, you did technically ask me to bring something sexy.

CARTER: Pres?

PRES: Hmm?

CARTER: You're so lucky you're not at my place right now.

PRES: How come?

CARTER: Because I'd have to stop that overthinking mind of yours somehow.

PRES: And how might you have done that?

CARTER: Oh, I can think of a few creative ways to keep you so preoccupied you won't be able to think at all.

PRES: Promises, promises.

CARTER: I don't make promises I can't keep.

PRES: Pinky promise?

CARTER: I am not typing that back. I have an image to uphold.

PRES: Okay. Then nothing sexy for you, Mister Stand-In.

CARTER: . . .

PRES: . . .

CARTER: God I'm pussy whipped already.

PRES: You did not just say that!

CARTER: Meow.

PRES: . . .

CARTER: Okay. Okay.

CARTER: I pinky promise I will ravish you so much this week that you won't be able to overthink.

PRES: I pinky promise I'll bring something so sexy you will need a forklift to pick your chin up off the floor.

CARTER: Girl, why didn't you just lead with that? I would've pinky promised my life away five minutes ago!

PRES: Just helping you with your self-control, Carter.

CARTER: You're working toward a spanking . . .

PRES: Promises, promises.

CARTER: Why are we going again? Sure you don't want to just come over and interview me tonight instead?

PRES: Is that what they're calling it these days?

CARTER: You can call it whatever you want, princess.

PRES: Self. Control.

CARTER: Fine. See you in the morning.

PRES: Night, Mr. Stand-In.

CARTER: Night, Miss Moneybags.

PRES: Who's getting the spanking now?

CARTER: Promises, promises . . .

PRESLEY: 😃

CHAPTER TWENTY-ONE

CARTER

"I'M REALLY GONNA miss her," I said, scratching Baby Yoda's favorite spot.

"There will be others. I promise," Dex reassured me.

"Shh," I said, "not in front of her."

Dex laughed.

"So, have you heard from Lauren and Richard? How are they doing on their honeymoon?"

"Yeah, it kinda got cut short. They're actually coming back tonight."

"Man, that's too bad," I said. "How come? Everything all right?"

"Yeah, just some work stuff. We opened a few charitable organizations, and the legal side's been a bear, especially in terms of structuring the way we manage and allocate contributions. Richard's creating a whole new finance group just for that division of Montague Enterprises, so there's no questions about our ethics, and everything's transparent. You know how bad things were when I first took it over from my father."

"I get it. You had to do things your own way. I respect you for how you've turned that company around."

"Thanks. It's an adventure every single day, but I love it."

I set Baby down and let her join her park friends for the last few minutes before we headed back. I needed to go pick up Presley, and Dex had to get back for a meeting.

"Hey, I have a question for you. Didn't Bianca interview you when you first met?"

Dex chuckled. "Yeah. It's how we met actually." He shook his head. "Never met a woman who asked me to hold her balls before."

"What?" I nearly choked out.

"Stress balls. They broke the ice. We were stuck in an elevator."

"Stress balls." I nodded. "So, how did you get from that to dating? Did she interview you before or after you started hooking up?"

Dex narrowed his gaze at me. "This is about Presley, isn't it?"

I glanced out over the dog park, acting like I was searching for Baby. But really, I couldn't look Dex in the eyes yet. How could I explain how much had happened, so fast. And why I was freaking the fuck out, because I knew right away that Presley wasn't the kind of girl you got over.

"Yeah," I admitted. I scuffed my sneakers in the dirt, watching a cloud of dust kick up. "Did Bianca tell you what happened at the wedding?"

"Something happened with you and Bianca?"

"No! God—no. I meant, regarding Presley. Apparently, Lauren got this big idea in her head as a way to say thank you to me, an 'old family friend.' So, she threw my name in the ring for the *Finance Times's* "Thirty Under Thirty" list. And get this—she somehow convinced Sylvia to consider me for the featured article online."

"That's great news, Carter!"

"No, it's not," I muttered.

"How come?"

"Because I don't want everyone to know my business model. It only works because of the fact that no one knows I'm hired unless the person wants them to know. I don't want to come across as an escort, and then embarrass any past clients. Not to mention, I just don't want everyone in my business, man."

"I hear you, Carter. I really do. But I've got no clout when it comes to axing an article. I couldn't even do that when I was pursuing Bianca. She was going to publish the article regardless of whether I filled in the blanks for her or not. And I wanted to do it my way, on my terms. So, I did."

"Did you hook up while she was writing it?"

"Why? You thinking of hooking up with Presley?"

I shrugged but couldn't stop the smirk. Just the sound of her name brought up so many memories from the past week.

"Shit, Carter."

"What?"

"You already have, haven't you?"

I shrugged again. I wasn't one to kiss and tell.

"I can't speak to the ethics part of the article if you've already done the deed. That'll be between her and her editor. But I can say this. The more you're involved in the story, the more you shape your own narrative. Period. And you have to be okay with that, even if things between you and Presley don't outlive the article. You feel me?"

"Yeah, man. Thanks." We gathered up the dogs and were walking back to the shelter when I remembered something I wanted to tell him. "Oh, hey, I meant to tell you, my dad's not doing so great. He's getting some precancerous polyps removed tomorrow."

"Oh man," Dex said. "I'm really sorry to hear that. Is there anything I can do?"

"I don't think so. He said it's pretty common. I'm hoping that's true."

Dex nodded. "If it changes, just let me know."

"Definitely," I said. "Presley and I are actually heading down this afternoon. I had a job there this week anyway, and we're gonna use the time together to bang out the article."

"I have no doubt you'll be banging something out," he said, smirking.

"Funny," I said. But honestly, it took my mind off my dad and I needed that.

"You want to stay at my place while you're there?"

"You mean at the big house?"

"Sure," Dex said. "Why not? Bianca and I were just down there, so it's still fully staffed, clean, and has a ton of food. I can have them get some rooms ready for you."

"Today? Just like that?"

Dex nodded. "It's better than the resort. I promise. No matter how much money was dumped into that place, you're still sharing walls. And if you and Presley do end up banging something out, you'll love the extra room and private amenities at the house."

Damn. In all my years, I'd never been in the big house. It was in a gated part of the island and was just for the Truitt family. I'd snuck back there when I was a kid, of course. But we'd never had the balls to sneak into the house itself—or any of the other private family "cottages."

"Sure, man. If you're cool with that."

"No problem. You can let me know how everything's looking while you're there."

I couldn't wait to tell Presley where we were now staying. Maybe I'd let it be a surprise. I wondered if she'd ever been back there in all her years on the island.

We'd soon find out.

THE FLIGHT WAS short, but the drive to the island would take about forty-five minutes. Everything was connected by old coastal highways, forcing us through other small beach towns before getting to the bridge that went over to The Grove. All this slowed the speed limit down, which I didn't mind since I had Presley all to myself in the back of the limousine I'd hired to pick us up from the airport. If it had been just me, I'd have rented a Jeep and been done with it. But Dex told me the house was stocked with fun cars to drive and not to waste my money on a rental.

That, and Presley deserved to arrive in style. I don't know why it felt important to me. Maybe because the last time we'd been on the island together, it hadn't ended so well. I wanted to erase any bad memories she had left of The Grove.

"Pretty swanky," she said, climbing into the back of the black stretch Lincoln sedan. The interior was two different tones of beige, and the seats were as soft as melted butter. "You didn't do this on my account, did you, Carter?"

I slid in beside her and closed the door behind us, grateful for two cold waters already waiting for us. I always forget how hell has nothing on the south's level of heat and humidity. I guzzled gratefully, handing the other to Presley.

"Of course I did. I couldn't let the princess return in a broken-down pumpkin, now could I?"

She grinned. "Very funny."

"Look, it's a forty-five-minute drive. I wanted us to be comfortable."

She glanced shyly at the darkened window separating us from the driver. "Any other reason?"

"Why, Presley, are you suggesting what I think you're suggesting?"

She ran her hand up the thigh of my distressed jeans, and I could feel the soft brush of her skin as it slid over the ripped parts of the material. She squeezed my upper thigh, then dipped her hand lower, nestling it in the heated crevasse between my legs.

"It's such a cliché, I know. But it's on my short list of places I've always wanted to make love."

I sputtered on the bottle of water I'd been downing. "You—have a list?" God, my cock was growing rock hard just thinking about crossing off every single place on that list with Presley.

"Yeah, doesn't everyone?"

"For a woman who was a virgin just a few days ago, you sure have a lot of surprises up your sleeve."

"You have no idea, Carter."

My dick kicked, already revving to go.

"So, tell me a few," I said. I ran my fingers up her bare legs until I found the hem of her short, lemon-printed wrap dress. How Presley managed to make a sundress full of large, bright yellow lemons look sinful as fuck was beyond me. But I'd never seen anything sexier as she leaned back against the seat and closed her eyes under the soft featherlight strokes of my fingers on her bare thighs.

She swallowed as my hand roamed farther under her skirt and brushed the hem of her panties. Lace. They were fucking lace.

"Well, a limo to start with. A hot tub. Another cliché, I know. Outdoors, like maybe while on a hike. Maybe at an overlook. The Eiffel Tower, though that one may be harder with security and cameras. The beach, of course."

"Of course," I groaned, imagining her naked on the beach now. "Anywhere else, little Miss Adventurous?"

"Ooh, I like that better than Moneybags."

"Don't get used to it. You'll always be Miss Moneybags to me," I teased. I slid my fingers past the hem of her panties and leaned over, sprinkling her neck with soft kisses. "Go on."

"How am I supposed to concentrate when you're doing that?"

"You're supposed to get out of your head this week, remember?" I teased, running my finger up and down her opening. The bottom of her dress was hiked up high on her thighs now, and I could see her fighting the war between keeping her knees together for some level of modesty, and letting them splay apart so I could get better access. I wiggled the tip of my finger in to get it wet, then circled her clit with it a few times.

Her legs parted for me, her need winning out.

"While camping," she continued, my fingers catching speed as I rubbed her clit. "In an office building. An elevator. On a desk," she said, blushing. Her breathing started getting heavy, turning into a half pant, half whimper as I scooped a finger between her wet folds. "Uh, on an airplane."

"You should've told me," I said, peppering her ears and neck with warm kisses. "I would've flown us down on a private jet."

"You have one?" she squeaked out, now pressing her pussy against my hand.

"No, but I know a guy," I said as I slid my second finger all the way in.

"Oh, fuck," she cried out, raising her hips to meet my palm.

"Where else, princess?"

I sucked her earlobe between my lips as I slowly slid my fingers back and forth now, fucking her with them. She gripped my wrist, her eyes rolling back as I increased the pace. Her hips were jerking in small, short spasms now.

"I—fuck, Carter. I can't think when you're doing this to me."

"Good, that's the point."

I slid from my seat, kneeling on the carpet in front of her, my fingers still pressed deep inside her. Her nostrils flared, her breathing hitching when she realized what was coming. I bowed my head, inhaling her fresh, clean scent of oranges and vanilla, mixed with the musky scent of her excitement.

"I'm gonna fuck you in all those places, Presley. Every last one, if you'll let me."

I flicked my tongue over her clit and she gasped, arching off the limo's seat.

"I have a few of my own I'm gonna add, though . . . because I've always wanted to fuck on a poker table," I said, then closed my lips around her swollen nub and sucked harder. "In Vegas."

I was rewarded with a moan as her fingers sought out my hair. I buried my face in her pussy and sucked on the outer lips as my fingers worked her over inside. She lifted her mons, pressing it against my warm mouth as I worshiped her with my tongue and brought her closer to release.

When she was almost there, I kneeled back, letting my fingers continue to slowly scoop back and forth inside her. I glanced up and was met with the most intense, passion-filled gaze. I wanted to draw out her release, though.

"At the movie theater," I said, adding to my ever-growing list as I grinned up at her. "In a lake, on a floating dock. On a tractor. In a pool."

"Fuck, Carter! A tractor? Really?" she cried out as I used my tongue to flick her swollen clit again.

"On a boat, too," I said, pulling it in and gently sucking on it to ease the building tension. "In a backyard looking up at the stars. On a balcony with people partying below, none the wiser."

I couldn't hold back any longer. I buried my face between her thighs, increasing the speed of my fingers and lapping at her sweet pussy with my tongue. She pressed her legs together, gripping the sides of my head as I sucked harder. It didn't take long for them to begin shaking as her insides tightened.

"God, Carter! I'm so close."

"Come for me baby," I said, sitting up. I took her mouth in mine and crushed my lips to hers. She was so fucking pliable and soft. They parted for me, her tongue hungrily searching my own. I thought of the night she'd surprised me by taking me in her mouth in the bathtub. My cock was swelling to the point of erupting it was so hard.

Presley sucked my tongue in—it was a hard, demanding, needy kiss as she finally peaked. Her head dropped back, her chest arching forward as she pressed down against my hand and released. Her warmth flooded my fingers as her legs spasmed. A soft giggle escaped her lips when she was done climaxing.

I pulled my fingers out, cleaning the evidence of our sex play with my mouth. "Do you have any idea how hot you are?"

"Me? You did all the work," she said, pulling her panties back into place and straightening the bottom of her dress. "Can you tell?"

"Tell what?" I asked, sitting back against the comfortable seat, fully pleased with myself.

"You know," she said, looking directly into my eyes. "Will the driver be able to tell we did anything?"

A smile curled my lips to one side. "If we didn't do anything, I think he'd be disappointed, princess."

Her ears burned a bright pink and she looked adorable as hell. Yeah, the driver would know we fooled around. And I was all right with that. I wanted the whole damn world to know this woman was mine.

CHAPTER TWENTY-TWO

PRESLEY

"UH . . . " I SAID eloquently, "do you have more money than you're letting on, Carter?" I looked up at the mammoth, three-story, dusky blue house with white colonial-style hurricane shutters. There was a two-car garage beneath the elevated beach house and a set of wooden stairs to a grand front porch. While pretty, I suspected it would pale in comparison to the back porch, overlooking the Atlantic Ocean.

"I wish," he said, grabbing my suitcase and heading toward the elevator doors beneath the house.

"This doesn't look like a Grove cottage," I said, looking around and noticing jet skis, kayaks, and paddle boards lined up neatly under the porch. "And here," I said, taking my suitcase back. "You have enough to carry, I can handle my own bag."

"Of course you can," he said. "I was just trying to be a gentleman."

Oh. I smiled sheepishly.

"Okay, then," I said, handing the suitcase back. "Thank you. Sorry, I'm just not used to guys doing something like that for me."

"What kind of guys do you date, P?" he asked, arching a brow. "I'm not claiming to be the best thing out there, but you know you deserve better, right?"

I laughed as we stepped into the elevator and ascended to the main floor. It was sweet of Carter. Of course he didn't know my dating history. Or lack thereof.

"You don't have to worry about that with me, Carter. Lauren taught me well in that arena. I know the kind of man I'm worthy of. I just haven't found him yet. So, I guess I can't let someone be a little gentlemanly if there is no someone."

He pressed his lips together while holding the elevator door open with his arm. "After you, princess," he said. I exited the elevator and set my laptop bag onto the floor. Carter reached out, grabbing my elbow so he could turn me to face him. "By the way, you do now."

I swallowed, my tongue inadvertently swiping over my upper lip out of habit.

"Lord, woman, stop that. And get all the way inside. Otherwise, I'll be tempted to fuck you right here in the entryway. And while that appeals to me—there are many better options on your Down and Dirty list that we can start crossing off," I said, glancing back at the elevator suggestively.

I blushed, unused to how forward he was. So sure of what he wanted sexually from me—and would deliver, no doubt. It wasn't that I'd been a prude just because I was a virgin. I'd just never found someone before Carter whom I wanted to give it all to.

The thing I loved about Carter was he didn't treat me like some delicate flower he had to protect. In fact, just the opposite. He recognized the fire that burned deep in my belly, and he was more than happy to stoke it for me.

Any time I wanted.

And after the car ride from the airport, I wanted even more. Badly.

"Let's start with the kitchen, then," I said, sashaying in the general direction I suspected it would be in. It didn't take long for Carter to drop our suitcases, chase after me, and make all my filthy countertop fantasies come true.

———

"SO DEX OWNS all this then?" I asked in awe. We'd had a chance to shower, and now we were eating dinner on the back deck. Our reclaimed wooden table sat ten and overlooked a bright blue pool that glowed warmly from the interior lights. Candles were set on the table, and in hurricane lamps around the pool, helping bring a little light to the area. It was pitch black out here, with a smattering of bright-white, far-off stars flung across the canvas of the night sky.

"Is that the Milky Way?" I asked, pointing.

"Yeah," Carter said, sitting back in his chair and sipping a long-neck beer. "One of my favorite things to do as a kid was go lay out on the beach on a blanket and look up at the sky. It makes me feel more at home than almost anywhere else on this island."

"I didn't know that," I said, twisting my napkin in my hands on my lap. But then, why would I? We were kids the last time we were here together, and he never spent much time with me then unless he was forced to. "What was it like growing up here?"

"It was hard some days," he said, looking out at the water rolling in, and then being gently pulled back out by the tide. Large sand dunes separated the house from the water, but from our height, nothing obstructed our view. And, honestly, my eyes weren't fixed on the same spot as Carter's because I couldn't take my mind off the handsome man sitting across from me.

"How come?" I asked gently. We'd had such different experiences here. I never thought about how much until now.

"Pres, you know we didn't have a lot. Yeah, The Grove paid my dad far more than he would've earned elsewhere without a college education. And I am grateful for the unusual lifestyle I had growing up on a resort island. But I still had to cross the bridge and go to school with the locals. And I never fit in, really. To the visitors, I was just an island kid. But to the local kids, I was an outcast because I wasn't around enough outside of school. I always had to come back here to help."

"I'm sorry, Carter."

"I'm not asking for your pity, Presley. I'm simply answering your question honestly." He took another long pull from his beer.

"You had plenty of friends, though, it seemed like."

"I had a few," he said, "but my life was mostly helping dad out here."

"Is that why you wanted to join the military after college?"

Carter laughed. "I couldn't wait to get the hell out of here. Not that it's not beautiful," he said, sweeping his hand at the view before us. "But this wasn't exactly how I grew up."

"But you can afford this lifestyle now," I said.

"Is this an interview question or a you question?"

Ouch. "I was asking because I'm trying to get to know you better, Carter."

He took another impressive sip, finishing off his beer. Then he stood, stretching his arms into the night air. "I'm gonna go grab another beer. You want anything?"

I could tell he'd shut down, but I didn't understand why. "No thanks. I think I'm just going to get some sleep if that's okay. I'm exhausted."

Carter nodded. I half expected him to make a comment about *why* I was so tired and maybe offer to help me fall asleep. Disappointment flooded over me when he sauntered back into the kitchen alone and pulled open the refrigerator door. I stood, too, looking out at the calm water. It was so quiet here—something I never experienced back in New York. It's not called "the city that never sleeps" for nothing.

Tomorrow I would get up early and walk along the shoreline, looking for seashells. It was something my father and I used to love doing. Lauren wouldn't come out of their bedroom suite until almost eleven each day, and by then she was pulled together and looked country club fabulous. Meanwhile, my dad and I had already been out shell hunting, swimming in the pool, and bike riding. We'd be hot and sweaty. She always let him wrap her in a wet hug, though, and kiss her on the neck. It was the same greeting almost every morning.

But I felt like I got the best part of him every day. It was our special time together, and something I looked forward to all year long. The summer after dad died, Lauren and I tried to come here alone, and it ended up being a disaster. Instead of coming out of her suite by eleven, I wouldn't see her until almost three. Dinner at the club was lonely without dad. I could tell the staff who had known and liked him felt pity for us as we ate alone, not talking. It just wasn't the same without his light to hold us together.

A shooting star flashed across the sky over the ocean right in front of me, and I smiled, closing my eyes and making a wish for Carter's dad.

I was so glad we weren't staying at the resort, after all. Being out here—well, maybe I could breathe and focus on my job. And maybe, just maybe, not drown in the memories of my father while we were here.

I looked back over my shoulder and Carter was nowhere to be seen. Yeah. I needed to pull my shit together and remember why I was here in the first place.

I locked the French doors to the back patio, then turned off the lights downstairs before heading to my bedroom. I was surprised that Carter had given me my own room while we were here. But, suddenly, I was grateful. It was too soon to be spending every night together. If I'd been in his bed, there would be no rest for the wicked. Carter was like a drug, and I was scared I wouldn't know what to do when I couldn't get my next hit. Or that, after Carter, everything else would feel like taking a Tylenol when what I really needed was something much stronger.

And worst of all?

I was already craving my next high.

Carter, meanwhile, was nowhere to be found, and I had no idea what I'd done to close him up like that. I tossed and turned all night long, barely sleeping a wink. Finally, like the desperate junkie I was becoming, I snuck out of my room and went in search of my fix.

CHAPTER TWENTY-THREE

CARTER

I WAS DREAMING of Presley. She was sun-kissed, standing in a small, coral bikini facing the water. Only it wasn't her today—it was Presley at thirteen. I'd been surfing all day, and the boys had gone home already. I was dragging my board back down the beach to get to the spot where we always stashed our things. That's where Presley was, her eyes shifting from the water to me as I drew closer.

"What do you want, brat?" I said, not sure why I felt the need to ruin her peaceful moment. Only, she didn't belong here. This wasn't where resort guests normally swam. It was behind our house and all the maintenance buildings on the backside of the golf course. "Don't you have a dance to get to?"

The dance was a stupid, end-of-summer tradition. All the kids loved it because locals usually came. And it was one night when they could be completely free, with no parents looking over their shoulders. Resort staff chaperoned the dance, so dad always made me show up for a little bit of it. But this year, I refused. I was heading off to college in a couple of weeks. He couldn't make me do that kind of bullshit anymore.

Presley shook her head. That's when I noticed a tear sliding down her cheek. I dropped my board and pulled on a long-sleeve T-shirt. The sun was setting, and it was cooling off by the water. "Why the long face?"

She bit her bottom lip, crossing her arms over her nonexistent chest. Well, I couldn't say nonexistent anymore. She'd started to fill out since last summer, but I felt like a perv for even noticing.

"My dad," she said, then plopped down onto the sand, her head falling to her bent knees. Her whole body shook as she cried, and I had not one clue how to comfort her.

"Is he . . . okay?" I asked, sitting beside her. I glanced down the beach, making sure my friends were long gone. I'd never hear the end of it if they caught me with Presley. She made it well known that she was mooning over me all summer—even though her bratty behavior would say otherwise. We'd all caught the way she looked at me sometimes. But she was just a kid, and there was no way I was touching that—no matter what lewd things my friends suggested.

She shook her head. "No. I think he's going to die. I overheard him talking to Lauren today when they thought I was at the pool."

Oh, fuck.

"Man," I said, running my hand in the sand in front of me, "that sucks."

"You think?" she said, her voice dripping with sarcasm. She looked directly at me, and I noticed for the first time that her eyes were green. She still had braces on, though, and her hair was pulled back into a long French braid that hung down her scrawny back.

"Hey, look," I said, knowing I would regret this later, "I wasn't going to go to the dance tonight, but maybe I could go with you to get your mind off your dad. You know—as friends."

She squinted at me, suspicious, before standing and brushing the sand from her legs. "Really, Carter?"

What did I say wrong?

I stood up and almost laughed when Presley put her hands on her hips and glared at me—like the child that she was.

"Never mind, *princess*. I was just trying to do you a favor."

There was ice in her eyes as she glared at me. They softened for just a fraction of a second, though, as I studied her. Maybe she was going through puberty and was just overly hormonal.

"I have no desire to hang around a bunch of little kids and sweat all night. But if you *really* want to do me a favor, I have a different one I'd like to ask."

Little kids, huh?

"And what's that?" I asked, crossing my arms over my chest. I didn't know how she wasn't cold by now. That's when I noticed the goose bumps racing up her thin arms. I pulled off my T-shirt and tossed it to her. "Put this on."

"Thanks," she said, tugging it over her head. The sleeves dangled past her hands it was so big on her.

"What?" I finally spit out. "What favor could you possibly ask me that I'd actually do?"

She lowered her eyes to the sand, and I knew that I was in trouble. She took a deep breath. I watched as her chest rose and fell as she gathered the courage to ask me whatever was on her mind.

My subconscious knew what was coming in my dream because I'd already lived it once.

"I want you to kiss me," she finally said, looking up at me.

I didn't even know what to say to her. Her green eyes were filled with vulnerability and hope. And I'd be the one to crush it. There was no way I could kiss Presley Kincaid—not in a million years. I couldn't because of who her father was and his relationship to my dad's boss. I couldn't because, secretly, I tossed off almost daily while thinking about her stepmom's large, round tits.

But most of all, I couldn't because—*fuck!*—Presley was only thirteen. No matter how horny I was, it was a line I wouldn't cross. I was going to college this year, and she was going into the eighth grade. Yeah, some guys might've done it. But I wasn't some guys. And Presley wasn't just some girl I'd never see again. If I came home for breaks, I'd have to face her and her dad next summer. That is—unless what she said was true.

I shook my head, trying to figure out how to let her down easy. Presley didn't seem like the kind of girl who fooled around at thirteen. In fact, she was usually out shelling with her dad, skimboarding the waves, and giggling with her friends as they ate popsicles by the pool, playing stupid, babyish games like Marco Polo.

"Why me?" I asked.

"Because, Carter, I may not be back again after this summer if it's true. And, I'm pissed, okay? I'm pissed that they're keeping something from me. And that I can't do a damn thing about it." Her chest was heaving now.

"I've never been kissed before, okay?" she admitted. "And I just—I don't know," she said, twisting my sleeves into her palms. "I feel like I can trust you. You know, with something like that."

Shit! I ran my hand through my hair, feeling like a dick.

"I can't, Presley."

"Why not?" she demanded, taking a step toward me. "Your stupid friends aren't here. No one will know, and your *cool* reputation won't be ruined because of me. I just—please, Carter?"

I shook my head no again, but I felt a sexual pull in my dream that I didn't have as a teenager while turning her down. When I glanced back at her, her breasts were larger. She ran her tongue over her top lip and batted those big, green eyes up at me.

"Carter?" she whispered.

I wanted to. God, did I want to now. What was happening to me? My dick swelled under my surf shorts, making them uncomfortably tight. Presley reached down and stroked my cock, and I groaned. *I shouldn't be doing this,* I thought.

Then, teenage Presley stood on her tiptoes and brushed her lips across mine. It wasn't so bad. It was kind of nice, actually. I looked down at her, and the sadness was still in her eyes, but now they were blazing with lust too. How did she know what lust was?

Fuck it.

I reached my hand down and wrapped it under her hair and cupped the back of her neck. She whimpered, pressing her tight, little body up against me. "Is this what you wanted, princess?" I asked, my other hand cupping her breast. It had grown considerably and was now a nice handful. Her nipple was rock hard, and I ached to wrap my mouth around it.

"Yes," she breathed out. "Oh god, Carter. Yes!"

The images were blurring between Presley then and Presley now.

Warm lips parted mine, pulling me from my twisted dream. Presley had crawled into my bed at some point and was now in my arms, kissing me back. I knew I wasn't still dreaming, but it sure felt like I was. I pushed images of younger Presley out of my mind and blinked a few times, trying to wake up more fully.

"Sorry," I said, groggily. "I had the weirdest dream."

"I'm not," she said, huskily. "You woke me with the hottest, most urgent kiss."

"I did?"

"Mmm-hmm," she said, nuzzling even closer. She suckled my lower lip, tugging at it, as she pressed against me. Then her mouth left mine, and she made her way down my chest and under the covers, leaving a trail of kisses along the way

The sensation of her warm, wet mouth flicking the head of my cock and then swallowing me into her throat was enough to confirm I was, in fact, wide awake now and no longer dreaming. I palmed her soft, blond hair, buried somewhere under my comforter, and closed my eyes. I knew I should stop her, pull her up so I could give her pleasure in return, but her mouth was like a fucking beacon, and my dick was happy finding its way home. Her hands cupped my balls, just as they were tightening. I knew I wouldn't last. I had to pull her up.

"Presley," I ground out between clenched teeth. I was about to explode. "Get your sweet ass up here."

"I want to taste you, Carter," she said, sucking me all the way in and running her tongue up and down my shaft.

I couldn't have stopped myself if I tried. I arched my hips up, and after a couple frenzied thrusts, my body spasmed as my cock constricted and then released. I was still holding onto Presley's hair, and she never lifted her head as she drank me in. It was the things dreams are made of, but this time, thank god, I was wide awake. Presley slowly made her way back up when I was done, my legs shaking from the torrent of my orgasm.

"Jesus, that was hot as fuck," I said, pulling her into my arms. I kissed her lips, tasting myself on there and causing my dick to flex again. Damn that was fast.

"I'm glad you liked it," she said, suddenly yawning.

"To what do I owe this pleasure?" I asked, my voice still husky from sleep. I couldn't figure out how or when she'd crawled into my bed. Especially after how I'd treated her earlier. I'd been an ass, and I knew I had to apologize.

"I couldn't sleep," she said, her eyes closed. She snuggled into my chest deeper and spooned into me. "All I could think about was you."

"I'm so sorry about earlier, Presley," I said, whispering it into her hair as I cradled her in my arms.

She mumbled something incoherent about me being a drug as her arm softened across my chest as she fell asleep. I stroked her hair softly and watched as she sunk deeper into a heavy slumber. Only when I was sure she was out hard did I close my own eyes, falling back into a blissful dreamland where adult Presley was begging me for a kiss again.

This time, I gave it to her. I gave her everything I had.

CHAPTER TWENTY-FOUR

PRESLEY

"DO YOU WANT me to come with you?" I asked Carter the next morning. Well, mid-afternoon, actually—because we'd spent all morning checking off spots on what I now referred to as my "Down and Dirty" list, thanks to Carter giving it a name. Then we showered and grabbed a quick bite to eat before he needed to scoot to the hospital.

"If it's okay, I think I'd like to go alone. It's been a couple years since I've seen my dad. And I have no idea what kind of shape he'll be in or if he'll want visitors. Why don't you hang out by the pool or something? Relax."

"Well, because technically this is a work trip for me, Carter."

"True, true. But you can't exactly interview me until I get home, right? So, why not make the most of your day? When was the last time you took time off? Loosened up?"

"You think I need to loosen up?"

Carter stared at me as if his eyes alone were saying, "Duh!"

"Fine!" I said, throwing my hands up in the air. I put the cream cheese back in the fridge and turned to say goodbye to Carter. I watched his back as he scooped up his wallet and keys from the entry table. I still couldn't believe the guy I'd embarrassed myself with on this very island was standing here with me now—a full-fledged man. A hottie at that. I needed to figure out a way to write this article in an unbiased way, and I was afraid the more I slept with Carter, the harder that would be.

"See ya later, princess," he said with a disarming grin before stepping into the elevator.

I stood there, not sure what to do with myself. I wandered around the house, checking out the other rooms we hadn't explored yet. For an architecture lover, Dex's beach house was like a wet dream. It was mostly a traditional-style home inside, though the kitchen was open to the great room and dining room. And you could see the ocean from the entire bottom floor. There seemed to be no bad view from this house.

I explored the other two bedrooms on the second floor that Carter and I weren't using. Then I made my way up to the third floor, where there were four more—along with a library/office combo and access to a small, sky-viewing porch with a railing. It was only big enough for a couple of lounge chairs, but the view from up here at night must be breathtaking. I wondered if Carter knew about it. I couldn't wait to share it with him. Gazing up at the night sky together sounded like heaven to me, and I knew it was one of Carter's favorite things to do.

I went back to the library to look around. I was torn between working up here or on the back patio. I was afraid the heat of the day and the lull of the ocean would either pull me in for a swim or send my ass to the hammock for a nap.

My phone rang, startling me. I rarely got calls these days as almost everything could be done over text. I glanced down, seeing it was Rico. I answered right away.

"Did you find anything out?"

"Hello to you, too, Presley."

"I'm sorry," I said, laughing. I sat down at the desk and propped my feet up, making myself at home. "Hey, Rico. How's it going? You and Artie doing okay these days?" I asked with sincerity.

"We're great, thanks. The adoption is actually going through! Her mother is scheduled for a C-section at the end of next week, so we're hoping to bring baby Amalie home right after that. I still can't believe I'm finally going to be someone's dad."

"Rico! That's great! We really need to do something to celebrate. Is anyone at work throwing you a baby shower?"

"I haven't thought much about one, to be honest. We were just so focused on whether we'd even get her or not."

"Well, let me ask Bailey. If one hasn't been organized yet, I'll make sure she puts a bug in Sylvia's ear. I know how long you've waited for this, and how many hoops you had to jump through until you found your surrogate. It's definitely worth celebrating!"

"That'd be great, Presley. We're kind of in shock that it's happening so fast now," he said, chuckling. "Artie's running around like a mad man trying to get the crib built and installing car seats. I told him to slow his roll since we both take the train everywhere, but he has this three-page checklist that I swear is going to be the death of me."

I laughed with my friend and coworker for a few moments more, then remembered the reason for the call. "All right, so lay it on me, Rico. I'm assuming you found something out?"

"I did. I'm going to send over some files of the original image blown up. It was from the local paper down there. The article talked about the original builder, a man with the last name Cartwright—that's the name on the builder's board in the background of the picture. It was unclear if he was just the builder or the original owner. The island was purchased from its original owner outright in all cash as part of a closed estate auction. The deed went to this Cartwright fellow for a short time, but he was the builder, so I'm not sure why. Not long after that, he went missing. Just—disappeared. Off the grid. No one has heard from him since. No known living relatives."

"Damn," I said. Why would Carter have a picture of him? How did his dad fit into the picture? "How did the Truitt family come to own the property? Did anyone suspect foul play?"

"According to the article, everything was transferred to the Truitt family before The Grove opened. It was never in the other man's hands as a finished resort. He never saw the project of a lifetime come to fruition. It's kind of sad if it was truly his."

"Yeah," I agreed. "And there's a legal paper trail to the Truitts?"

"Yep. Everything is in their name, uncontested all these years later. There were some fishy things happening on the work site though—police reports filed for vandalism, arson, that kind of thing. Seemed like they all clustered around the ribbon cutting, but then died down eventually. Maybe once it switched hands."

"Was there any connection between these crimes and the Cartwright guy's disappearance?"

"Not that the police found. They chalked it up to local kids partying there after hours. Once they installed twenty-four-hour security, those crimes disappeared. Back then, that would've been armed night guards, I suppose."

"So, who all was in the picture?"

"That was Keaton Truitt, Dex's grandfather. The other man was the builder, Pennington Cunningham Cartwright. The kids were Dex Truitt Sr., Robert Wright, Catherine St. Germain, and Davison Rockefeller."

"Holy shit. Why was he there?"

"No clue. The family's name is on nothing else, so he could just be the kid of a family friend."

"Nice friends," I muttered.

"Right? There's something else we found out, too. I doubt it's related, but I'll let you decide."

"What is it?" I asked, swinging my legs down, now on the edge of my seat.

A stack of papers went flying everywhere. "Shit!"

"You okay over there?" Rico asked.

"Yeah, just clumsy," I sighed, looking down at the mess I'd made. "Go on. I'll take care of it after our call."

"Well, it's just weird. Even though the deed for the property and the resort itself is in the Truitt family name, there was also a substantial trust set up at the same time, tied to the sale. It's closed, though. So only the family's attorney would be privy to the details, or whoever's name is on the trust. But it doesn't make much sense, as far as I can tell."

"How'd you even find out about it?"

"Presley, haven't you learned not to ask me that by now?"

"Fair point," I said, laughing. "I doubt it has anything to do with my current article, anyway."

"Oh yeah, who's that on? The Truitt family?"

"No. That's been done. And done again," I said, laughing. "This is on the son of the other boy in the photo. He had this picture up in his home, and I got curious."

"You know what they say about curiosity," he warned.

"Ha-ha," I said dryly. "Duly noted. Thanks, Rico."

When I hung up, I immediately texted Sylvia's assistant, Bailey, about Rico and Artie's baby shower. Luckily, she was all in and told me not to worry about a thing.

Looking down at the mess on the floor, I sighed. What a klutz! I started picking everything up and trying to organize it back into its original neat stack when something caught my eye. I didn't mean to snoop, but the legal paperwork was clearly for an established trust. That's when I saw it was the same Limited Liability Company that was listed on The Grove's website, which in and of itself wasn't shocking.

But my hands began to shake when I saw a name I recognized as the beneficiary of said trust. *Holy crap!*

CHAPTER TWENTY-FIVE

CARTER

"I DON'T UNDERSTAND," I said, looking between Veta and my father. "I thought you said this was just routine surgery, removing a couple polyps."

Dad cleared his throat, reaching out for my hand. "It was, son. And I'll still be okay. I promise. But they found a small mass when they were in there that was hidden during my initial exam. The camera found it when they were removing the polyps."

"A mass. A fucking mass? What does that even mean?" I didn't mean to, but my voice was getting louder with each question. I let go of his hand and ran my fingers through my hair as I paced the small hospital room. "Like, cancer? Is that what you're saying?"

I glanced at Veta and saw her head lower, a lone tear sliding down her brown cheek. Then I looked back to my dad, and when I saw his stoic eyes, I knew.

"Pops," I said, my voice catching. This could not be happening.

"Look, son, it's not a death sentence or anything, okay? One step at a time. I meet with an oncologist tomorrow.

We'll go from there. Try not to borrow too many worries, okay? We don't know what we're facing yet."

"Yeah, but Dad—"

"Get over here, Carter," he said. And I did. I leaned over the hospital bed and wrapped my arms around the man who had been the one constant my whole life. *My* rock.

Now I needed to be his.

I straightened up, grabbing his hand again. "Just let me know what you need," I said. "I'm doing all right for myself now, and I can help with hospital bills, home care, whatever you need. I can come stay here for as long as you need, too, if you need any extra help. I just—"

My throat caught and I had to bite back tears. I would not do that to my dad.

"Carter, I'm fine. I promise. One day at a time. Okay?"

I shoved my hands in the pockets of my jeans and fiddled with Dex's car keys. "All right, Dad. I'll be on the island at least through the end of the week and will head over to your house after your oncology appointment if that's okay."

"Sounds good, son." He looked tired, and that pissed me off. I needed the strong dad I remembered. The one who had energy for days and single-handedly ran the wealthiest island resort in the United States. The one who played ball with me for hours on end when I was twelve. And worked out with me when I was sixteen and wanted to beef up for the girls. The man who ran laps around me, even after I'd gotten out of the military.

"Where'd you say you were staying while you're here?" he asked, gratefully taking the cup of ice Veta handed him.

"I'm actually staying at the Truitt's place," I said. "I was gonna stay at the resort because I have a job there tomorrow night. But Dex offered, and I couldn't pass it up. Have you ever been over there?" I asked, then felt stupid. Of course he had. He knew every inch of this island. Nothing escaped "Mr. Bob."

He nodded. "It's something else, isn't it? I call it 'Truitt Estates.' They have several houses back there. You must be staying in the main house?"

"Monster, three-story, blue one?"

"That's the one," he said, chuckling. "You like it?"

I shrugged. "What's not to like?"

"Not a damn thing," he said, laughing. "Look. While you're here . . . there's something I need to talk to you about. You have a birthday coming up, and—"

He started coughing, and Veta grasped his hand. "You okay, Robert?"

He nodded.

"I'm not worried about my birthday, Dad. And neither should you be. We just need to get you treated as aggressively as possible to kick this thing's ass."

"We'll talk about it later," Veta said to my dad. "Carter, I'll call you after we're home from the oncologist appointment. Maybe you and your lady friend can come over for a nice, homecooked meal?"

I glanced at Pops. He didn't look too well. "We'll see. I don't want to put any strain on either of you. But I appreciate the offer, Veta."

Dad started to doze off again.

"Take good care of him, okay?" I said quietly. I wrapped Veta in a hug and held her so long I was no longer sure who was holding whom up. All I knew was I needed to get out of there. Go to the one place where I felt most at home on the island.

IT WAS DARK by the time I pulled into Dex's driveway, and I felt guilty as hell. I hadn't called Presley all day. The afternoon had gotten away from me once I got on my board. The waves lulled away the deep ache in my chest, helping me forget about everything else for a few hours.

The downstairs lights were off, so I left them that way. Just because I couldn't sleep didn't mean Presley shouldn't. Instead, I grabbed a couple beers and headed outside. Even though I'd been in the water for hours, my muscles were sore, and my mind was wide awake. A dip in the hot tub under the stars before bed might be just the medicine I needed.

When I rounded the corner, I inhaled sharply. Presley was there, leaning back against the hot tub's edge, her body mostly submerged. But the bubbles weren't enough to hide her glorious breasts that peeked above the surface in a tiny yellow bikini top. Her hair was wet, hanging in long ropes over her shoulders. Her eyes were closed, and her face was relaxed, giving me pause as to whether or not I should join her.

"You going to stare all night or come join me?" she asked quietly, never opening her eyes.

"Sorry, you just looked so peaceful. I didn't want to disturb you."

"I'd love the company, Carter. It's been a long day."

Oh, right. I'd left her alone—all fucking day long. What a gentleman I was proving to be. "Pres, I'm really sorry."

"Relax, Carter. You don't owe me an explanation. I'm just here tagging along for business, right? You're here taking care of your dad. It's not like we're dating or anything."

Right. I swallowed, still unsure if I should join her.

"How is he?" she asked, finally opening her eyes to look at me. I couldn't help but notice the tiny beads of sweat that trailed down her face and between her breasts. My dad was the last thing I wanted to think about. All I could think of now was burying myself inside Presley and having her kiss away all my pain.

I offered her one of the beers and climbed in beside her, watching as she gratefully took a sip from the bottle. "It's kind of hard to think about my dad when I'm watching that sexy as fuck mouth of yours," I said. I knew I was being a prick. I needed to ask her about her day. Open up about my dad. She knew him and was concerned in her own right, after all.

But all I could think about was sliding inside her.

She swallowed, understanding the feral look brewing in my eyes. She licked her lips, then nodded ever so slightly, giving me the okay. I took a long pull from my beer before setting it into a cupholder outside the water. She was so fucking beautiful I could hardly breathe.

"Presley," I growled, standing over her, "I've been an ass today. You sure this is what you want?"

I had one hand beside her head, the other one already dipping below the water. I found the hem of her bikini bottom and traced my fingers along it, brushing her inner thigh. She bit her bottom lip, and I had no choice. I was a weak man.

My mouth crashed down on hers, drinking in the taste of her beer, and the chlorinated smell of the water. Her mouth parted easily, giving me access that I didn't know I deserved. But I swallowed greedily, lashing her tongue with my own. There was nothing gentle about this. I needed her to be the one to shut this down. I felt out of control. Damaged. And I didn't want to hurt Presley, but I couldn't get enough of her.

When she reached for my cock and rubbed me through my board shorts, I knew there was no turning back. "Is that what you want, princess?"

Her moan against my mouth confirmed she was just as turned on as I was. I didn't have to check. I knew she would be ready. I undid the strings on her bikini bottom and slid my hand between her legs, cupping her hot sex. She lifted her hips to me—giving me access and permission. I slid two fingers deep inside her and felt her gasp against my mouth. She bit my lower lip hard, and my animalistic side took over. "Fuck, Presley. Be careful."

"I trust you, Carter."

"Maybe you shouldn't," I said, sliding my fingers back and forth. She squirmed beneath my hand, her mouth parting as her eyes closed and her head fell back.

Her legs started to shake around my hand, but I didn't let her finish. I lifted her hips up out of the water and heard her gasp as she gripped the sides of the hot tub just in time. I brought my hungry mouth down to her wet pussy and buried my face there, feeling peace for the first time all day. I trailed my tongue up her hot center, then went to work on her clit. Her legs were over my shoulders, and I could feel her thighs shake against my head. It was hot as fuck, and I was just getting started.

I wrapped my arm around her thigh, so I could work her clit with my thumb while I licked her clean.

"Fuck! Carter," she cried out. Her hips bucked against my mouth, and I knew she was close. I reversed my hand and mouth position, this time sliding my fingers back inside her slick opening while sucking down hard on her clit. Her scream of pleasure ripped through me, just as the walls of her sex clamped around my fingers. Her body started to shake, so I palmed her lower stomach with my other hand and let her orgasm flood over her.

I didn't give her time to recover before I set her hips down and flipped her over. "Trust me still, princess?"

She nodded, bracing herself on the side of the hot tub. I ran my fingers between her cheeks and up her wet slit. My cock throbbed in my hands. I didn't have a condom, but I would pull out in time. I pressed my thick head to her opening, closing my eyes as I pushed my way inside. She pressed her hips back for more, before I was even all the way in.

I smacked her backside and heard her moan as I drove in as deeply as I could. Good god, she was tight. I gripped her hips and closed my eyes, relishing in the warmth of Presley wrapped around me and the building tension in my balls. Everything was on fire, and I just pounded into her, taking, taking, taking until I couldn't anymore. She was matching me thrust for thrust, and I nearly lost my fucking mind. I grabbed her hair into a ponytail and tugged, eliciting a moan as I thrust my hips even faster. I was so close.

"Fuck, Presley!" I pulled out at the last second, releasing warm torrents onto her back. She groaned, collapsing against the wall of the hot tub as I squeezed my cock dry. I ran my hand over the narrow of her back, in awe of this woman who had given her whole self to me physically over the last week. I definitely didn't deserve her.

I let go, grabbing my beer and sitting back in the large bucket seat. I watched as Presley sank into the water, dipping her head back to rewet her hair. The smile on her lips surprised me when her eyes finally met mine. She winked, grabbing her own beer and settling into the seat next to mine.

"Did that help?" she asked.

"Jesus, P," I said, glancing at her from the corner of my eyes. "I'm sorry. That was too rough, wasn't it?"

She laughed, shaking her head. "Honestly, Carter? It was really hot. I would never do anything I wasn't comfortable with. Trust me. I've been down that road before, and I'll never let that happen again."

"I'm sorry to hear that," I said, my fist gripping my bottle at the thought of anyone pushing Presley too far. "College?"

She sighed. "No, actually. It was my first real boss, the one at the paper I was interning for."

"Fucker," I snarled. "Do I need to go rearrange somebody's face?"

Presley laughed. "No, though I appreciate the offer. It wasn't that bad—but he'd heard the office gossip and knew I was pretty inexperienced. He made it clear that he wanted to be with me, though he had no business doing so, being my boss and all."

She sipped her beer, looking out over the ocean. "But he was also handsome and charismatic. And very married. I told him I wasn't interested several times, but he just wouldn't take no for an answer. He found me at the Christmas party, alone, and cornered me . . ."

"You don't have to tell me, Presley, if you're uncomfortable. I didn't mean to pry."

"It's okay. It's more embarrassing than anything else. He kissed me without me giving him the okay. I told him to stop, but he just deepened his kiss. It was confusing, honestly, because I'd never been kissed like that by an older man. He knew what he was doing, unlike most of the guys I'd fumbled around with in college. So it shocked me when I felt turned on by his kiss— even though I didn't respect the guy or want to be with him."

"It's completely understandable, Presley."

"Is it though? That's what I struggled with. I kissed him back, Carter. It just encouraged Victor in a way I didn't mean to. Before I knew what was happening, he put his hand under my skirt and rubbed me, through my underwear. I was frozen in place. I knew I should stop him. I wanted to. But he was still kissing me, even though I'd stopped kissing him back. I told him to stop, but maybe I didn't use those exact words. I think I just said I didn't think we should be doing that. Someone could walk in. Your wife's in the other room. We need to go. That kind of thing."

"He assaulted you, Presley. You get that, don't you?" I would find this man and kill him. "Who was it, P? What's his last name?"

She shook her head. "It's fine, Carter. I'm over it. I was madder at myself for not shoving him away or yelling in his face to stop. For not being more vocal about my needs. He was just—so high up at the company. I was afraid to make a scene at the Christmas party and look like a child."

My teeth were clenched, but I didn't say anything. I could tell Presley wanted to get the rest off her chest.

"He kept rubbing me until I got wet. I was mortified. And scared. I didn't want anything to do with this man. Yet I'd kissed him back and was obviously turned on or my body wouldn't have responded that way."

"Yes, Presley, it can. That wasn't your fault. You were young, and he took advantage of your inexperience and position at the company to assault you. But your body is a network of sensory nerves, and it can respond, even if you don't want it to. That wasn't your fault. That didn't signal in any way that it was okay. He was an asshole."

"I know that now," she whispered. "I'm sorry, I didn't mean to bring all this up. I just—I didn't listen to my instincts then, which is how I found myself alone with him in the first place. And then I didn't stop something I was extremely uncomfortable with. He ran his finger, under my underwear, when he was done. When he pulled back and looked at me in the eyes, I didn't like what I saw. He patted me down there, with his sticky finger. Then told me to come find him after the party, and he'd take care of my little problem for me. Meaning my—"

"I know what he meant, Presley. Did you punch him?"

"No," she said, chewing the corner of her lips. "I was shocked. I went home. Then called in sick the next day. I had the holidays off. I talked to Willa about what happened. She offered to rearrange his face, too," she said, laughing. "But I told her no—it was partially my blame. I put my notice in at the company after the break and didn't go back. It was a good opportunity, a good starting point at a place I could've seen myself writing for a long time. But I wasn't going to put myself in a position I didn't feel safe in ever again."

"Well," I said, offering my hand to her, "I'm proud of you. I'm really sorry men can be such selfish assholes sometimes."

She came over to me and curled up on my lap. "You're not, though, Carter. You surprise me. I pegged you as arrogant, and you keep proving me wrong."

"It's you," I murmured, warm against her mouth. Our lips were inches apart, and she was straddling my lap now, her arms around my neck. "You've bewitched me or something."

She laughed, low and throaty, then wiggled her nose like Samantha from the old TV show. "If I do, do I get anything I want?"

"Maybe," I teased. "Depends on your demands."

She leaned forward and whispered into my ear, nibbling it gently when she was done.

I stood up, ready to haul her ass from the hot tub and back to my room for the night. "Your wish is my command, princess."

CHAPTER TWENTY-SIX

PRESLEY

I HAD TO talk to Dex before I drew any conclusions. And I had to start my interview with Carter today, too. Since he had a work event later, it was imperative to get through my questions, so I had something to start with when I began writing. But first, I wanted an update on his dad. He'd blown me off last night, instead focusing on our physical connection. I helped him work off whatever pent-up energy he'd been carrying early into the morning hours. He was still asleep upstairs, so I used the time to call Dex, instead.

"Hey, Presley! How're you enjoying the beach house?"

"It's amazing! Thanks so much for letting us stay here."

"Yeah, no problem. Anytime. What's up?"

I could hear the clack of his keyboard in the background as he multitasked. I took a deep breath. How did I start a conversation that began with, "So, I was accidentally snooping . . ."

"I have something important to ask you, Dex, if that's okay?"

"Sure. Does it have to do with the story you're doing on Carter?"

"Maybe? I'm not sure. Have you ever heard of Pennington Cartwright before?"

The clacking of his keyboard stopped.

"Why do you want to know?"

I swallowed. That wasn't the yes or no answer I was expecting. "I found a picture of him in Carter's house. He didn't seem to know who he was, but his father was in the picture, too. Your dad, as well."

Dex cleared his throat. "What does this have to do with the story you're writing? Carter wasn't even alive then."

"No, nor were you. But it seems as if your fathers knew each other."

"Is there a question in there somewhere, Presley?"

There were so many questions, but I wasn't sure which I had the nerve to ask. "Your family owns The Grove outright, doesn't it?"

"Yes, we do. Why?"

I could hear the agitation in his voice, and I knew I was tiptoeing a very narrow line right now. One question the wrong way could blow up a friendship I wasn't willing to risk losing. I thought of Bianca. She'd been so brave pursuing the article she'd written about Dex, back in the day when she was still at *Finance Times* full-time. Surely, he'd understand where I was coming from?

"I couldn't let the feeling go that there was more to that picture than met the eye, so we did a little research, and—"

"I'm sorry, who's *we*?"

"You know," I hedged, "my guy at the *Times*."

"What's your question, Presley? I have a one o'clock."

"Why is Carter's name on a trust that's tied to the deed of The Grove?"

"Talk to my assistant and get a meeting on my calendar for the day you get back in town. Tell her to move whatever she needs to make it happen," he said curtly. "Have you spoken to Carter about this yet?"

"No, I—"

"Don't."

Okay, then.

"Can you just tell me—"

"No, Presley. I won't. It's a bigger conversation than this. We'll talk in person when you get home. Just do me a favor. Don't share this information with anyone else at the *Times* yet, okay? And for god's sake, don't say anything to Carter until we've had a chance to talk. Got it?"

What in the world had I stumbled into?

"Sure, Dex."

"Good. It was nice chatting with you, Presley. I'll tell Bianca you said hello."

Then the line beeped and his secretary's soft voice greeted me. She set an appointment for first thing Monday morning. I'd have to sit on my questions for several more days, and I wasn't sure how I could do that while juggling my interview with Carter and sleeping in his bed at the same time. I put my head in my hands and closed my eyes. Did I really want these answers? Were they even important to the interview at hand? I didn't think so if I was being honest. So why couldn't I just let it go?

Then it hit me.

I cared about him. *Really* cared about him.

Fuck.

A warm palm resting on my back nearly had me flying out of my chair. I squealed as I turned and saw Carter standing there, looking all sexy and rumpled in his cotton sleep pants and nothing else. "Jeez, Carter, you scared the crap out of me!"

"Got a guilty conscience or something?" he teased.

"What? No! Why would you ask that?"

He put his hands in the air. "Calm down. It was just a joke," he said, kissing my forehead. "Good morning, beautiful."

He nodded toward the coffee pot. "Mind if I steal some?"

My heart rate slowed as I watched Carter stride across the kitchen, every step so confident and . . . masculine. His round ass filled out the pajama pants, and I suddenly had an urge to run my hands over them. But I *had* to stay focused today.

"You ready to sit down and chat?" I asked.

"First thing?" he asked, a lazy smile creeping over his face. "I could think of a better way to ease into the day."

He sipped his black coffee and looked at me over the rim, his eyebrows raised. THIS. This was how Carter had gotten into some of the most elite circles in New York City. He had a way about him that just charmed the pants off everyone.

"Have you ever slept with a client before?" I asked.

"Really, Presley? You have to ask that?"

I shook my head. "It just seems like it would be so easy. You have some pretty big doors opened for you with the clients you keep. And it's no secret how good-looking and charismatic you are—"

"You think I'm good-looking and charismatic?" he asked, stalking toward me.

I stood, putting my arms out straight in front of me. "I do. You know I do," I said, walking backward around the table as he followed me, smirking. "God, Carter! Stop that. I have to interview you, for heaven's sake."

"What if I answered every question in bed? You ask a question. I answer. You get a reward."

It was tempting. Too tempting. There was already a significant chance my article would be majorly biased. If I was taking down his answers with his face pressed between my legs, I'd never be in a sane enough state of mind to write this damn thing. And it was a possible game changer for my career if I nailed it. I was up against three others for the front story, I'd found out. It wasn't a given that mine would make it. I had to stay professional. Focused.

I glanced down at Carter's abs and the walls of my pussy clenched. *Shut up!* I told it, silently. I made it to the couch and picked up a pillow. "Don't come any closer," I warned.

"Or what? You're going to smother me to death?"

"Smart ass," I said, laughing. "Seriously, Carter, I can't think straight with you half naked and looking all, all—"

"All what, princess?"

"Delicious and shit."

Carter full out belly laughed. "Rain check? If I answer every question you have, you'll go swimming naked with me later?"

"Wait—what? Out there?" I asked, pointing over my shoulder. "In the day? No way. Anyone could see us."

"But no one will. They're paid to not notice things that go on around here, Presley. And no visitors can access this part of the island, or this beach."

My eyes glanced over my shoulder at the blue waters, the gentle waves crashing into the shoreline. It *was* on my list. "Fine. But only if you answer every question I have first."

"Deal," he said, coming closer.

"From a distance!"

"I thought we'd just seal the deal with a kiss?"

"Nope. No way. That's how my panties get wet and I can't think straight, and then I wind up bent over the side of a hot tub," I said, rolling my eyes.

"You fucking loved it, though," Carter said, stepping closer.

Without thinking, I threw the pillow at him and ran back around to my side of the table. Carter grabbed my wrist before I made it all the way and twirled me into his chest. I was laughing, looking up into his dark brown eyes when the knowledge sucker punched me right in the gut.

I was in love with Carter Wright.

CHAPTER TWENTY-SEVEN

CARTER

SHE ASKED VERY insightful questions, and I answered them all, though I was still uneasy about the prospect of this interview. How could I celebrate being a millionaire, while possibly outing my clients? Our relationship was based on trust, and I couldn't help but worry that this would break it every way to Sunday.

"So, no, I don't sleep with clients," I reiterated. "It's a hard line I never cross. Now, and this is off record, but I want to be honest with you on a personal level, Presley. I have slept with a client's friend or relative before. We go to a lot of high-profile events, and the adrenaline is unlike anything I can explain. And sometimes, that adrenaline, along with a couple of drinks . . . well, I've had a couple lapses of judgment. But never with a client. It's important to me to distinguish that line. I would never do that for money."

"I was just kidding, Carter. I would never put anything like that in the article, either. I just realized, I guess, how easy it would be for a client to fall head over heels for you."

"I don't let that happen, Presley. I'm more careful than that."

"Okay," she said, nodding, "I believe you, Carter. I'm sorry I asked."

"It's all right. What's next?"

"Well, I was wondering why you have so many concerns about your business getting more exposure. I would think you'd be proud of the fact that you've built this niche company into a multimillion-dollar business in such a short amount of time. Wouldn't more exposure mean more work?"

"Yes and no," I said. I leaned back in my chair and crossed my hands over my stomach. "Let me start with a story. Bear with me."

She nodded, turning up the volume on the voice recorder she used.

"When I was in the military, my commander came to me one day. We were friendly, even though he scared the shit out of me, too," I said, chuckling. "He confided in me that his daughter was getting bullied a little in school because of her Down Syndrome. Pissed me off, and I didn't even know her. Kids can be so cruel."

Presley nodded, concern softening her gaze as she listened intently. "When I left the military, I asked after her. I hadn't heard him talk about her again, but then, he was a quiet kind of guy. Kept his emotions to himself. He looked surprised that I'd remembered. Her prom was coming up, and he and his wife were torn about letting her go. She wanted to, badly. But the bullying hadn't gone away, even with school intervention. That only seemed to make it worse, despite the fact that her father was a decorated five-star general."

I took a sip of my coffee. "I offered to take her to the prom, so she didn't have to go alone. And I'd certainly never let a soul bully her while I was there."

I could tell Presley was surprised.

"Her dad took me up on it, and the rest is history. I took Val to the dance. I made sure she had a great time. And I made sure no one bullied her at school ever again."

"Do I even want to know?"

"Nah," I said, winking. "But they left her alone after that. I didn't care so much about that part as I did helping her get a normal experience of going to prom. She deserved that."

"Once again, you surprise me, Carter. But, how does this affect you today?"

"Presley, my clients come to me for so many different reasons. Val's dad made an off-handed remark that night about standing in for his daughter when she had no other friends in her corner, and something just clicked. Maybe I could help others, too. Her dad was very wealthy, and despite me protesting, he paid me for taking her that night. I hadn't done it to make money. I did it because I knew what it was like not to have friends in high school. Hell—I didn't even go to my own prom."

"What?" Presley asked in disbelief.

I shook my head. "You saw what I wanted you to see, Presley. A cocky, too-cool-for-school kid with a run of the island. But my inner circle was small for a reason."

"Carter, I didn't realize."

"It's not a big deal," I said, blowing it off. "I don't give a shit about any of the kids I went to high school with. But it taught me compassion for those who weren't in the in-crowd. I got into a lot of fights standing up for others. Almost got expelled."

"Why didn't you?"

"My English teacher saw something in me. Made me keep fighting. Encouraged me to go to college first before joining the military."

Presley nodded, jotting down notes even though the recorder was still going.

"Anyway, Val's dad referred me to other clients, and word of mouth took off quickly. It seemed there was quite a need for someone to step in and save the day."

"So, that's what you do as Mister Stand-In? Save the day?"

I bristled. I knew she wasn't being mean, but I also didn't know if she really understood. "Presley, a lot of my clients are assholes. Let's be honest. I'm not too picky, and I follow the money. I'm not gonna lie. I charge a decent amount to be someone's stand-in. It's not always altruistic."

"Then why do you keep doing it?"

"Because after that day, I also promised myself I wouldn't take money for jobs like that again. I'd charge big for the times I draped myself on some model's arm for a charity ball or served as an heiress's date to piss off daddy or make an ex-boyfriend jealous. It pays the bills. I've done things as simple as chaperoning a dance for a private school, to walking the red carpet with A-list celebrities. But I've also walked a bride down the aisle because her own family didn't want to be there when she met her bride at the other end. There are so many reasons why I do what I do. But it's not all for money. That's why I hate to focus on that side of it. I do what I do so I can help others who can't spend daddy's money to hire me."

"You—do pro-bono work? As a stand-in?"

I shrugged. "Yeah. Though it sounds weird when you say it like that. Just as much as I have a network of rich bastards who are willing to throw money at me, I also have a network of clients who are less fortunate. Who are bullied or discriminated against. Who just need an ally on their arm to feel normal. To feel strong. That's why I do what I do. That's also why I don't advertise my business. It's all word of mouth."

Presley sat back, staring at me. "Wow. Carter, I had no idea."

"Why would you? You hadn't seen me again until your mom hired me. I mean, how weird was that?"

Presley laughed. "Pretty weird. I didn't know it was you at first when she told me she was doing that. But then she explained it to me, and I have to admit, I jumped to conclusions. Made assumptions. A lot of people must do that with you."

"Every day," I said. "But I don't really give a shit. I'm confident in who I am and what I do. I don't owe a single one of them an explanation. They hire me. I show up and look good. Sometimes I help them make a better impression or smooth the way for a client to gain entry in a way they might not have been able to before. I have a lot of wealthy clients, Presley. But not all of them want others to know they've hired me."

"I see," she said, though she didn't look like she really did.

"Have you ever thought of separating the businesses? Making one a nonprofit?"

"Yeah, one day. I'd like nothing more than to volunteer to be a stand-in for kids in need. Be the big brother they never had. Walk them down the aisle when a parent's too shitty to care. That kind of thing."

Presley stopped the recorder, her eyes slowly raising to meet mine. "I'm ready for your end of the bargain."

She stood up and took my hand, leading me to the back door.

When we got there, she peeled off her sundress and walked outside, butt naked. I hurried to step out of my pajama pants and chased after her as the hot afternoon sun beat down on us and the tide pulled us out above our heads.

Interview over.

———

"I'M SORRY I can't get out of this," I said, my forehead pressed against Presley's. We'd spent the afternoon swimming naked and crossing another sandy spot off her Down and Dirty list. We weren't going to have too many more left at this rate, though I had a few more places I wanted to add now that I'd had more time to think about it.

"It's okay," she said. "I had a wonderful day, Carter."

"Me, too. That interview wasn't too bad after all."

Presley chuckled. "I'm not through with you yet."

"I was hoping you'd say that." I tipped her head back and kissed her soft lips. "I don't know what time I'll be back."

She nodded. "I understand. Your wealthy socialite awaits you," she said, referring to the woman who hired me for the charity auction she was hosting on her yacht. I might've forgotten to mention that she was Lauren's age, and was only bringing me to make her ex-husband jealous.

"She will dim in comparison to you," I said truthfully.

And when I finally met her a few hours later, she did. Vivienne Vanderbilt was a pretty woman with too much makeup and a hard edge. She eyed me critically and licked her lips as she circled me like a piece of meat. "Amber wasn't wrong. You *are* a fox."

"Uh, thanks?"

She trailed a finger down the front of my tux. "My ex-husband will be here tonight, even though he was not on the guest list. Let's just say a petty former employee of mine is trying to make a statement. One I care nothing about. Nonetheless, I appreciate you joining me. I have no interest in dating these days, after what he put me through," she said, sounding genuinely upset. "But I will not give him the satisfaction of seeing me alone at my own event. I want him to choke on what he lost."

"May I ask why he lost it? So I know how to help you this evening."

She turned on her crystal heel, making her way to the closest bar. The yacht was bustling with servants and volunteers, but the guests wouldn't arrive for a bit. She had the bartender fix her a dry martini with extra olives and ushered me over. "Your poison?"

"Whiskey, neat."

We headed up top, the views of The Grove stunning from the deck of the yacht. It twinkled majestically, surrounded by the green of palm trees, thick, lush grass, and a variety of colorful flowers and shrubs. The waves lapped at the shoreline in front of it, and guests mingled poolside with drinks in their hands. From here they looked like ants, but soon, they would board a smaller boat and be brought to the yacht, where we would gamble offshore for charity.

Vivienne sat on a bench and crossed her long, tan legs. She was wearing a black, satin evening gown that dusted the floor. The slit up the front revealed a lot of bare leg, and if I looked hard enough, I might just get more than I bargained for. But I wasn't interested. Vivienne adjusted the scalloped arches of her strapless gown, as if purposefully drawing my attention to her breasts. My eyes never left hers.

"My ex-husband was a bastard, if I can be blunt," she said, sipping her martini. "Let's just say his indiscretions weren't kept quiet around his office. Everyone seemed to know he couldn't keep his dick in his pants, including me. It was just a matter of time before I couldn't take any more. We have kids together, you see. And I came home one afternoon early from a tennis match. Mr. Vanderbilt should have been at work, so I crept quietly upstairs to our bedroom, so I didn't wake the twins from their nap. Their nanny, Anfisa, kept them during the days. Turns out she took care of a lot more than just my kids."

"Oh, man," I said. "What a douche bag. How old was she?"

"Eighteen," Vivienne said, pursing her lips together. "He was fucking an eighteen-year-old Russian girl we'd hired from an international nanny service. They train their whole lives to come to America and nanny for wealthy families," she spit out. No wonder there was a bitter edge to her. She'd been hurt and betrayed. "Turns out they encouraged their nannies to get in good with the husbands, who they believed controlled the money and could offer them a better life here."

"Vivienne, I'm so sorry."

"No need. I was better off. There were sexual assault allegations filed against him at work, too. He managed to buy his way out of those before the paper finally let him go. But he just took a higher, more prestigious job with its sister media company and never got a scratch on him. He makes me sick, and if we didn't have the girls, I would never talk to that man again for the rest of my life."

"Can't say I blame you, Vivienne. So, do you want just arm candy tonight, or do you want to make his skin crawl with jealousy?"

A feral grin broke out across her painted red lips. "Is that an option?"

"It is now," I said, determined. What a piece of shit. "I don't kiss clients or cross any lines like that. But it doesn't mean I can't make him jealous as fuck."

She nodded. "Thanks, Carter."

Guests poured onto the boat and the evening was in full swing by the time Vivienne's ex made an appearance. The smug bastard had his black hair slicked back and wore a white tuxedo coat over his black pants. He had a cigar lit and air kissed several women before zeroing in on my date.

She held my arm tight, her back stiffening like a rod. I acted like I didn't see him, turning into Vivienne and stroking her bare arm as I leaned down and whispered in her ear. "Pretend I just told you how I wanted to get on my knees and pull up that dress beneath one of the poker tables, while you wiped your ex clean of all his money."

Her face flushed bright red as she looked up at me, her mouth forming a perfect O. I lifted my brows suggestively. Then I dipped her back, away from him, in what looked like a kiss. I pressed my face into her hair, just inches from her mouth and said, "Grip my bicep, and dig your nails in."

She did, and when I brought her back up, she had the good grace to run her fingers over her hair, smoothing it back into place. Just as her ex reached us, she was adjusting the top of her gown, making sure the fabric was still covering her voluptuous breasts.

"Vivienne," he said low, looking at me, "always making a scene, I see."

The dick had ice blue eyes that held no light.

"You would know, wouldn't you? How's Anfisa doing these days?"

"Who's the kid you brought tonight?" he asked, ignoring her dig as he flicked his cigar ashes in my general direction.

"Mr. Vanderbilt! It's so good to see you again," said a man standing nearby, taking his attention away before I could say anything. The two men clasped hands and Vivienne's ex stepped away and got lost in the crowd.

"He's a piece of work, isn't he?" She sighed. "Come on, let's make the most of the evening. We're raising money to help fight child sex-trafficking. I want to encourage lots of drinking and lots of gambling," she said, laughing.

The rest of the evening went by as expected. I played a couple hands myself and donated all the winnings to Vivienne's charity. We were laughing together over roulette when I glanced up and caught a set of icy blue eyes staring our way. I lifted my chin, then made a show of dropping my hand below the table. I leaned into Vivienne and told her to make a face like I was pleasing her under the table.

On cue, she blushed, bit her lip and closed her eyes, as if keeping them open was painful. Her chest rose and fell gently, and she reached over and grabbed my arm. I stared at nothing else in the room but Vivienne. The dealer spun, and I didn't give a shit about winning or losing—I just wanted nothing more than to stick it to that prick of an ex.

Vivienne made a little whimper, playing the role perfectly. She clutched my sleeve discreetly, as if she were doing everything in her power not to lose control. I pulled my hand from under the table and smelled it, glancing up at her ex. His eyes were murderous. I winked at him, then grabbed Vivienne's hand and pulled her away.

"But, sir, you won!" I heard as we darted through the crowd.

"Donate it!" I hollered back.

By the time we made it down to the lower deck, we were laughing, Vivienne's face alive with excitement. "Oh, Carter, I can't thank you enough!" she said, throwing herself in my arms. I swung her around.

"He looked like he could kill me," I said, laughing.

"Can I get you a drink? You've earned it."

"Sure," I said gratefully. "I could use another one."

I watched Vivienne make her way to the bar, stopping to mingle with friends along the way. She was a beautiful, older woman, like Lauren. It made me wonder if they knew one another. Probably. But she wasn't Presley, and I found myself missing her.

I pulled out my phone to text her when I sensed someone standing in front of me, blocking my view of the party. I glanced up, as if bored. Of course he'd come to find me. Insecure prick.

"May I help you?" I asked.

"Who the fuck do you think you are?" he asked, pressing closer.

Was he really doing this, here?

I stood my ground. "You're gonna want to take a step back."

"Or what, you little shit?"

I put up two hands. "Whoa. Someone's emotionally volatile."

"Yeah, well, I don't like punks like you who glom on to my wife."

"You mean, your ex-wife, right?" I said, taking a step toward him now. "Don't you have an eighteen year old to go fuck or something?"

He snapped, grabbing the lapels of my tux in his hands and shoving me back toward the wall I was standing near. "Why you little—"

"Victor!" I heard Vivienne cry out. "Stop it!"

The man's nostrils flared as he stared at me.

"Victor is it?" I asked calmly, even though red was flashing before my eyes as my brain made the connection. *Married man. Paper. Assault allegations.*

"Leave my date alone!" Vivienne shrieked, tugging at her ex's sleeve. "For god's sake, Victor, you're making a scene."

He shoved me again, then smoothed his lapels down. "You talk to me about making a scene? Really? When you let your little boy toy finger you under the table in plain sight? I wasn't the only one to see that little display, you fucking slut," he spat.

Vivienne gasped, taking a step back.

I grabbed Victor's shoulder and spun him around, slamming his back against the wall. Somewhere behind me a guest gasped, but I didn't give a shit. All I could see was Presley, pressed up against an office wall, with her boss standing over her, taking advantage of her innocence and inexperience.

I pressed my hand into his chest hard, keeping him at arm's length. "You want to talk about inappropriate behavior? At least she's not married anymore," I said. "And at least she's a consenting adult. You wouldn't know about that, would you, *Victor*?"

"What the fuck are you talking about?" He made to brush by me, and I shoved him back.

Vivienne touched my arm. "It's okay, Carter. He's not worth it."

I turned to look at her. "No, he's not. But someone he hurt is," I growled. I turned back to the asshole who was taking up too much air. "Does the name Presley Kincaid ring a bell?"

I saw the recognition flash across his eyes and he grinned, thrusting his chin out. I grabbed his jacket and slammed him against the wall again. "I wouldn't look so smug, you piece of shit."

"My, my, my. Seems like Miss Kincaid strikes a chord for you," Victor said. He glanced over my shoulder at his ex. "Guess you like them young, too, and don't just go for the cougars."

"Fuck you," I spat. "Presley's my age, you dick. Unlike you. What are you? Fifty? Sixty? You fucking piece of filth. You're lucky you aren't arrested right now."

He leaned forward, so Vivienne couldn't hear. "She wanted it, kid."

Rage blurred my vision, and before I knew what was happening, I was punching Victor in the face. His head snapped back when my fist connected with his jaw. He stumbled, having caught him completely by surprise. It wasn't until the second or third punch that he finally tried to swing back. He wouldn't have gotten one in on me, but two men finally pulled me off him, and that opened up the space between us, leaving me unguarded.

Victor got one good punch in before someone pulled him off, too, yanking him back into the crowd.

"Oh my god, Carter! Are you okay?" Vivienne asked, rushing forward. I shook the two men away and ran a hand over my face.

"Yeah, I'll be fine," I said, taking a few calming breaths so I wouldn't run after Victor and beat him to death. I wasn't usually a fighter, but my training and desire to protect had kicked in, and I wanted blood.

"Sorry to have caused a scene at your event," I said, looking around. But everyone had gone back to minding their own business, sipping drinks, and pretending nothing that lowbrow had occurred.

"Carter, don't be sorry! This was the most fun I've had in a long time. And you left Victor far worse off than he did you," she said, clapping her hands together. "Now let's go get some ice on that eye."

CHAPTER TWENTY-EIGHT

CARTER

I STAGGERED INTO the beach house at nearly three a.m. and tried my hardest not to wake up Presley, even though every instinct in my body told me to. In all my time standing in for others, nothing had ever happened like what went down on the yacht tonight. My blood was still boiling as I tossed and turned in bed, Victor's cruel words playing on repeat: *She wanted it, kid.*

If I had to do it all over again, I wouldn't change a single thing—except maybe fight harder to get free from whoever pulled me off Victor so I could finish what I started. Only then, while thinking of getting revenge for Presley, could I finally fall asleep.

I felt like twenty shades of shit by the time I made my way to the kitchen sometime after noon. I was sure I looked it, too, judging by Presley's expression when she stopped typing to openly gape at me.

"Morning, beautiful," I said groggily.

"Carter!" she gasped, jumping off her stool and making her way over to me. "What in the world happened? I wish I could say the same about you, but you look like a swollen, purple, mess."

I laughed, then groaned. "You should see the other guy."

"Do I even want to know?" she asked, getting a bag of peas from the freezer and wrapping them in a towel. "Here, sit."

She pressed the bag to my temple. In all honesty, he'd gotten a fairly good hit in for an old man who was being pulled off me. My left eye was bruised and turning purple, but it wasn't as bad as Presley was making it out to be. It was just a little tender.

I sat down while Presley poured me some orange juice. I knew I should probably come clean about what happened, but I didn't even know where to start.

Presley's phone vibrated on the counter, and she grabbed it. "Sorry," she said, grinning. "It's Willa."

Her smile quickly faded, though, as she read through the text, lifting a hand over her mouth. She tapped the screen and read some more, her face void of any expression.

"Pres? What is it?"

"Have you seen the news today?"

"Nope. Don't really care for it."

"You might today," she said, handing me her phone. "And I think we need to have a chat."

I couldn't read her expression, but I grabbed the phone from her. Everything stood still for a moment when I realized what had happened. Someone from the party had taken pictures. Lots of pictures. There was a photo of me sitting with Vivienne at the roulette table, her hand grasping my arm. Then there was another picture of me scooping her back into what looked like a kiss. But the worst was the headline: "Lovers Quarrel Breaks Out Over Billionaire Media Mogul Victor Vanderbilt's Ex-Wife and Playboy Escort, Carter Wright."

There was a clear picture of me throwing a punch and connecting with Victor's jaw. "Fuck!" I said, slamming Presley's phone onto the quartz countertop. "Fuck!"

Presley sat completely still, her hands in her lap, while looking down.

"Pres, I'm so sorry. It's not what it looks like."

"How do I know that, Carter? Do you even know who that man is?"

"Yeah, I do. Why'd you think I was punching him?"

"I don't know, maybe because he caught you getting chummy with his ex-wife and didn't like it?"

"It's not like that, Presley."

"Well, that's exactly what it looked like," she whispered. "A picture says a thousand words, doesn't it?"

"Yeah, but it doesn't tell the whole story, and you know that," I said. "She's a client."

"Right. And you don't sleep with clients." She stood, making her way toward the stairs. "You just finger them under the roulette table. So, technically, guess you're not a liar."

"Presley!" I yelled after her.

She turned. "Don't, Carter. I was stupid. So stupid for letting myself get personally involved when I should've been focused on the story. I never should've let myself get swept up by you again."

"Come on," I yelled out. "That's not fair. Let me at least explain."

"I can't, Carter. I need some space."

I watched helplessly as Presley made her way up the stairs, then immediately called Dex because I didn't know who else to turn to.

"Nice, quiet, little trip to the beach, huh?" he said when he answered.

"Fuck, man, it's not how it looks."

"I believe you. But I can't wait to hear how it really is."

"I wish everyone was that understanding," I grumbled. Then I told Dex everything.

"Carter, I wouldn't worry about it. Shit like this happens all the time. It'll blow over. And everyone knows what a slim ball Vanderbilt is."

"I need a lawyer, just in case."

"Sure thing. I'll get you in touch with mine. Anything else?"

"Could you maybe ask Bianca to put a good word in for me with Presley? She was so hurt when she saw the news this morning. Can't blame her. It's a fucking mess. But she won't even hear me out."

"I didn't think things were that serious with you guys. It's only been, what, a couple weeks?"

"I don't know what it is, to be honest," I said, walking to the back patio and sitting down to stare out at the ocean. I needed to surf. To get my mind off things. To give Presley time to cool down before I went upstairs and tried to talk some sense into her. "All I know is she went from being a brat I couldn't get rid of when we were younger, to a woman I'd do almost anything not to lose."

Dex whistled. "Well, shit."

"Yeah. Shit. I've really fucked this up."

"Vivienne was just a client though, right?"

"Of course she was! You know I don't do that, Dex. Which is why the headline pisses me off. And so much for anonymity now. Everyone knows about my fucking business. FUCK!" I yelled, standing to pace the length of the patio.

"Then let Presley write her piece. Help her shape the narrative you want with the media. This was a sensationalistic article written by a rag magazine. Help Presley understand what really happened, then work together to help people understand what it is you really do, and how you'd never cross ethical lines like sleeping with a client."

"That might be a little hard if anyone finds out I was sleeping with the writer of the article," I said. "I won't let Presley lose any credibility over me."

"She won't, Carter. Bianca and I won't let that happen. I promise you. Besides, you know better than anyone—everyone in New York has their secrets. Find out Vic's, and you won't need a lawyer."

I nodded. Damn if I didn't know that truth in my line of work.

"Thanks, man. I appreciate everything."

"No problem, Carter. By the way, how's your dad doing?"

"Not good. I need to get over to see him. I was supposed to go today to check in on him . . . and bring Presley for a nice family dinner. Those plans have been blown to hell."

"Give her time. She'll come around. She's a reasonable woman. She thinks more logically than with her heart. She'll hear you out eventually."

"I hope so, Dex. I sure hope so."

BY THE TIME I got out of the water and made my way back to the house, my whole body was finally relaxed. I would find Presley and hash things out. Then we'd swing over to my dad's place so they could meet her. Well, as an adult this time. He would be so surprised and happy to see Presley again. She'd always been one of his favorites.

The house was quiet when I entered, and my heart ached for Presley. It's weird how fast these feelings had come. I craved her. Absolutely needed her to feel whole these days. When we were together, things just felt right. And not only because of the sex—though it was the most mind-blowing sex I'd ever had. And it wasn't because of the things we did. I'd done far more and far worse with other women.

It was the connection I felt when I was with her. It was like she saw my soul, and I saw hers, every time our eyes met. I sounded like some love-sick schoolboy, but it was true. Presley made me feel safe in a way I wasn't sure I'd ever felt. I *had* to make this right.

I bounded up the stairs, two at a time. Her door was closed. I knocked, stepping back to give her space, and waited. When she didn't answer, I knocked again.

Still getting no response, I cracked opened the door. Maybe she'd run out. "Pres? You in here?"

I looked around. There was nothing there. The room was as spotless as the day we arrived. I went to the bathroom and it, too, had been cleared out. I couldn't stop myself from opening drawers and the closet, torturing myself with the truth of what had happened.

Presley left me, and there wasn't a damn thing I could do about it.

CHAPTER TWENTY-NINE

PRESLEY

I GOT HOME late that night and was grateful to Willa for picking Jar Jar up from the kennel for me. She stood over my crockpot, a spoon in one hand, a glass of wine in the other.

"You're a sight for sore eyes," I said, dropping to the floor to pet the cat. "The tabloids would go crazy right now if they could see you in this getup," I said to my friend, waving at her "Will Cook for Sex" apron.

"And don't think I'm putting out just because you made— what exactly did you make?" I said, sniffing the air.

"Turkey chili in the crock pot, corn bread in the oven."

I stood up and walked over to Willa, wrapping my arms around her. "I don't deserve you."

"Of course you do, Pres. You're fucking fabulous, and so am I."

I shrugged. "You have a point."

"Dish up," she said, pouring me some of the mystery red wine she'd already gotten into. We carried our bowls into the living room off the kitchen. It was smaller than the front sitting room of my brownstone, making it the cozier choice to curl up, have a bowl of chili with my best friend, and cry.

"I think you need to hear him out," Willa said after listening to my sob story. "Carter doesn't really seem like the kind of guy who would do something like that."

"And I don't seem like the kind of girl who would go from zero to sex goddess in a couple of weeks—but here we are. Anything's possible."

Willa laughed, but then sobered up when I shot her my stink eye. "I'm serious, Willa! What possessed me?"

"The Cock of Carter Present?"

"Really funny," I said, crossing my arms over my chest. But then I burst out laughing. "Though, to be fair, I guess it is better than Loneliness of Virginity Past."

"But not as good as Relationship with Hottie Future," she pointed out.

"Ugh," I moaned, hugging a pillow to me as I sank into the couch. "Can I tell you something?"

"What?" she asked, smearing butter on her bread. I don't know how she did that and maintained her figure.

"I thought I loved him," I said sadly.

"Thought?"

"Well . . . how can I love him if I can't trust him? If I feel like I don't know who he really is."

"But you *do*, Presley. That guy in those pictures—that was a man doing his job. You said he stood in for people who needed to keep up appearances, right? So maybe that woman needed to make her ex jealous. Did you ever think of that?"

No, actually, I hadn't.

"But if he's that good of an actor, then how do I know he's not playing me?"

"God, Presley! You're so damn logical sometimes. Love isn't about logic. It doesn't play by your timeline. It doesn't wait till the fourth date—"

"Well, technically, neither did I this time," I said, rolling my eyes.

"But that was a good thing, in this case!" she insisted. "Presley, I know he hurt you. I know you've had shit for a run with guys in the past. And Victor really did a number on you—even if you insist it was nothing. It caused you not to trust and prevented you from getting close to men for a while. So, here you are," she said, waving her hands around the space. "All I know is you've seemed happier with Carter in this short amount of time than I've seen you in years."

"That's so cliché, Willa," I huffed. "I don't need a man to make me happy."

She leveled me with her warm, brown eyes. "I didn't say happy, Presley. I said *happier*. There's a big difference. And you know what? Sex makes a girl happy, okay? That's empowering—not something to use against yourself. Men do that enough for us. We don't need that garbage," she said, clearing our plates. When she came back, she stood over me for a minute, quiet.

"What, Willa? Spit it out. I know you have something else to say."

"Did you ever stop to consider that with Carter, it was the first time you got out of your head and listened to your heart?"

I don't know why the tear fell, but it did. I swiped it away.

"Then, at the first sign of doubt, you closed right back up and tried to go all left brain on the situation," she pointed out. "That doesn't work with love, Presley. To make this right, you need to soften a little. Listen to what your gut is telling you about Carter, and not what the pictures or the tabloids are. Then listen to what *he* has to say. Hear him out, girl."

I considered what she said. I would have to sleep on it before deciding how to move forward, though. Because this heart was exhausted and battered. And I needed to make things right with the past before I could look forward to the future.

I MOVED UP my appointment with Dex since I was home early, but I had a few hours to kill. I needed to get out of the house, or I would be tempted to answer one of the dozens of texts from Carter. And I could not bring myself to read them quite yet.

I met Lauren at Lumières for lunch. She was running late, of course, which gave me time to read some of the articles and comments online. I shouldn't have. More pictures had come out from the Sail for Freedom charity cruise. I rolled my eyes. Vivienne Vanderbilt needed some serious help with her marketing team. Though, I'm sure she and a group of her upper crust friends probably just sat around over tea, thinking themselves brilliant for coming up with their "clever" little title. Barf. Yeah, it was an amazing organization they were donating to. But did it really require a yacht full of drunk gamblers to help keep children safe?

I sighed, triple checking the time on my phone. If Lauren didn't get here soon, I'd have to eat lunch alone so I could make it to Montague Enterprises in time. As if on cue, Lauren swept into the dimly lit French restaurant. I couldn't overlook the irony of a café named after something that gives light being one of the most dramatically lit restaurants in all of New York. Fresh candles burned around the open room, lending little ambient light. Antique wall sconces added a little more, but not much.

"Really, Presley? Are we attending a funeral? What's with the lighting in this place?"

I gaped at Lauren. "Have you really never been here?" I asked. "It's rumored that Stefani Germanotta owns it."

"And I'm supposed to know who that is?" she asked, shaking her cloth napkin and settling it onto her lap.

"Uh, yeah. Lady Gaga?"

"Oh lord. No wonder the dramatics," she said.

"I think it's cool," I said, looking around and admiring the decor. "And, they have some of the best French food in New York."

Lauren sniffed her nose at the menu. "I doubt that," she muttered.

"Something bothering you today, Lauren?"

"No, why?"

"You don't seem like a woman fresh off a honeymoon."

"Maybe that's the problem," she said, setting her menu down. She sighed. "We had to cut it short."

"I know. I heard from Dex that there was some big finance summit or something."

"Yes, for the charitable arm of Montague. It's exhausting."

I rolled my eyes. "Perhaps not more exhausting than how hard the people have it who need their charitable help?"

"Oh, Presley, you know what I mean."

I didn't. But I left it alone. "Well, it's good to see you again," I said with false cheer. Stress had gotten the better of me today.

"I know, darling. I'm sorry to be such a downer. I'm sure after lunch I'll feel like myself again."

We placed our orders and sipped wine over small talk. When the food came, we ate mostly in silence, savoring every bite. "I concede, it is marvelous," Lauren said, pushing her half-eaten dish of shrimp and mushroom risotto aside. "The salad filled me up, though."

I was still devouring my herb-roasted salmon and fingerling potatoes when the server brought a cafetière for Lauren to sip. That was a fancy name for the strong French press coffee Lauren preferred. I couldn't help but remember the way Carter looked the last happy morning we spent together. He'd been in his cotton pajama pants, with bed head, and those piercing brown eyes gazing over the rim of his coffee mug at me. That was before shit hit the fan.

I missed everything about him.

"Presley?"

I glanced over at Lauren. "I'm sorry, did you say something?"

"Where are you today?" she asked gently. "Is everything okay?"

"No, it's not. But it will be. I hope."

"So, what are you working on right now?" she asked, switching gears.

"Oh, do you mean the article about Carter that you basically bribed Sylvia to hand me on a silver platter?"

"Don't be crass, Presley. It was simply a favor. And he did meet the criteria for their 'Thirty Under Thirty' list. Did you get the feature story?"

I sighed. "I don't know yet, Lauren. I'm still writing the article, and—" How could I explain any of this to her?

I couldn't.

"It's complicated. But it's still a work in progress."

"Speaking of a work in progress," she said quietly, "how about that Carter? He certainly grew up nicely, didn't he?"

"Lauren!" I said.

"What? I'm married, dear. Not dead." She sipped her coffee. "So, have you had a chance to interview him in person yet?"

I almost spit out my sparkling water. How did I unwrap that one?

Luckily, I was saved when my phone buzzed. I glanced down to see who it was. Unfortunately, Lauren did too. And it was Carter.

She smiled, lifting a brow. "I see you have."

"No, he's just trying to get a hold of me about something. Following up."

"Well, why don't you answer it then?"

"Because," I said, slowly, "we're still having lunch."

"Okay, be evasive then," she said as she paid our bill. She gathered her purse but paused before she stood. "Presley, it would be nice to see you smile more."

"Thank you, Lauren. But I smile quite often enough."

God! What was it with people? I hurried from the restaurant and caught an Uber to Dex's office. While sitting in the back, listening to the driver sing along to the Four Tops, I checked my emails from Sylvia and some follow-up leads about the island sale. By the time I was dropped off in front of Montague Enterprises, it was hard not to have a pep in my step.

I hummed "I Can't Help Myself" all the way up to Dex's office.

"Hey, Presley," he said, taking a seat at his desk after I sat down. "I have to make this quick. We're kind of short in the finance department right now, and things are blowing up left and right."

"It's okay. Thanks for seeing me so fast."

"I'm glad you could make it, actually," he said, taking a swig of water from a bottle on his desk. "Before we start, have you talked to Carter since coming home?"

"No, why? Is his dad okay?"

"No, actually, he's not. The cancer is worse than they thought, and it's spread to other organs. But I'll let you ask Carter about that. I was talking about what happened the other night on the charity cruise. Wanna talk about it?"

"Not really. And if I do, I'll find Carter about that, too."

Dex nodded. "Taking the stubborn route, I see."

"Dex, look, it's complicated, okay? And it was probably for the best anyway. I mean, I have an article to wrap up this week, and I wasn't exactly in a position to be unbiased."

Dex folded his hands over his stomach and leaned back. "And, you really think that being apart from him will make you unbiased?"

"Yes, I do," I said. "Bianca managed to write a professional article about you, didn't she?"

"Not without its ups and downs."

"But it all worked out in the end," I pointed out.

"Is that what you want, too? For this to work out with Carter in the end?"

"I don't know. It's too soon to be thinking long term. Carter and I—we were just having fun. Getting to know each other again. That was all."

"Okay," Dex said, looking unconvinced, "if you say so. I'll let it go. But, Presley, for the record, I think it meant a little more than that to Carter. In case it matters."

I swallowed, willing myself not to cry. I was going on very little sleep and a whole lot of emotions. "So, you wanted to tell me about the trust I found in your office at the beach?"

"Yes, I did. First of all, how did you come across it, if I may ask?"

"I wasn't snooping, if that's what you want to know. It was on your library desk, and I took a call in there. I, uh, accidentally might've put my feet up on your desk during the call, and when I got off, my legs must've caught the stack of papers. I'm really sorry, Dex. But I promise I didn't go snooping for it."

"And why do you think his name might be on a trust that also talks about The Grove?"

"I don't know. That's why I'm here, isn't it?"

"You have to promise me you won't print any of this. And you won't share it with Carter unless he shares it with you first."

"Okay."

"I'm serious, Presley. It cannot go in your article."

"Okay! It won't. I promise."

Dex pulled a large, stapled document many pages thick from his desk drawer. "Is this what you saw at the beach?"

I looked down at the paperwork. It was the same quality, same letterhead, same law firm, same signatures. I nodded. "I think so. I know it's not any of my business, Dex. I was just setting it back on the desk when I happened to glance down and saw Carter's full name on there as key beneficiary," I said, clearing my throat. "Why would he be a beneficiary of The Grove?"

"The short answer is because in less than two weeks, it's going to be his."

"Excuse me?" I said, not understanding. "What's going to be his?"

"Everything," Dex said, steepling his fingers.

"I'm sorry, Dex. I guess I need the long answer because I still don't understand what you mean."

He grinned. "That's okay. It took a while for it to sink in with me, too. Hang on," he said. He called his secretary over the intercom and told her to move his next meeting. "I don't care. It can wait. Do not let anyone interrupt me until I walk out of this office, okay?"

He looked down at the document and swallowed. "Just so you know, Carter doesn't know anything about this yet. His father wanted to be the one to tell him—and it was supposed to be on his thirtieth birthday. But with his dad's health declining so fast, he notified me that he was going to be talking to Carter about it this week."

"Okay," I said slowly. "So, how long have you known?"

"Not long at all. In fact, that's where I was the week before your mother's wedding. I went down to The Grove to meet with my dad's lawyers."

"Did your dad tell you about this? Before he passed away?"

He shook his head. "I had no idea. His lawyers showed me all of the original files, legal paperwork, binding agreements, old journals with testimony and background, and each generation's signature's acknowledging the transfer."

"The transfer of what? And why?"

"A long time ago, it was Carter's grandfather who owned the land off the coast of South Carolina. It's not huge, as you've seen, but it's prime real estate. Back then, not so much. It was hardly accessible. It was mostly marshland overrun with alligators, I've been told. But Carter's grandfather was a builder, and he had a vision. He also had the pocketbook to make it happen. Keaton Truitt, my grandpa, and Carter's grandfather, Pennington, were best friends. 'Thick as thieves' as my mother would've said.

"Turned out, Pennington had, uh, acquired some of his wealth in a way that made others a little butt hurt, to say the least. A few of those men who felt cheated by Pennington came after him. They were relentless. They set fire to the contractor's trailer. They ran off good workers by luring them with more lucrative work. And there was a car accident. I think that was the straw that broke the camel's back."

"Oh no. That's how Carter's grandmother died!"

"Yes, you know about it?"

"I, uh, may've seen a picture at Carter's house of a ribbon cutting. Carter told me about his grandmother's passing and how his grandfather deserted them. Rico, my guy from the office, ran a check for me on a few things. But Pennington's last name wasn't Wright if I remember correctly."

"No, it was *Cartwright*. Pennington Cunningham Cartwright. Notice anything?" he asked, smiling.

"Carter Wright. Cartwright. Well, I'll be damned."

"When they killed his wife, Penn lost himself. He was devastated, and he didn't want to bring any more pain to anyone else. He had a son, Robert Wright, already, and he didn't want his death on his hands, too."

"Mister Bob," I said quietly.

"Yes," Dex said.

"So, Penn did what? Changed his name? That doesn't seem very sneaky. Surely men like that could figure it out. Why didn't he go to the police?"

"Have you ever stopped to consider that maybe the police knew about it, and maybe they looked the other way? These men Penn owed money to, they weren't exactly of the gentile south variety. These were men he'd made serious enemies of. Penn might've thought he was being clever, but it caught up with him in the end. So, yeah, he changed Robert's name and sent him to live with a young family who worked for him on the island. He was originally Pennington Jr."

"He doesn't look like a Pennington." I was at a loss for what else to say.

"No, he doesn't," Dex said, smiling.

"I still don't understand how he could just leave his son behind. I could never do something like that. I think I'd move heaven and hell to make things right."

"We think that sometimes, Presley—until we realize we love someone else so fiercely we'd do anything to protect them, first and foremost. He did it to protect Robert, and everything he'd worked legitimately for all those years."

"Is that how you feel? About Bianca and the kids?"

"I'd walk away from everything tomorrow if it meant keeping them safe, Presley. There's not a single thing in this world that's more important to me than protecting them."

I nodded. That kind of love was something I wanted someday. I felt like I was falling *in love* with Carter. I loved so much about him and the man he'd become. *Shit.* I'd fucked up royally.

"Then what happened?"

"Penn took off. Got out of the country. Completely changed his identity. He sold everything—the island, his properties, his business, his cars, his home—to my grandfather."

"No shit," I said.

"It gets better. He sold it to him for one dollar."

"Come again?"

Dex nodded, letting that sink in. "Penn and Keaton agreed that Keaton would see to the completion of the resort. They'd already had strong interest while in the design and build phase, and they knew it would make money hand over fist. The deal was that the Truitt family would always provide work for Robert when he became old enough, to keep him close to the business. Penn didn't want to pass his legacy directly onto Robert, because he was afraid for him still. He didn't want him to end up like his mother. He knew those guys would be too suspicious if the Truitt family immediately sold off the business. Everyone assumed they were business partners anyway, so there was no suspicion when Keaton took over after Penn's disappearance."

"Makes sense, I guess. But why a dollar? Why not sell it for face value and skirt out of town loaded?"

Dex laughed.

"He was loaded enough without it. But it was also hard to move that kind of money around that fast back then, Presley. Technology allows us to hide money much easier these days," he said drolly. "Penn wanted to ensure that future generations of his family would be taken care of. So, the agreement was made, between Keaton and Penn, that on the thirtieth birthday of Robert's firstborn child, the entire kit and kaboodle would be transferred back to the Wright family, for the amount of—"

"Let me guess, one dollar?"

"Exactly."

"But why would the Truitts do this all these years? Honor an old deal between two friends long dead?"

"They were like brothers, Presley. It was a pact our family intended to keep. My dad, he wanted nothing to do with the business after grandpa died. He enjoyed the profit from it, and the prestige of owning it. But the day-to-day operations? It wasn't his style. He was the one who enjoyed being pampered, not the one doing the pampering. Honestly, I think he never really saw it as his, but while he had it, he was going to make a fortune from it. That's the Truitt way."

"And that was the deal?"

"Yes. Anything we made while in possession of the assets was the Truitt family's to keep and invest. It wasn't completely altruistic. We've done quite well adding to our family's portfolio because of this. But in order for it to be the legacy that Penn envisioned, it needed to have someone close by who remembered the property and had a deep love for it while it was in someone else's hands."

"Bob."

Dex nodded. "Yes. Bob."

"So, he knew about it all these years? Knew he was busting his ass, but would never see a dime or be able to enjoy the luxuries of the resort?"

"Presley, don't you see? He did though. He lived there, in paradise, all year long—doing what he loved. He made that resort his in his heart a long time ago. He lived the life he wanted to all these years. He's excited to finally pass it on to Carter now. Well, I'm sure he'll still run the place, but everything financially reverts to Carter as the sole living heir."

I sat in silent disbelief.

"Does that mean the house we stayed in—"

"Everything, Presley."

I swallowed. This changed everything. Carter wasn't just a millionaire before thirty. He was now well on his way to becoming a billionaire. "Carter's not going to like this attention."

"No, probably not. But it doesn't have to be made public. We can try to keep the trust quiet for as long as we can. Though with public land transfers and property deed records, it's a little harder to hide. But with enough money, almost anything is possible these days."

"Is there still a concern about these men? Their children's children? What if they come after Carter?"

"They think Penn and his kid were killed in a hurricane that hit Florida that year, after fleeing. That was the news they made sure got back to the island."

"And they just left Keaton alone? Didn't find it suspicious that the operation was now his?"

"They didn't have a beef with him. He was squeaky clean. Like I said, I'm guessing they believed Keaton was a legitimate business partner on the venture from the get-go." Then Dex chuckled. "Kind of ironic, huh? Ethics must've skipped a generation, I guess."

I knew a little of Dex's history with his father, mostly from the stories Bianca shared. But it was hard to be in finance and not study what happened with Dex Sr. and Montague Enterprises back in his day.

"Keaton smoothed things over enough to keep the hitmen at bay, but he made it clear he was not his friend's keeper and they were never allowed on the property again."

"Well, shit." I stood and started pacing Dex's office. "So, your dad never told you?"

"No. He had a heart attack a few years before he died. We thought he was doing better, but the next one took us by surprise. He never had time to. But Myra knew about it."

"What would've happened if Robert never had kids?"

"Then it would've stayed in the Truitt family line."

"Wow. I guess it's lucky for Carter that your family is so squeaky clean again, then, huh?" I took a deep breath. "So, you're really just going to transfer everything back over to Carter? Just like that?"

"Well, he'll owe me a dollar," Dex said, suppressing a grin. "But, yeah, just like that."

I looked at him in disbelief.

"Presley, it was never mine to begin with. Just like it was never my father's. If Carter wasn't a factor in any of this, I'd probably sell the entire thing off and reinvest the money elsewhere. There's a lot of maintenance with a place like that."

"And a lot of profit though, right?"

"Sure," Dex said, shrugging. "But I've got enough of my own. And I'm learning that the older I get, the more I'm interested in reinvesting what I've got into the community. Giving back."

"Is that why Richard Brash is expanding the financial department for the philanthropy division of Montague?"

Dex nodded. "After we opened the Arts and Cultural Center in Jelani's memory, we realized we wanted to give back even more. That was just a stepping-stone for Bianca and me. Richard's still staying on as CFO for all of Montague Enterprises, but we need to hire an executive to officially lead the charitable division."

"That would probably help Lauren relax," I said, laughing. "If Richard were to get the support he needs."

"Yeah, I already apologized to her about that one."

"So, wow, Carter's life is about to change, big time."

"Yep," Dex said. "Hey, has he talked to you since, you know, the whole party went down?"

"No," I said quietly. "He tried to, but it was a lot to take in. And I was hurt."

"Just do me a favor, okay? Carter's not that guy. He's the farthest thing from *that* guy. But the media's doing a good job of painting him in a way that sells papers."

"Yeah, no thanks to Victor, I'm sure."

"He has a hand in it, no doubt. So, could you do me a favor? Carter, actually?"

"What is it?"

"As honestly as you can, help him rewrite his narrative, okay? He busted his ass to get off the island and go to college. He served his country, for god's sake. And I'm pretty sure he explained how his business came to be, right?"

I nodded.

"He's as altruistic as they come. He took the easy jobs to bankroll his volunteer work. Put up with all that bullshit and being called 'arm candy' by the same rich fucks who hired him. But Presley . . ."

"Yeah?"

"He does more volunteer work these days than not. He made his millions, and that was enough for him. All he wanted to do, being Mister Stand-In, was to stand *with* those who had to stand alone. Don't let the media bury that truth. You know Carter by now. At least, I hope you do. Just hear him out."

I nodded, then gathered my purse from the floor so I could leave.

"One last thing," Dex said.

"Yeah?"

"Bianca tells me you have a dual degree in business and finance?"

"I do."

"Ever want to manage a charitable division as a finance executive?"

My mouth fell open. "You mean—"

"Yep. You'd be reporting to Richard, but we'd make sure that didn't affect pay or performance. You would report directly to me for those because of your family ties now."

"I don't know what to say, Dex. You really think I'm qualified enough?"

"I don't know. Why don't you send me your résumé and let me see?" He stood and came around the desk. He leaned back against it, looking every bit the sexy business mogul that he was. "Bianca put in a good word for you, Presley. She thinks you're wasting your talent at *Finance Times*."

"How come she's never said any of this to me?"

"She's your friend. I'm sure in time she would've encouraged you to spread your wings. I'm just offering to help you spread them sooner."

"Thanks, Dex. Does that mean I'd have to call you Mr. Truitt now?"

He laughed. "No. Dex is fine."

I gave him a quick hug, then headed to the door. At the last minute, I looked back, taking everything in that I'd learned today. It wasn't just going to change Carter's life. It would change mine, as well. "Dex?"

"Yeah?"

"Thanks," I said.

"For what?"

"For reminding me of the type of man Carter really is. For trusting me with this information. We're going to look like asses featuring him as a 'Thirty Under Thirty' when a week later he'll be worth significantly more than that. But that's for another article, I suppose. And maybe not my worry anymore," I said, grinning.

"The *Finance Times* won't look like an ass if you clear his name and talk about his bright future as a philanthropist, rather than focusing on where he is today."

"I don't really know what he plans to do with his future," I said truthfully.

"Then I think you better go make a phone call. You have a deadline, I hear."

I grinned. "That I do."

CHAPTER THIRTY

CARTER

"ARE YOU PUNKING me right now?" I asked in disbelief, staring back and forth between Veta, my pops, and his lawyer after a lengthy, unexpected conversation.

"No, son. Legally, I was supposed to wait until your thirtieth birthday to tell you all this, but with the way my health's been going, we didn't want to wait another day. And I didn't want you to hear it from anyone other than me."

"And I wouldn't, Dad, because you're going to be just fine. I'll get you the best health care money can buy."

He grimaced. "Sometimes, money's not enough, Carter. But family is. And this was what your grandfather, Penn, wanted. It's what he sacrificed everything for."

I paced my dad's small house, trying to wrap my head around what they'd just told me. I didn't even know how to dissect everything, or how to feel about it yet. If what they said was true, I was about to become wealthier than I ever could have imagined. On the other hand, what did I really know about running a resort? I couldn't wait to leave the property all those years ago. Would I have felt differently if I'd known that it would all be mine one day?

I shook my head, glancing at the lawyer. "Am I required to manage the property? Or can I hire that out like the Truitts?" I wasn't sure what I wanted to do yet, but I needed to understand my options.

"It's yours, Carter. You can do whatever you want with it after it's transferred over to you. But I suggest getting a personal financial manager immediately."

"That's an understatement," I snorted. "Dad, why haven't you taken more for yourself all these years, knowing this would all be passed down to me anyhow. You should've had more."

"Carter, I had everything I wanted. I had a life I love in a place that's always felt like home. With the woman I love," he said, affectionately squeezing Veta's hand. "By the way," he choked out, holding Veta's hand up for me to see, "we made it official while I was in the hospital."

"Huh?" I looked at Veta's hand and saw a small eternity band surrounded by diamonds. "You guys got hitched? Why didn't you tell me? I could've been there!"

"Not everything's about you, son. We've been wanting to do this for years. And I want Veta taken care of when I'm no longer here to do it myself. It wasn't anything big. We just had a justice of the peace come to the hospital and do it bedside. Not the sexiest honeymoon, though," he said, laughing.

"Dad," I said, looking between them, at how happy they looked, "does that mean Veta's finally going to move in?"

"If you'll let her," Pops said.

"What do you mean? It's not my business where she lives."

"But it will be. When I'm gone, I want her to stay in my house on the island. That technically belongs to the Truitts, which means it'll belong to you in a few days."

I ran a hand through my hair. *Fuck* There were a lot of trickle-down implications I knew I had to think through.

"What if I don't want it?" I asked the lawyer.

"Why wouldn't you want it, Carter?" my dad asked, incredulous. "Your grandfather left everything and everyone he loved so you *could* have it."

"Yeah, but if he'd done everything on the up and up, he wouldn't have had to, right? So, he should be praised as a hero after all this time?" I shoved my hands in my pockets. "A real man would've earned his money the right way. He wouldn't have left those he loved behind. He would've cared more about people than money."

"Wow, Carter, that must be easy for you to say, not knowing what your grandfather went through. Have you even bothered to read his journals yet?"

He knew damn well I hadn't. Otherwise, I would've known about my inheritance a long time ago. "I grew up with nothing, Pops. I was made to feel less than by everyone. I just can't help but wonder how different things might have been if The Grove was always ours. If I'd grown up running it, instead of running away from it."

The room was quiet. My dad sat up in his bed, though it clearly strained him. "Son, you're still young. You don't have the benefit of looking back yet like I do. All I can say is you grew up exactly as you were meant to, and it's made you into the capable, strong man you are today. Don't just think about this inheritance from the money perspective. That's never been what motivated you—which is why it's definitely going in the right hands after all these years. Think about what you can *do* with the money, son. All the people you can help."

I closed my eyes and rubbed my temple.

"When you love someone, there's nothing you won't do for them. Penn did what he thought was right after making one wrong decision with the wrong men. It cost him everything. But he loved and trusted the Truitts. And they've honored this legal agreement all these years instead of contesting it. You will damn well appreciate the sacrifices made on your behalf. And you will hold your head up high and do whatever your heart calls you to do with your new wealth. But, please, don't disrespect my father's name."

I hung my head in shame. He was right. Of course, he was right. "I'm sorry, Pops," I said, going to his bedside. "I'm just processing all of this. It's a lot to take in."

"I know, son."

"So, Dex—he's the last Truitt, other than his kids. Does he know about this?" I asked, worrying how it would change our friendship.

"Of course he does, Carter. He was given copies of the trust a few weeks ago when he came down. The transfer paperwork has all been drawn up. There's a board that over-sees The Grove's operations. You can be as much a part of that, or as little, as you want. I will stay on as the property manager for as long as I can, but I think you might need to have the board start looking for a replacement soon," he said.

"Dad! Don't say that."

"Carter, be realistic. Cancer changes everything. I'm going to need treatments until I get this under control. *If* I'm able to get it under control. I don't have the pep anymore to run around the property and be the Mr. Bob everyone expects. No one wants to come on vacation and see a broken-down old man hobbling around the property. It breaks the illusion of perfection and excess. I have a young man in mind I'd like to recommend. He's been under my wing for a while now.

He's family through my adoptive parent's siblings. I'll put a good word in for him with the board. He has a lot of heart and works like a bear. He loves this place, just like I do. Been running around here since he was a kid."

"You mean Scottie?"

"Yeah," my dad said, "that's him."

I nodded. "I trust you, Dad."

"Good. Then trust me when I say everything is as it's meant to be now."

I thought of Presley. The one thing I wanted more than anything else in my world and couldn't have. She wouldn't answer my calls. She ignored my texts. And I didn't know how to make this right. I just knew that she was worth figuring it out for.

"Not everything, Pops. But it will be, soon."

"Is this about that lady friend of yours?" Veta asked.

"Yeah. But she's more than just a friend. And I lost her."

"Then get her back," Pops said, as if it was as easy as that.

"I was actually hoping to reintroduce you to her today, but I kinda messed things up," I admitted, shoving my hands in my pockets. "Remember when I told you I ran into the Kincaids again, Dad? At Lauren's wedding? Well, it turns out Presley's not so bad after all."

"Of course she's not," he said fondly. "I know I don't have to tell you this, but Presley was always a special little girl. She had a light and kindness to her that not many other kids in her social group had. She was one of the few with parents who actually set a good example. If she turned out anything at all how I imagined she would, then I can see why you'd want to hold on to her."

I was trying not to get too choked up, knowing my dad approved of Presley. I was determined to make sure he got to see her again before his health deteriorated any further. "I think I love her, Dad."

"I know you do, Carter. You've never been like this over a woman before."

"I'm gonna do everything I can to bring her home soon," I promised.

As I drove back to the beach house, all I could think about was how it would soon be mine. But it didn't even matter if I didn't have Presley back there with me. It was too damn empty without her. Memories of our time together haunted me. And I was tired of living with her ghost.

That night I sat on the patio, staring up at the stars and dissecting my future. One thing was clear: I would move heaven and earth for another chance with Presley. All the money in the world didn't matter if I didn't have Miss Moneybags to spend it with.

I grinned.

All this time, and my future circled right back around to The Grove, and to bratty, little Presley Kincaid. What were the odds of that?

Even more, what were the odds that nothing in the world made me happier?

CHAPTER THIRTY-ONE

PRESLEY

"THIS IS EXCEPTIONAL writing," Sylvia said as I sat across from her in her spacious office. "I have to say, I was a little skeptical about running this piece after Carter made the news in such a splashy way," she said.

That was the understatement of the year.

"But I can see why you fought so hard not only to keep him included in the feature, but to use it as an opportunity to clear his name. It helped that Victor didn't press charges."

"Thank you," I said. I'd finished Carter's piece and was glad I'd listened to my heart. I still hadn't spoken with him yet about what happened, but I did know Carter's heart. And my article reflected that while protecting his business as much as I could.

"I've reviewed the top three contenders, and I'm pleased to let you know that yours was selected for the lead article."

I was excited. I truly was. This meant more positive exposure for Carter, and it would hopefully make things right there and set the record straight on what it meant to be a "stand-in." But it didn't make me as happy as I thought it would, professionally speaking.

"Thank you, Sylvia."

"Well, aren't you excited? This is a bottle-popping moment for your career, my dear. Feature stories are extremely hard to come by, especially at your age."

She got up and uncorked a bottle of champagne, pouring me a glass. "Let's toast to your future here, shall we?"

"Sylvia, I want to be upfront with you about something," I said, not sure if I was shooting myself in the foot by being so honest. I hadn't gotten the job yet at Montague, but the more I talked to Lauren and Richard about what it entailed, the more I wanted it. *Badly.*

"What is it, dear?" Sylvia asked, perched on the corner of her desk, her blood-red heels crossed at the ankles.

"I'm applying for another job," I said. "I hope that doesn't change your decision on the article. I think Carter's story deserves to be on there. But I think there might be a better fit for me elsewhere after this."

"I see," she said. But she didn't look like she really did. "You know you have a noncompete clause, right?"

"It's not with another publisher," I said truthfully.

"Do you mind me asking who it's with then?"

"I'd rather not say. Not until I'm sure I got the job."

"Does that mean you're leaving either way?"

I hadn't thought about it before now. But there was a spark of hope that burned through my chest when I thought about leaving and finding another place in the world for myself. Yes, I was helping people with my writing. But it wasn't as numbers intensive as I'd thought it was going to be. I didn't want to just *write* about finance, I wanted to live and breathe it. And the fact that I'd also be able to help charitable organizations in the process was a win-win for me.

"It does, Sylvia. I'm truly sorry. I know you put your neck out for me because of Lauren and my relationship with

Bianca. I appreciate all of the opportunities you've given me here. I think maybe it's just not my calling."

"Well, you're young enough to still follow your heart, aren't you?" Sylvia said wistfully.

There was a story there, but stories were no longer my business. The only story I wanted to focus on was the one with me and Carter. And I had a happy ending I needed to go write.

———

"I GOT THE job!" I squealed over the phone to my stepmother a week later, even though she probably already knew—being married to my new boss and all.

"That's wonderful, darling. When do you start?"

"Right away, I think. They are so short staffed, and Richard wants me to be a part of building my own team and laying out my thirty-, sixty-, ninety-day objectives for Montague Philanthropy's financial division."

"Well, if anyone can do it, I know you can, Presley. Your father would be so proud of you."

"Thanks, Lauren. That means a lot to me."

"I'm proud of you, too, for what it's worth."

"It's worth a lot," I said honestly.

"So, have you heard from Carter lately?"

"No," I admitted. "He's been down in South Carolina taking care of pressing business at The Grove. At least, that's what Bianca and Dex are telling me."

"Is he moving down there, then? To take care of his father?"

"I—I don't know. He answered my last interview questions that I emailed to him for the article, but it was more on a business front than a personal one."

"Presley, have you ever considered going to him?"

"What do you mean?"

"I mean, sometimes we have to fight hard for what we want. You've been miserable since everything went down with Carter. I know the past few weeks have flown by with Rico's baby shower, finishing your article, and then getting a new job on top of that. But do those things really mean that much if you aren't happy?"

"Why does everyone keep saying that?!" I nearly shouted into the phone.

"Presley Baker Kincaid," Lauren said over the line, "there is no need to take a tone with me. That's beneath you."

I sighed in frustration. "Look, Lauren, I've never needed a man to make me happy, okay? I'm just not built the way you are."

Oops.

"Is that what you really think of me, Presley?"

Yes. "No, not really." *A little, maybe?*

"Presley, I loved your father so much, but I wasn't the one who pursued him. He came with a lot of baggage—and I don't mean you," she clarified. "He loved your mother so damn much. How could I compete with that? But the more time I spent with him, the more joy I felt from being a part of a family. Did I have joy before that? Of course, I did. I was a successful interior designer. I loved my career. But I loved your father more. We were happiest when we were together."

"I remember," I said, trying not to get too emotional.

"He believed in love so much he was willing to open his heart again, even after he was devastated over the loss of your mother. You have a whole life ahead of yourself, Presley. I know you don't need Carter, or any man, to make you happy. But ask yourself: Does he enrich my life? Am I more joyful when he's around? Can we be happier, live our best lives, if we were together? Do we lift each other up?"

"Wow, Lauren . . . I didn't know you had this in you."

"There's a lot you don't know about me, Presley," she said coyly.

"Are you happier with Richard now?"

"I am," she said truthfully. "Your dad taught me a lot about the human heart's capacity for more love. I owe it to myself to experience it again. A life with love is never wasted."

"I hear you, Lauren. And I really appreciate the pep talk. I needed this today."

"That's what moms are for, dear. Just because your dad isn't with us anymore, and I'm Lauren Brash now, doesn't mean my heart isn't big enough for you, too."

Oh. Wow. I will not cry. I will not cry.

"Thanks, Lauren. I've got enough in mine for you, too," I said. "And Carter. Definitely Carter."

Lauren laughed, then we spent the next half hour plotting.

CHAPTER THIRTY-TWO

CARTER

"HAPPY BIRTHDAY TO you," they sang. "Happy birthday to you. Happy birthday, dear Carter. Happy birthday to yooooou!"

I closed my eyes and blew out my candles. All thirty of them.

I glanced around at all the people in my life who meant the world to me. There was only one person missing—perhaps the most important one of all.

"What are you going to do now that you're almost a billionaire, and just a hair over thirty?" Dex asked, clapping me on the back.

"Send out eviction notices?" I teased.

"Fair enough."

"I'm just kidding, Dex. You know you, Bianca, and the kids are welcome to keep the house here. Or any other house at The Grove if you want."

"There's actually one near the main house that I've always loved," he said. "We could be neighbors. Maybe our kids could grow up together and vacation here in the summers."

"Unless there's a modern-day immaculate conception, I don't see that happening."

"Still no word back from Presley?"

I shoved my hands in my jeans and stepped back from the cake so Veta could cut it. Dad was doing a little better with his chemotherapy, though his doctors cautioned us that at this point, because of the spread to other organs, it was more to treat the cancer than to cure it. In other words, it was buying us some time. I wanted every minute I could get with him, which is why I'd been staying at Dex's beach house—scratch that. I guess it was my beach house as of today.

"I've left her a ton of messages apologizing, saying hi, just wanting to make sure she was okay. Even if I didn't do anything wrong, she's still hurt over this. And I get that. It just kills me to know she's hurting because of me, and I can't do a damn thing about it."

"Can't you though?"

"Unless I literally sit on her doorstep in Chelsea, I don't know how else to get her to respond. She emailed me a list of follow-up questions for the interview, and I took your advice."

"What wonderful advice did my handsome husband give out this time?" Bianca asked, curling up to Dex's side with a glass of wine in her hands. Scottie had the kids out on the beach watching a movie on a huge blow-up screen so they could be here for my party. The guy was already doing an amazing job stepping into his new role. Dad would technically stay property manager in name, to help make critical decisions. But Scottie had jumped into the deep end and was learning the day-to-day ropes as quickly as he could. We suspected it wouldn't be long before the job would be all his.

"He told me to take back my narrative with the media. To not let them bulldoze my reputation just so they could sell a few papers. So, that's what I did, with Presley's help."

"The article was amazing, Carter. Presley has gotten a lot of positive feedback from it."

"I'm glad," I said, meaning it. "I didn't want her to write it at first—I even fought her on it. But then I realized it could really raise some awareness about the social issues behind why some people hire me to begin with."

"I'm glad you let *Finance Times* run with it. If you ever want a spread on your newfound wealth and what you're doing with all this money, just let me know. I may know someone who could write it," she said, winking.

"I'm sure Presley won't want another thing to do with me after that fiasco on the yacht," I said, grimacing.

"I didn't mean Presley, Carter. She actually doesn't work at the *Times* anymore. Didn't you know that?" she asked, looking pointedly at Dex.

"Uh, no?" I said, turning toward my friend. "Is there something you're not telling me?"

He pulled up his phone and opened the *Finance Times's* website, then handed it to me. The top article was an announcement about Presley Kincaid signing on with Montague Enterprise's philanthropy division as their new finance executive.

"Well, holy shit. Good for her."

"Good for us," Dex said. "She's already started her onboarding process, and that girl is smart. She's running circles around poor Richard and has a dozen process improvement and innovation ideas that she wants to integrate not just in the philanthropy division, but at a corporate level, as well."

"That's wonderful," I said. But it also left a huge hole in my heart. I just wanted a real and honest shot with Presley. Without any of the drama from our pasts getting in the way. I'd missed my chance with her twice. I wasn't doing it again.

"Look—I gotta go," I told Dex and Bianca.

"You can't leave," she said. "It's your party!"

"It's my party, I can leave if I want to, leave if I want to," I sang as I backed away from them and headed toward the door.

"Carter!" Veta called out. "Get some cake at least!"

"Can't, Veta!" I said over my shoulder. "I've got something much sweeter in mind."

I made my way back to the beach house to pack an overnight bag. I'd sit on her damn stoop as long as it took to get her to listen to me. It was such a stupid mix-up. Yeah, maybe I'd taken it too far, but Vivienne's ex was such a douche bag. He'd tried to make things worse for me, too. But Dex's lawyer slapped the paper with several defamation of character cease and desist notices. And when I received a threatening phone call from Victor one afternoon, I calmly made some phone calls first before getting back to him.

See, the thing about working with a close circle of wealthy people in the dog-eat-dog metropolis of New York City is that everyone is willing to turn on someone else eventually. And everyone has secrets they want to keep. It didn't take long for Dex's lawyers to get some of the women Victor had assaulted over the years to agree to speak out against him. Presley's testimony wasn't even needed, he'd had that many allegations filed against him during his run at the paper. Conveniently, all the internal investigations found him not guilty and were originally dismissed. But women speaking out in volume would be hard to silence.

I was surprised he didn't press charges against me for the fight I started on the yacht, but something told me Dex might've had something to do with that, too. It didn't stop Victor from threatening to bring me down, though, when I told him what was coming with his own pending assault charges in the form of a class action lawsuit. I'd do it all over again, too, if it meant protecting other young women like Presley.

When I approached the house, I was surprised to find the downstairs lights on. I could've sworn I'd turned them off. I took the elevator up, rehearsing what I'd say to Presley in my head when I finally saw her.

All coherent logic left my brain when I realized that flesh-and-blood Presley was standing in my living room, and she wasn't a mirage. She had a small cupcake in her hand with a solitary candle and a cute blue gift bow on her head. She looked ridiculous and adorable all at once.

Neither of us knew what to say. But I could tell there was forgiveness in her eyes. Just as there was passion. Thank god that hadn't died when she looked at me. I walked toward her, never breaking eye contact. I was eager to have her in my arms again. Talk, that could come afterward. First, I just fucking needed to hold her again so I could finally breathe.

"Happy birthday, Carter," she said. "Make a wish?"

I looked down at the cupcake and the lone candle. I closed my eyes and made a wish. When I opened them, there were tears in her eyes.

"My wish has already come true," I said, setting the cupcake down. "You're really here."

"Carter, I'm so sorry—"

"Presley, you don't owe me an apology. I should've realized there would be photographers there and how you might feel seeing me with a client. I did nothing to prepare you for that. If I could do it all over again, I would've woken you up that night after the party to tell you what went down. That way, you could've heard it from me first. I never dreamed it was going to go down like that."

"I understand that now, Carter. I guess I just panicked when I saw Victor in the papers, and you kissing his ex-wife. I was so confused. Especially since we'd just had a conversation about how you never crossed that line with clients. Everything in me wanted to believe you, but the pictures were so hard to unsee. They brought out a lot of insecurity in me. I think maybe because Vivienne looks so much like Lauren, too," Presley admitted.

I wrapped my arms around her and finally pulled her against my body, enveloping her shaking frame. I wanted to soothe the tears away. Kiss them away. Make love until she could cry no more. But I knew we had to put the past behind us before we could build a future. And that was exactly what I wanted with Presley Kincaid.

"Come here," I said, leading her upstairs.

She didn't question me. She held my hand tight and walked up all the flights of stairs with me until we were on the stargazing balcony.

"I was wondering if you knew about this," she said, smiling.

"I found it after you left," I said. "I've spent many evenings up here, just looking up at the sky. It's like a sea of infinite possibility. I've had a lot of time to think, Presley."

"Me too."

"Let's sit," I said. I pulled her onto my lap on one of the lounge chairs. Her back was to my chest and my arms were where they belonged—around her. I'd waited weeks for this, and I was almost overwhelmed finally having her in my arms again.

"Cute bow, by the way," I said, booping the bright blue bow on her head. "Does that mean you're my birthday present?"

"If you'll have me back," she said quietly.

"Let's talk first. Then you can let me know if you want me back, as well."

She nodded, relaxing against me.

"Presley, Vivienne asked me to stand-in as her date that night because she had a very slimy ex-husband, as you now know. Vivienne knew about his work indiscretions and let a lot of them slide. But when she caught him red-handed with their nanny, she couldn't look away anymore. So, she divorced him. That was a several years ago. She did not invite Victor to the party, and she wasn't looking for trouble. But she found out he'd managed to weasel in as someone's plus one. Which is where I came into the picture," I explained.

"When I got there, I didn't know who her husband was. I just knew he was Mr. Vanderbilt. And yeah, looking back, I could've probably put two and two together sooner, but I honestly was just worried about helping Vivienne not feel insecure around the man who'd hurt her so badly. When he walked in, he was such a smug bastard. Really flaunting it in her face—you know?"

Presley murmured, "Yeah, that sounds like the Victor I remember."

"So, I told her to trust me. To follow my lead. It was just an act to make him jealous. And boy did it ever. We paid him no attention, but I made sure he got an eyeful of what looked like me romancing Vivienne. I swear to you, Presley,

I *never* once did anything inappropriate with her. She doesn't hold a candle to you, anyway, princess."

She turned in the seat so she could look at me. "I was so foolish, Carter. We weren't exclusive. We'd never talked about being exclusive. Just because we were having sex didn't mean you owed me a damn thing. I—I was jealous. And that wasn't a good look for me. But I realize now how much I overreacted. I should've been there as a friend, instead of blowing what we had so far out of proportion," she said.

I grabbed her wrist and pulled her closer to me. "We were more than friends, and you damn well know it, Presley. We may not have had a talk because it was all so new, but I wouldn't be sleeping with you and messing around with anybody else. Especially with you."

"What does that mean?"

"It means I have feelings for you," I said. "Deep feelings. You weren't some random hookup for me. I'm sorry if you felt like you were. That was never my intention."

"You didn't make me feel that way," she whispered. "Which is why it caught me so off guard, I think."

"I never touched her intimately. I just made it look like I was. And I never kissed her. It was all slight-of-eye for Victor's benefit."

"Is that why you ended up with a black eye?" she asked, giggling.

"Oh, is that funny to you?" I was so ready to kiss those damn lips silent.

"A little? It was kind of nice to see how much worse off Victor was."

"That part wasn't about Vivienne, Presley."

"Oh," she said, growing quiet. "What was it about then?"

"I'd put two and two together by then. About who he was. You mentioned Victor's name the night you confided in me. And when I got him alone, he confronted me about Vivienne. So, I confronted him about you."

Presley gasped. "You didn't!"

"Yeah, I did. I'm not sorry either, because he was a complete dirtbag and had what was coming."

"So, he punched you?"

I shook my head. "Nope. I threw the first punch."

Presley took my face in her hands and leaned forward, gently kissing my lips.

"Thank you, Carter."

"I wish I could've done more," I admitted.

"I think you did enough," she said. "Nobody's ever done anything quite so chivalrous for me before. It's kinda sexy."

"Oh, it gets better," I told her. I filled her in on his threat and the women who had come forward, thanks to Dex's attorney and Vivienne's promise to protect them. We'd be taking Victor all the way down.

"Oh, Carter," she said, hugging me, "a part of me is so relieved to hear this. And another part of me knows I can't hide from it anymore."

"What do you mean?" I asked.

"I want to be a part of the defense team against him."

"Are you sure? That kind of intense examination isn't easy."

"It adds to the pressure though, doesn't it? The more women who come out. I never would have done this on my own though. Hell, I didn't even realize it was this bad."

"Unfortunately, Vivienne suspected. It wasn't until Dex and I had some friends start asking around about her suspicions that even more cases came to light than we anticipated, too."

"Well, I'm sorry that's the case. But I won't be sorry to see them all get justice."

"To see yourself get it, too," I reminded her.

She nodded, then curled against me. "So, now what? It's easy for me to forgive you, but you have no reason to forgive me, Carter. I didn't believe in you when I should have. Instead of trusting, I ran. And then, when I should've listened, I avoided you. I'm really sorry."

"Pres, we both made mistakes. I don't blame you. I know what it all looked like. I can just promise you that I won't put you in a position to question me again."

She looked up at me. "What do you mean?"

"I want you more than I need Mister Stand-In."

"No, Carter. Did you read my article?"

"Yes, I did. It was really good, Presley. I appreciate what you did for me."

"I didn't *do* anything. I just told the world who you really are. I got your flowers, by the way," she said, resting her hand against my chest. "Thank you."

I lifted her chin. "I have so much more I want to talk to you about, princess. But more than anything, I need to feel you in my arms. Are we okay?"

"More than okay," she said, stretching up and kissing me. "In fact, I have a special surprise in honor of your birthday."

"Oh yeah? And what's that?"

Presley stood, grinning as she removed her clothes slowly, piece by piece. Once again, she was completely naked underneath—no panties, no bra.

"In honor of your birthday, I wore my birthday suit," she said, grinning.

I stood and faced her, taking off my jeans and sweater in between kisses. "I couldn't ask for a better birthday present,

Presley. Now get back down here," I said, yanking her in my lap. Her adorable squeal turned me on to no end, the effects ricocheting straight to my cock.

"I have one more surprise," she said.

"Oh, yeah? And what's that?"

She slowly lowered herself over my cock as I leaned back against the lounge chair, the evening sky lighting our way. Presley leaned forward, her long, strawberry blond hair brushing my naked chest and sending goose bumps across my skin in the cool October air.

"I'm on the pill now," she said, sinking all the way down until she could go no farther.

"Fuuuuck," I said, finding a slow and steady pace as I drove myself deep inside her, my face buried in her hair.

This was officially the best birthday ever. I got the girl, I got the money, and the bad guy was going down. Life couldn't get any better than this for a guy who started out with next to nothing. Now, with Presley in my arms, I had everything I never knew I needed and more. She wrapped her arms around me, and we stayed molded like that together, our bodies making up for lost time as our love was baptized beneath the stars.

EPILOGUE

PRESLEY

"MISS KINCAID, ISN'T it true that—"

"It's Mrs. Wright, now," I said, correcting the reporter. We had Dex to thank for that. We were officially the second wedding he officiated, before he decided to retire that hat.

I looked toward a young, timid woman in the back of the crowd. "How about you?"

She looked around, unsure if I'd called on the right person. She smiled gratefully, even as her male counterparts tried shouting over her.

"Thank you, Mrs. Wright. Can you please tell me about Montague Enterprise's new philanthropic initiative partnering with the LGBTQ community to make sure no one feels alone again?"

I smiled broadly. "Thank you for asking the questions that matter, Ms. . . . ?"

"Silverstone."

"Well, Ms. Silverstone, my husband and I have joined forces to open The Stand-In, a nonprofit organization staffed with many compassionate volunteers who will be there to help support the LGBTQ community in any way they need—whether it's to be an advocate for them at their school to make sure their voices and needs are being heard, or to stand-in as a big brother who walks his sister down the aisle when a parent has turned their back on them. Connection, empathy, and equality are the cornerstones of The Stand-In, and we hope to not only be there for those in need, but to also partner with existing nonprofits to help further educate the community about the diverse and beautiful LGBTQ community here in New York City.

"We'll be working closely with The Center, The New York Anti-Violence Project, and the LGBT Bar Association of New York to further push the agenda of equal rights for everyone. We want to make sure that more impactful fines are levied against those businesses that continue to discriminate against this community."

A round of applause broke out around me, and I smiled out at the crowd. "Any other questions?"

"Is it true that Montague Enterprises is also funding The Stand-In, and does that make it a conflict of interest?"

"My husband is the primary CEO of The Stand-In. As you know, he created the business model with his successful previous business. I will help provide funding, access, and resources, through Montague Enterprises, with the blessing of Dex and Bianca Truitt and the board of directors. We will have transparent and frequent audits of allocations of funds. Most will be used to help support other initiatives that help this community, like the classes provided at the Jelani Okiro Arts and Cultural Center, as well as to support federal legislation that further expands rights to the LGBTQ community nationwide.

"If that's everything, I thank you for joining us today. We'll be cutting the ribbon on our new facility in just a moment, and I invite you join us for our celebration afterward."

I was just about to step off the podium when a man called out from the back of the pack, "Mrs. Wright, isn't it true that you're only speaking up against Victor Vanderbilt in the upcoming trial because you have a vendetta to clear your husband's name after last year's scandal?"

A year ago, this kind of question would have intimidated me. But a year has made a big difference. Every day I drew more and more strength in myself because of the happiness I shared with Carter and our newborn son, Pennington Carter Wright.

I smiled at the crowd, not letting one man's venom affect me. I'd experienced that enough already this past year becoming one of Montague's youngest senior executives, and the financial executive of one of the most influential nonprofit consortiums in New York—because Montague wasn't just about furthering its bottom line, it was about making impactful change to the communities that needed it most.

"Unfortunately, I am not allowed to discuss an open case. However, I will say that no matter the outcome of the trial, there will be no real winners here. Over twenty women have come forward with claims of sexual assault against my previous employer, Victor Vanderbilt. He'll have his time in court to defend himself, just as I'll have a chance to share my story. Thank you all for being here today," I said, before exiting the stage.

Dex, Bianca, Willa, Lauren, Richard, and Carter all met me at the bottom of the podium. Carter handed Penn over to me, and I greedily snuggled him against my nose. I was met by the adorable cooing sound he was now making.

"Very well played, Mrs. Wright," Bianca said, winking. She, too, had a new baby on her hip—their third and final, according to Dex. Keaton Dexter Truitt may've been a surprise, but he'd been a welcome blessing to our little extended family. And that's what it felt like these days.

When we weren't in New York, we were at our second home in South Carolina at The Grove. The gorgeous blue beach house that held so many good memories—and a few not so good ones—was now ours. We'd already "initiated" just about every room in the house and had already gone through my entire original "Down and Dirty" list. We were now working our way through a new one, too. Though, admittedly, Pennington made it a little harder these days. Turns out you have to be on the pill for at least thirty days for it to be effective. Who knew?

He was a blessing, though. And we were excited to have our two families grow up, side by side, in both business and love. I could see Keaton and Penn becoming fast friends one day, just as their namesakes had been. We would protect them fiercely though, just as you do with the ones you love.

We also added onto our family in another way I never expected. We were now the proud owners of a rescued Borzoi named Chewie, thanks to Forever Grey. The fluffy Russian greyhound was white with beautiful tan spots, and Jar Jar mostly loved her. They're still feeling each other out.

At the ribbon cutting ceremony, I stood by my partner and best friend, holding his hand. Willa held Penn in her arms next to me, and Lauren and Richard stood behind us. I glanced over, smiling at Bianca. She, Dex, their girls, and Keaton joined us for the start of an exciting, brand new chapter in our lives.

I let the Truitt's oldest daughter, Georgie, do the honors. She laughed with delight as she confidently cut the bright yellow ribbon in front of the new offices for The Stand-In. I gave her a high-five.

I couldn't wait to rewrite history and put this new ribbon-cutting photo on our wall beside the original one at The Grove. Over the past year, Carter had quickly become the husband and father I knew he could be. There was so much more to him than the cocky, arm-candy façade he'd portrayed as Mister Stand-In. When he opened his business, and his heart, to the world by being completely transparent in the interview he did for me, he realized the freedom that came with honesty.

Though, our families did agree to keep *some* things personal, for the safety of Keaton and Penn. I understood now, as a parent, the lengths you would go through to protect the ones you love.

"So how does it feel?" Carter asked, swooping down and planting his lips against mine. I swooned. This never got old.

"How does what feel?"

"Standing in your power," he said, winking. "I am so proud of you, Presley."

"I'm pretty proud of you, too, Carter. I guess we're gonna have to retire Miss Moneybags and Mister Stand-In, huh? Those two don't really exist anymore, do they?"

"They're in here somewhere," he said, biting at my lower lip. "They just don't run the show anymore."

"No, I guess not."

"Are you happy, Presley? Really happy?"

It no longer made me angry to have people ask me that, maybe because for the first time, I understood what true joy felt like.

"I am," I said, standing on my tiptoes to kiss him. "And I have a surprise for you later."

"Oh, no," Carter said. "The last surprise you gave me led to a surprise pregnancy."

I laughed. "But you wouldn't change it for the world, would you?"

"No, I wouldn't," he said, grinning that cocksure smile he was so famous for these days in the news. "So, what's my surprise?"

I leaned over and whispered into his ear. His strong arm wrapped around my waist, and he grabbed a handful of my ass.

"Inside. Now," he growled.

"Carter! We can't leave our own party!"

"We're not leaving," he said. "We're just efficiently working our way through our new D&D list."

I giggled, grabbing my husband's hand as we ran inside the building, found Carter's new office, closed the blinds, and locked the doors. We could hear people on the other side of the wall mingling and laughing, music playing in the background.

But all I could see as Carter wiped the desk clean and tossed me onto the top was my man. The man who stood by and stood up for me time and time again. The man who made me a woman and a mother. And most of all, the man I would love for the rest of my life.

"I love you," I said, quietly, holding his face in my hands.

"I love you, too, princess. Now get your ass over here," he growled, yanking my hips to the edge of the desk as my laughter bubbled over. "Goddamn, you get even more beautiful every day."

"Why thank you, Mr. Wright."

"Stop talking, Mrs. Wright, or I'll give your naughty little mouth something to silence it with."

"Pinky promise?"

He cupped my breast, made much fuller after Penn's arrival. His other hand traveled under my pencil skirt and found me already wet for him.

"Fuck, Presley," he said, running his fingers up my center, "I'd pinky promise my life away in this moment for a taste of you. You ever going to wear underwear, woman?"

"I don't plan to," I said honestly.

"Good," Carter said, chuckling.

We made good use of his new desk, crossed off the first location on our new list, and might even have accidentally made Pennington a big brother.

Yeah, I couldn't get any happier than this.

Want to keep up with all of the new releases in Vi Keeland and Penelope Ward's Cocky Hero Club world? Make sure you sign up for the official Cocky Hero Club newsletter for all the latest on our upcoming books:

https://www.subscribepage.com/CockyHeroClub

Check out other books in the Cocky Hero Club series:

http://www.cockyheroclub.com

OTHER BOOKS BY C.M. ALBERT

ARDEN'S GLEN ROMANCES
Faith in Love
Proof of Love
Visions of Love

STAND-ALONE ROMANCES
Last Night in Laguna
The White Room
Consumed by Love – A Written in the Stars novel

LOVE IN LA QUARTET
The Stars in Her Eyes
The Fire in His Touch (2021)
The Lies in His Head (2021)
The Songs in His Heart (2021)

ABOUT THE AUTHOR

USA Today bestselling author C.M. Albert writes heartwarming romances that are "sexy and flirty, sweet and dirty!" Her writing infuses a healthy blend of humor, high-heat romance, and most of all—hope. When not writing or kid-wrangling, she's either meditating, kayaking, reading, hugging a tree, or asleep. But first, coffee. #TonyStarkForever

Join C.M. Albert online at:

WEBSITE: colleenalbert.com

COCKY HERO CLUB READER GROUP:
facebook.com/groups/CockyHeroClub

FACEBOOK: facebook.com/cmalbertwrites

READER GROUP:
facebook.com/groups/ColleensAngels

INSTAGRAM: instagram.com/cmalbertwrites

TWITTER: twitter.com/colleenmalbert

GOODREADS: goodreads.com/cmalbert

BOOKBUB: bookbub.com/profile/c-m-albert

PINTEREST: pinterest.com/cmalbertwrites

NEWSLETTER: subscribepage.com/w5x4p1

ACKNOWLEDGMENTS

TAPS MIC.

For the three people who made it this far, I lovingly want to acknowledge, thank, and send big, socially-distanced air hugs to the following people for either enriching my life, inspiring me, offering a hand, or being general, all-around bad astronauts (as my daughter would say):

- My wizard editor, Erin Servais of Dot and Dash, LLC
- My patient, taco-loving cover designer, Marisa Wesley of Cover Me Darling
- The wickedly talented, adorable panda bear, Reggie Deanching of R + M Photography
- The man who's not just a pretty face—my inspiration for Carter Wright, Aidan Stewart
- All of my naughty "Angels" in the Colleen's Angels Readers' Circle
- My uber private Beta and ARC readers . . . You're mine, all mine!
- All the bloggers, bookstagrammers, and influencers who love on my books (I see you!)
- Jackie James, my Oz and just an incredibly uplifting, kind, and positive human

- The friends who keep me sane on a daily: Deena, Heather, Jacque, Jen, and Sheila
- The funny, ever-growing gamer who hoards food and soda cans in his room, Evan
- My creative star girl who sings and dances light everywhere she goes, Gillian
- The only man I'd want to be quarantined with, my rock, my BFF, my heart, Derek

An extra special thanks to Vi Keeland and Penelope Ward not only for inspiring me with their own amazing books, but also inviting me to write in their world. I fell in love with Dex and Bianca in *Mister Moneybags* and knew right away that was the world I wanted to play in. Thanks to you and Brower Literary & Management for all of the opportunities you've created for us Cocky Hero Club authors, and for going to bat for us to get our books into as many hands as possible. I'd also like to thank Dan and Alyssa for keeping me honest and helping a girl out when I should have already known the answer.

I was able to breathe life into Presley and Carter because of you, and I am forever grateful!